TEARS
IN THE
DESERT

KAREN V. ROBICHAUD

TEARS IN THE DESERT
Copyright © 2020 by Karen V. Robichaud

ISBN: 978-1-4866-2003-6
eBook ISBN: 978-1-4866-2004-3

Word Alive Press
119 De Baets Street Winnipeg, MB R2J 3R9
www.wordalivepress.ca

WORD ALIVE
—PRESS—

Cataloguing in Publication information can be obtained from Library and Archives Canada.

For my precious granddaughters,
Cierra and Caylin, with all my love.

And for Mike, Candice, Chris, Linda and Kathy,
for your love and support.

He led you through the vast and dreadful wilderness, that thirsty and waterless land, with its venomous snakes and scorpions. He brought you water out of hard rock.
—Deuteronomy 8:15

PROLOGUE

Some say there is a moment in everyone's life that is so shocking, so frightening, that it blazes into your mind with the ferocity of a wildfire. And though you may seem fine to others, in your very core the horror of the moment has changed you forever.

Perhaps it's that fine spring morning when you're hiking on a path in the woods and inadvertently step between a furious mother grizzly bear and her two cubs. Or the bright summer afternoon when you're in an airliner flying over the Atlantic and thick black smoke begins filling the cabin. Maybe it's the splendid autumn evening when you leave the mall and jump into your car, glance up into the rear-view mirror, and see a masked face looking at you from the back seat. All moments that send your terrified heart rocketing into your throat with such force that you cannot release the scream bubbling up inside you.

For me, that moment occurred on a scorching summer night in northern Australia when I was eleven years old. The images of that horrifying night are seared into my mind forever. The shock on my sister's face, the terror in her voice as she begged me to save her, the metallic odour of her blood… these ambush me daily, as vivid as if it were happening right now. They petrified me then; they petrify me even now, two decades later.

PART
ONE

CHAPTER ONE

The desert region of northern Australia can be a forbidding, pitiless place. We arrive there, in the town of Desolation Creek, on a blistering Tuesday morning. Dad pulls over on the shoulder at the entrance to town. The sign off the road reads:

Welcome to the town of Desolation Creek
Population 3,727

"Perfect," my sister Natalie says with the biting sarcasm only she is capable of voicing.

Dad pretends he doesn't hear and drives into town, cruising through the main drag, called predictably, unimaginatively, Main Street. It's early, the crack of dawn and the street and sidewalks are empty, and the businesses not yet open.

"Oh, Dad, this is the middle of nowhere," Nat says with quiet despair.

"Now, princess, it is not the middle of nowhere," he reassures her. "It's the Outback. There are small towns just like this all around here."

My mom glances over the front seat at Natalie, and I can see by her expression that her heart, though not in complete despair like her eldest daughter's, has deflated a little.

Their shared reaction doesn't surprise me, for Mom and Natalie not only look strikingly alike, they have similar slow, thoughtful personalities. I, with my thick eyebrows, knife-like nose, jug ears, and hasty impulsivity, am pretty much the female twin of my dad.

I peer out the windshield. There isn't much to the town, but I find it exciting nonetheless. On the left are a bank, town hall, library, and drugstore. All are aged, flat-roofed, wood-panelled structures. On the right I see a grungy-looking pub, a grocery store, and a hardware store with a sign advertising guns, fishing rods, and bait worms for sale… and then another pub. Next to the pub is another bank, and next to the bank is a boxy-shaped lemon-yellow restaurant with a sign that reads *Louisa's Diner*, a pretty yellow rose among the thorns.

As we leave the centre of town, the businesses get dingier. I see a pawn shop, a tattoo parlour, and a place called Fast Cash Payday Loans. The businesses soon give way to residential homes, most of which are grey-sided and so dilapidated that they look more like shacks that have been there nearly a century. We don't stop.

At the westernmost edge of town, Dad pulls over on the shoulder again. A sign on the dirt to the right reads *Blue Rock River Road*. There's a second sign behind that one, a yellow rectangular sign that reads *Dead End—No Exit*.

"Touché," Nat says.

Dad ignores her, turns right, and drives down the narrow unpaved lane. At the end of the lane, also on the right, is a larger wooden sign:

BLUE ROCK RIVER CHURCH
Pastor Cecil Ingram
Sunday School: 9:30–10:30 a.m.
Sunday Services: 11–12 p.m.
Wednesday Prayer: 6:30–7:30 p.m.
ALL WELCOME!

Dad looks out the windshield up to the sky and raises his hand. "Hallelujah, thank you, Lord, for bringing us here safely."

"Amen," Mom murmurs.

Nat lets out a heavy sigh.

Dad smiles broadly at Mom, then turns right and drives over the badly potholed and rutted dirt parking lot of the church. The car bounces from side to side, throwing me into Nat and Nat into Quinn. We all laugh, but I see Dad grimace and know he's concerned about possible damage to the shiny used SUV he bought from a dealer in Alice Springs.

Dad stops in front of the parsonage and kills the engine. We all stare at the dilapidated monstrosity that is the parsonage—and our new home.

"Is this it, Dad?" says six-year-old Quinn, squinting out the side window to the house.

Dad smiles at him. "Yes, this is it, little bud."

Nat's mouth drops open. "No," she says, aghast.

"Oh, yes," Dad says, cheerfully. "Home sweet home."

"I thought Deacon Taylor said it was recently renovated," Mom says in a quiet voice.

"I'm guessing he meant the interior. Don't judge a book by its cover, pet."

Mom nods but looks unconvinced.

I roll down my window, and instantly punishing arid heat fills the car like a blast from a furnace.

Dad rolls his down, too, and hauls in a big lungful of air. "Smell that, kids. Pure desert air. Now isn't that the most refreshing air you've ever breathed in?"

"It smells rotten," says Natalie, peering worriedly out the side window. "Like something's dead in the bushes."

Dad pays no attention to that. He slaps his palm down on the steering wheel, grins wildly, and says with exhilaration, "Come on, everyone. Let's go see the place, and then we'll head right over to the church."

We all climb out and stand facing the parsonage. It's a two-story, wood-sided house. The shingles remaining on the roof are brown and most are curled up. The steps to the front porch drop on one side and the white paint is so worn off that the boards are grey. The siding is twisted and the paint is peeling off everywhere, but it's heaviest around the sills. The bare wood is black from rot.

Dad scratches his chin. "Could use a fresh coat of paint."

Mom nods. "It certainly could."

He gives Mom a wry smile. "But then, it is thirty-seven years old."

She nods again. "True."

"Look, pet. There are two rocking chairs on the porch for us to sit out on warm evenings," my dad says, pointing to the shabby wooden chairs.

Mom puts her hands over her eyes to shield them from the sun and studies the rickety chairs. "I see that," she says, in a slightly subdued voice.

"Where is everyone?" Nat says, looking around. "There's no one here to meet us."

"Looks like we arrived a bit early," Dad says brightly, but I see a flicker of disappointment in his eyes. "I'm sure Deacon Taylor will be over later. He said if he wasn't here when we arrived, he'd leave the key under a big planter right at the side of the front step."

Nat catches my eye and mouths silently, *Well, that's just rude.*

Quit it, you baby, I mouth back. Though at eleven, I'm eighteen months younger than she is.

About a hundred yards to the left of the parsonage is the white-sided church Dad will be pastoring. With its boxy shape and no steeple or cross, it looks more like a bingo hall, although it appears to be in better shape than the parsonage. I wonder how many people attend. A while back, I overheard my parents talking about a family who lived next to the church and claimed that the land the church and parsonage sat on was theirs. They'd harassed the former pastor and talked about a scandal involving him. Apparently that had caused a nasty split in the congregation and the membership had dwindled. I'd also heard my parents talking about how a member of the congregation had been bitten by a poisonous spider during a Sunday morning service and died.

I can't help but think the townspeople would wonder why this Canadian pastor had uprooted his young family and moved more than seventeen thousand kilometres from Nova Scotia to Australia, why he would leave a decent-sized church to pastor a small church for little pay in an isolated town in the wild Outback. They'd likely believe my dad was running from a scandal, too.

But they didn't know my dad like I do. His passion is rebuilding, growing, and healing broken congregations… and he's always wanted to visit Australia. Thus, Blue Rock River Church seemed perfect for him. He could heal, rebuild, and lead a church while living in the country of his dreams.

A gust of scorching wind howls off the land. It's so hot and full of sand that it bites into the exposed flesh on my face and arms like tiny needles. The searing heat burns my mouth and singes my throat, making it hard to even swallow, let alone breathe. I turn away from it and pull in some air, try to get some clean oxygen into my lungs.

I shield my eyes with my hand and survey the property. Grass is sparse, and the lawn in front of the parsonage is mostly dirt, with weeds, clumps of brush and bushes, and a few scrawny-looking trees. There's a clothesline in the back of the parsonage that creaks in a hair-raising kind of way. The air smells of dust, dead brush, and baked clay. The buzz of insects from the bushes is as loud as a siren. There's also a small vegetable garden at the right side of the house; wilted tomato vines, bean, and pea shoots are visible among the weeds.

My mom loves gardening. She raises flowers and rose bushes, but her passion is growing her own vegetables. In Nova Scotia she had a huge garden and grew tomatoes, peas, squash, cucumbers, beans, potatoes, zucchinis, peppers, and pumpkins. Even after she canned and froze what she could, it was always too much for us and she'd give the rest away to friends, family, and the local food bank. Her eyes fall on the garden and light up slightly.

I look behind the church and parsonage and see only a flat unforgiving expanse of treeless land. There are little patches of brush and rocks here and there, but that's it. And hot does not describe it; the air is blistering, scorching my skin and frying my eyeballs. Heatwaves shimmer over the ground. Every few minutes, a fierce gust of wind sweeps off the desert and fills the air with a boiler-like blast of grit and sand that clogs our nostrils and ears and collects in the corners of our eyes. I'm hotter than I've ever felt in my life. It's like standing inside a kiln.

Natalie cants her head and uses a fingertip to clean the dirt from her ears. "Ugh, the heat is unbearable and the dirt is so gross, Dad."

He nods sympathetically. "Yes, but this is a hot subtropical desert climate, princess. It heats up rapidly once the sun rises. We'll have to plan our activities accordingly."

"Activities? What activities? The town is dead. I didn't even see a mall or movie theatre," complains Nat, who'd been anticipating days spent in town with lots of other teenagers, especially cute blond Australian boys.

He gives her an apologetic smile. "I'm sorry, sweetheart. But we're here to rebuild and grow this church, not to spend our days with recreational activities. We'll have enough activities at the church to keep us all occupied." He notices her crestfallen face. "There is the Blue Rock River not far from here, maybe a ten-minute walk from the house. There are shade trees there and we can go swimming or have a picnic when we have time. There'll be lots of privacy."

"Wonderful," Nat says, rolling her eyes.

Dad doesn't get that she didn't want *privacy*; she wanted teenagers and lots of them—if not at a public pool in town, then at the river. She most definitely did not want to swim with us, her lame, embarrassing family.

Dad reaches out and softly squeezes her arm. "It will be fine, princess, I promise."

Nat shifts her arm away and stares straight ahead, her eyes moistening.

She looks profoundly miserable and I feel a trace of pity for her.

"The church is a bit on the outskirts of town. There's not even a sign out on the main road to let anyone know it's here," Mom points out. "And the parsonage looks like it's falling to pieces. I'm not certain it's even safe for us to live in."

Dad merely shakes his head, unconcerned. "Oh, I'm sure it's perfectly safe, pet. The congregation would never allow us to live in there if it weren't. I'll talk to the board of deacons about putting up a sign. Look, we're here now, so why don't we all try to make the best of it?"

The parsonage is rundown, the heat blistering, and the dusty dry air isn't even close to the refreshing ocean air back home—no matter what my dad thinks. Despite it all, my heart thrums with eagerness at the promise of days filled with thrilling new exploration and adventure.

"It's awful, Dad." Natalie pulls her blouse away from her moist skin. "Why would they build the church down this horrid road at the far edge of town? It's like the boonies out here, and Mom's right, the parsonage likely isn't safe to live in."

"Your mother didn't say it wasn't safe to live in. She said she wasn't certain, and as *I* said, I'm sure it's fine,."

"Oh, Dad, have a heart. Can we please drive back into town and stay in a hotel until you talk to Deacon Taylor? At least a hotel would have a pool. It's so hot, I feel like I'm being roasted alive."

He gives her a pained look. "No, we can't do that, princess. Give it a chance. You'll see. Everything will be okay."

She lifts a brow towards me, indicating she wants a supporter. Always Dad's faithful collaborator and greatest defender, I scowl at her.

She turns to Mom, lifts her eyebrows and gets a sympathetic smile back. Mom steps over and puts an arm around Nat's shoulder, pulling her into her side.

"I know it's a little disappointing for you, sweetheart, but we can't go stay at a hotel," says Mom. "I'm sorry."

Dad steps over and encompasses them both in an embrace. "It will be fine." Then he turns and faces the house. "Now come on, gang. Chins up. Let's go have a look inside the parsonage. I'm sure the interior is in much better condition than the exterior."

"I'm not going in there," says Natalie warily. "It looks like spiders and snakes could be living inside."

"Not could be… for sure," I say, torturing her. "Australia has one hundred and seventy species of land snakes. They have the most snakes and spiders than any other country in the world. And the most venomous. Taipans, brown snakes, tiger snakes…" I look at the house and nod solemnly. "I bet the place is crawling with them. Watch out for the ceiling lights, Nat. They'll drop right off them onto your head."

"Dad," Nat says, near tears.

Dad narrows his eyes and gives me a long look. "No, no, there aren't any spiders or snakes in there," he says with a cautioning tone intended for me. "It likely just needs some cleaning up."

Nat doesn't look convinced.

Dad turns to my mom and beams, his intense blue eyes dancing with delight. "It likely just needs some good old TLC. Right, pet?"

Mom stares at him for a long time without blinking.

Oblivious, he then turns to her and repeats it: "Right, pet?"

Mom lets out a soft sigh. "Yes, some cleaning up should improve things," she says with feigned optimism.

But snakes and spiders don't bother me and my stomach flutters with excitement as we follow Dad down the driveway to the front porch. He stops at the side of the step, lifts a ceramic planter, and picks up a key. He sets the planter back down and bounds up the shaky wooden steps to the door to unlock it. He throws us a happy grin over his shoulder, then turns the doorknob with a flourish—and the door jams. He bumps into it hard, but without looking back at us he grabs the knob again, presses his shoulder against the door, and gives it a forceful push. This time it frees and opens with a spine-tingling creak. He steps inside with the four of us right behind him.

The wind kicks up, blows into the house, and the smell of the places hits us hard.

In the small foyer, Nat scrunches up her nose. "Ew, it stinks in here. It smells like a wet dog."

"It's not that bad," Dad says with an edge in his voice, beginning to lose patience.

Quinn scrunches up his nose. "It smells like a dirty dog."

"Well, that makes sense. The previous pastor and his wife had two big dogs, from what I've been told."

I have to smile at that. Nat and Quinn are right. The air reeks of wet dirty dog hair. But that doesn't bother me.

The wind dies as suddenly as it kicked up, and over the whirr of the insects outside I hear Mom let out a long, weary breath.

I survey the place. A narrow foyer leads into a narrower hall that leads into the kitchen at the back. There's a stairway in the middle of the hall that rises up to the second floor. To the left of the hall lies a living room and master bedroom. The bedroom has a queen-size bed and six-drawer dresser with a mirror. Sunshine pours in through the windows despite the grime on them.

We follow Dad across pale brown hardwood floors that have not a drop of varnish left on them. In the kitchen, we find that the grimy window over the sink casts the room in darkness. A bare, dusty lightbulb hangs by a chain. Dad yanks it and the bulb flickers on. The room lights up, dimly, due to a thick coating of dust on the bulb.

There's a tall stainless steel garbage can in a corner, and it's overflowing. The lid lies on the floor and a rancid smell comes from the can.

"Ah, there's one source of the stench," Mom says.

Dad crosses the floor and picks up the can. "I'll get rid of it and let some fresh air in."

"Watch for maggots, Dad," I tell him. "That garbage has been rotting there for a long time."

Natalie clamps a hand over her mouth, losing all colour.

"Ha, your face just turned as white as a maggot," I say, delighted.

Dad breathes out hard. "Raine, stop," he warns, then opens the door and carries the can out to the backyard.

I can't believe it. Nat whines for an hour, and he barely says a word to her. I say one thing to tease her and right away he's annoyed with me?

Mom opens the windows. Instantly, a gust of hot wind blows in, carrying a wall of dust that swirls around the kitchen before settling on the table, countertop, and floor.

When Dad comes back inside, we inspect the kitchen together. Four pale wood chairs are arranged around a dark rectangular table. Along the left wall is a fridge, and across from the counter and sink is an ancient-looking cookstove and pantry. We find mouse droppings on the floor and countertop. The cupboard doors are twisted and ajar, and inside I notice cans of soup and baked beans. Next to the cans is a sack of rice with a hill of mouse poo around a chewed-up hole.

"The pastor and his wife left us some food," I say.

"Haha, funny." Natalie makes a face at me. "Look, there's rodent poo in the rice. There's a mouse or a rat living in here. Oh, Dad."

I poke her with my elbow. "A mouse? I doubt it. Where there's one mouse, there is likely a thousand more."

She wraps her arms around herself and shudders. "Stop it, Raine."

Quinn looks hopeful. "If I catch one, can I keep it for a pet?"

"No, you cannot." Dad turns to Natalie. "Don't worry, princess. If there's a mouse, I'll get rid of it."

"It?" I say, grinning.

Dad winces and gives me a severe look that shouts, *That is enough*. Then he steps over and puts his arm around Natalie, leading her out of the room and back down the hall.

"We won't even be in here much," he says. "It's too hot to cook indoors. There's an outdoor kitchen and a barbecue on the back porch. We'll use those for the summer months, all right? Now, let's check out the rest of the rooms."

We step into the living room. Like the kitchen, the walls are bare—not a photo, not a print or painting of any kind. A brown and green plaid couch and matching armchair sit next to each other, their fabric worn thin. There's a mismatched coffee table and end table topped with a tan-shaded lamp. On a wobbly stand along the wall across from the couch is an old television with rabbit ears. A layer of dirt covers the screen.

Surprisingly, to the right of the couch I discover a green-shaded banker's lamp on a desk that's in good shape—an anomaly in this shack. I'm thrilled at the thought of sitting at this desk writing stories about all the adventures I'm going to experience in this parched and dangerous land.

Across from the living room is the master bedroom. Stepping inside, Mom smiles at Dad, her spirits lifted.

"The house isn't all that bad, is it, pet?" he says.

"It's nicer than I thought at first."

Dad reaches out and squeezes her hand. "Let's check out the second level."

The staircase is so narrow and steep that we go up single file, Dad in front, me next, and Mom, Quinn, and Nat behind. The steps creak horribly, the wooden planks so short that we have to turn our feet sideways to step off them safely.

Dad grumbles, his feet much longer than ours. "Be especially careful coming back down, gang. Pay attention and go slow."

We stop at the top of the stairs.

Nat looks around and makes a gagging motion. "It smells even worse up here, Dad."

"Just needs to be aired out," he says, smiling at us like a crazy man.

He goes into the nearest bedroom and opens a window. I step over beside him and gaze out towards the horizon. I can't tell where the desert ends and the sky begins. It all looks the same.

Dad looks at me and we share a smile.

"I knew you'd love it, tiger," he says, squeezing my arm.

"I do, Dad," I say, glad that we're so alike, so close. Privately, though, I've always disliked him calling me tiger; it sounds so much less tender than what he calls Nat (princess), Quinn (little bud), and Mom (pet). But then I overheard him tell Mom that he calls me that because he thinks I'm as fierce and bold as a tiger. That pleased me to no end.

There are two small bedrooms and a bathroom upstairs. One bedroom has a single bed made up with white sheets and pillowcase. On top is a pink blanket and multicoloured quilt folded at the end of the bed. A nightstand is next to the bed, and atop it is an open Bible.

"This will be your room, little bud," Dad tells Quinn.

I turn and look into the second bedroom across the hall. It's in better condition and has two single beds and a five-drawer dresser. This will undoubtedly be Nat's and my bedroom. I'm also thankful that, just like all the other rooms in the house, ours has a ceiling fan.

"Strange," Mom says, looking into what will be Quinn's bedroom. "Going by the pink-coloured blanket, it looks like a woman or girl slept here."

"I remember now… Deacon Taylor told me the pastor's mother lived with them," Dad says vaguely without turning from the window. He nods languidly, lost in thought as the hot breeze puffs the curtains and ruffles the pages of the Bible on the nightstand.

I step over and look down at the book, my eyes falling on Ephesians 5:17, which someone had highlighted with a yellow marker: *"Therefore do not be foolish, but understand what the Lord's will is."*

Mom comes up alongside me and follows my eyes to the same verse. Her light green eyes flick back and forth as she reads, and then she looks over to my dad who's still peering out the window at the austere land behind the house. His expression is one of pure joy.

"Amen, Lord, amen," she whispers.

She turns and walks out of the room. Nat and Quinn follow her.

Despite supporting Dad, I know she has doubts about his claim that the Lord has led us to this congregation to rebuild the church. I overheard them talk about it, and Mom asked if he was sure it was God's will and not his. After all, it had been his lifelong dream to live in Australia.

I don't know who's right and I don't care. Despite the heat, I like it here. I'm so excited that it feels like an electric current is running through my body.

I pick up the Bible and close it, then cross the floor and stand beside Dad at the window. He glances sideways, sets his hand on my shoulder, and squeezes it. We both stare into the sunlight blazing down on the baked desert.

CHAPTER TWO

A thin cry comes from Natalie's throat.

"Nat, what's wrong?" I ask, stepping into the bedroom behind her, carrying a taped cardboard box marked *Natalie and Raine's Clothing*. Her eyes are glassy, her face bloodless white and slack.

She points to a corner of the room. "S–s–ssss...."

I set the box down on the floor and move up beside her so I can see into the room better. "What is it?"

Her breathing is fast and shallow. "A... a..."

In the corner, I spot a slender, greyish-brown creature lazily sunning itself in a pool of sunshine.

"Oh," I say, with delight. "A snake!"

It suddenly stirs. Its head rises and its red tongue flickers in and out, tasting the air.

I grin. "Look, Nat, he's saying hello."

Natalie sways, suddenly light-headed, and I let go of the box to grab her arm and steady her.

"Whoa, it's okay, Nat. I don't think it's even a snake. I think it's a flap-footed lizard. It's actually known as the snake lizard because of its snake-like body. If it is, it's not venomous." Once I'm sure she isn't going to collapse, I release her arm and step toward the snake. "Let me take a closer look."

As I approach, the creature begins to slowly uncoil itself.

"Raine, no!" Natalie grabs a handful of my shirt and pulls me back toward the doorway.

"Nothing to worry about, Nat. Let go of me."

"Dad! Help!" she screams, hanging onto my shirt. "Dad!"

Mom enters the room, frowning. "What's wrong?"

I yank myself free from Natalie's grip and point to the corner. "Nat's all spazzed 'cause there's a snake lizard in here."

"A what!" Mom gasps.

"A flap-footed lizard," I tell her, peering closely at the reptile. "It looks like a snake but it's not one. Don't worry, it's just a lizard."

When Mom sees it, she stops cold. Her breath catches in her throat and her face blanches.

"That thing is not a lizard," she says. "It's a snake."

I shake my head. "No, Mom, it's a flap-footed lizard. Come up beside me here and have a closer look at it."

"I will not!"

"Okay, look from there then. See, it doesn't have front limbs, but you can see its tiny flap-like hind limbs. And it has outer ear openings. And watch its tongue when it flicks out. It's not forked like a snake's. That's just a harmless lizard. I'm pretty sure it is anyway."

"You're pretty sure?" Mom says, her voice quavering. "Where's your father? Go get your father."

"Why? I can get rid of it."

"Don't you go near that thing. Get your dad now!"

"But he's outside unloading the car."

"I don't care. Go get him now!" She touches Natalie's arm. "Come on, sweetheart. Raine, you, too. Let's all back out of the room slowly."

I sigh and walk past them as they nervously retreat. I set the box down in the hall and go outside, where I see Dad at the back of our SUV. He leans in and pulls out two large suitcases and a smaller tote bag. Carrying a suitcase in each hand and with the tote tucked under an armpit, he walks across the drive and up the path to the front door. Quinn follows with a smaller suitcase.

I see a spade lying in the grass below the kitchen window, then walk over to get it. The ground is so hot that it burns through the soles of my shoes, and my hand is nearly scalded when it brushes against the blade. Grabbing it by the wooden handle, I carry it into the house and up to the bedroom. I step past Mom and Nat, who have closed the bedroom door and are cowering in the hall outside it.

"What are you doing with that?" Mom says, looking at the spade. "Where's your dad?"

"He's too busy, Mom. Don't worry. I'll get rid of it."

She clutches my forearm. "Are you crazy? Do not go in there, Raine. I mean it."

"Oh, Mom, relax."

Despite her fear of the lizard, her eyes narrow. "Watch your mouth, Raine Hunter."

"I'll be fine. It's harmless. It's just a lizard."

She stares at me. "Just a lizard," she echoes in a whisper. "My soul."

I step past her, open the door, and enter the room. I cross the floor, holding the blade of the shovel toward the lizard.

"It's just a little-bitty thing. Aww, it's a baby, I think," I say over my shoulder to Mom and Natalie. They stand in the open doorway, watching me, eyes bulging.

"That thing is not a baby, not by any means," Mom says. "You be careful."

I stop three feet away from the lizard and gently prod it with the edge of the shovel. The lizard jerks its head back and then uncoils itself and begins to move toward me.

Natalie screams.

"Raine, stop that," Mom orders shakily, her face the colour of clay. "It's going to bite you. Leave it alone and get your father. Now."

I gently poke the lizard again and it lunges.

"Rainie, please, listen to Mom. Come out of there," Natalie says, near tears. Mom wraps an arm around her to comfort her.

"Nothing to worry about, Nat." Standing my ground, I jab carefully at the lizard again. This time it thrusts forward and I slide the edge of the blade under it.

"Got you," I cry, swiftly lifting the spade up into the air.

Natalie moans softly.

Holding the spade out in front of me, the lizard clinging to the blade, I walk toward the door. "Step aside, people."

Mom and Nat move like lightning out into the hall.

As I exit the bedroom, I look left to Mom and our eyes meet. I hold up the spade with the lizard draped over it and give her a triumphant smile.

She stares at me, and her expression, which I've seen more than enough times in my eleven years, says, *My youngest daughter is as bold as a wildfire, but she is not normal.*

Later that evening, we all gather in the living room, tired and sweaty. Except for some unpacked boxes sitting out on the back porch, we're all moved in.

"Now kids, I know we talked about this before, but now that we're here I want to go over it again," Dad says, his expression sobering. "We need to be extra vigilant around the waterways in Australia. There are about five crocodiles per one kilometre in the northern territory, but around here it climbs to nearly fifteen per kilometre. Most of the creeks in this area are known crocodile habitats."

Mom closes her eyes. "Oh, Rye, you never told me that we'd be in any immediate danger."

Dad pulls a white handkerchief from his back pocket and wipes the sweat from his face. "We aren't in any immediate danger, pet. Deacon Taylor told me there has only been one death by a crocodile around here in twenty years. An intoxicated young man who went swimming late at night with a group of young people in a known crocodile habitat." He smiles confidently. "There's really nothing to worry about. People have been living in the Outback for years. Tourists have been visiting these parts for years also, and have survived. We just have to be vigilant when we're hiking in the Outback or swimming in the river."

Natalie stares at Dad in disbelief. "Hiking in the Outback? Swimming in a crocodile-infested river? What are we? The Crocodile Dundee family?"

Dad chuckles softly, running his thumb over Mom's hand. "We are the Hunter family, and we are here to heal, restore, and grow the congregation of this church. Thus, we will be reaching out to people in and around Desolation Creek. That's our first priority. But when we have the time, we will visit the national parks, the historic and sacred sites, and experience Aboriginal culture. I want us to experience all the natural wonders of this magnificent country."

"Like the natural wonder we just found in the bedroom?" Mom says wryly.

Dad laughs, and Mom and I join in. Quinn is playing with a toy car and isn't paying attention. Nat still hasn't recovered from the ordeal and doesn't find it one bit funny.

Dad cups his chin sombrely. "Quinn, put the car down please and listen carefully. We need to be alert and cautious on land and around waterways, especially Curillin Creek, which is the closest crocodile habitat to our home. Look around you carefully at all times. Do you understand?"

Quinn, Nat, and I all nod vigorously, though I hear Nat swallow hard.

"My soul, Rye, they are children," says Mom in a low, rebuking tone. "You can't expect them to be on guard all the time when they're out playing."

"I *do* expect them to do just that when they're playing in the bushes around our property," he says with a stern tone. "As for the creek, you three must never go there for any reason. There's never been a crocodile attack at the river, but still, you are forbidden to go there alone to play or swim. Either your mom or I have to be with you. Understand?"

"Yes, Dad," Quinn and I say while Nat gazes at Dad in disbelief.

He nods toward a box sitting on the floor near the door. "I brought some books on all the animals, reptiles, spiders, and plants native to Australia, and in particular the Northern Territory. I want all three of you to read and study them. Memorize the pictures so you'll be able to identify and differentiate between the harmless and the lethal ones."

Quinn frowns. "Diff... Huh?"

"It means recognize, little bud. Memorize the pictures and pay special attention to the snakes and spiders so if you see one you'll know which ones are deadly."

Quinn nods. "Okay, Dad."

"I already did," I tell him.

Dad allows a small smile. "Look them over again."

I smile back. "Sure, Dad."

He looks at the three of us, his gentle blue eyes softening. "Chances are we will never see or encounter anything deadly. This isn't a lecture. I'm just reminding you all to be alert at all times. All right?"

We all nod soberly.

"I'm not afraid of snakes or spiders," says Quinn.

I shrug a shoulder. "Me neither."

Dad bobs his head in approval. "That's good, but never forget that the snakes and spiders here are not at all like the ones in Nova Scotia. The majority here are lethal."

By now, Mom looks stressed out and Nat looks like she's going to pass out. But I can't wait to see one of these lethal snakes or spiders—and I don't mean in a picture in one of my dad's books.

CHAPTER THREE

I'm studying the menu in Louisa's Diner and can't believe what I'm reading. The lunch special today is Louisa's Hot Kangaroo Dinner.

"That's odd," says Dad, coming up beside me and scanning the menu. "I thought Aussies weren't fond of eating kangaroo meat."

A woman in her fifties with long frizzy grey hair tied in a ponytail walks past us at the counter and overhears. She stops. "We aren't, but it's not always that easy to get beef or pork this far out in the bush."

"Right," Dad says. "I should have thought of that."

The woman's face gleams with a sheen of sweat. She's wearing beige hiking shorts, a white short-sleeved blouse with pockets on the front and white running shoes. Her nametag reads *Louisa*.

"Most of us try never to eat roo meat if we don't have to," she says. "But sometimes we have no choice. It's not wild, though. It's farmed. It's mostly just for the tourists."

Dad nods. "I see."

"You want some?"

He shakes his head. "No thanks."

"Good." The woman pauses, studies us, and there's a slight relaxing of her mouth. "You tourists?"

"No," Dad explains with a smile. "I'm the new pastor of the Blue Rock River Church."

"Oh, right," she says, nodding. But she doesn't smile back. "I heard some Canadian was moving here to take it over."

"Yes, that's me. I'm Rye Hunter." Dad tilts his head at me. "This is my daughter, Raine."

She smiles at us. "Well then, welcome to Desolation Creek."

"Thank you," he says. "So are you a member of the congregation?"

She narrows her eyes. "No, and I don't want to be," she says in a cool tone. "So let's just get that straight right from the get-go. Don't preach or quote Bible verses at me. And *do not* leave Bible tracts on my tables or in my bathrooms."

"Fair enough." Dad holds his smile, but I notice a trace of surprise and disappointment in his eyes.

She sees it, too, and softens her voice. "But don't let that stop you from trying others in town."

"It won't." He chuckles. "Wouldn't be much of a pastor if it did."

"I suppose not," she concedes. "You might be up against a wall here, though. So far no pastor has been able to keep that church going. This is a tough town, full of rough characters." She twists her mouth up wry smile. "The only places filled to the rafters on Sundays around here are the pubs. Don't know if you noticed, but there are six pubs and two liquor stores, and only two churches in this town, both of which are in danger of closing."

Dad nods but doesn't look worried. "I see."

Mom, Nat, and Quinn, who'd gone into the drugstore for a few items, come in then and join us. We walk across the room and sit in a booth along a side wall with a big plate-glass window overlooking the sidewalk and street. An old window air conditioner rattles and shudders, blowing warm, sticky air that doesn't do much to cool down the diner. I'm wearing shorts, and my thighs quickly stick to the vinyl seat.

Louisa comes over with a pad and pen in hand. "Nice-looking family," she says, smiling. Dad introduces the others. "Now what can I get you folks?"

Later, as we leave the diner, Dad walks through the tables and booths and invites each customer out to Sunday services. Louisa narrows her eyes as she watches him.

"Just inviting folks out, not handing out tracts," Dad assures her. She doesn't look happy but lets it go.

Outside, though, he hands out flyers to every person we pass. He even goes inside the shops and stores and invites the patrons inside to Sunday service.

I'm glad my parents never looked back as we climbed into the SUV and left town. When I looked back, I saw that nearly every person Dad had given a flyer either blithely or a little angrily tossed it into the air. The sidewalks were littered with his flyers.

Back at the house, it's still so hot inside that it feels like a wood furnace going full blast. The ceiling fans run constantly, but even after the sun goes down they provide no relief from the suffocating heat.

Mom lifts her blouse at the collar and shakes it to try to cool herself. "The fans are useless, Rye."

"I know, pet, but it's December, the dead of summer here."

"And there's an inch of dirt on every piece of furniture," she adds, dismayed. "No matter that I dusted today, the dirt came right back in. It's clinging to everything, including our clothes, skin, and hair."

"Well then, don't worry about it, pet. It's something we'll all have to get used to."

"I see someone already has," Mom says drily, noticing a Bible verse written in the thick dust on the coffee table. She reads aloud, "*For dust thou art, and unto dust shalt thou return. Genesis 3:19.*"[1] She turns and fixes her eyes right on me. "Now who wrote that, I wonder?"

I shrug. "You wanted me to memorize part of Genesis. I wrote it out to help me remember it."

Mom gives a weary sigh.

Dad frowns at me. "How about next time you're, ah, memorizing Bible verses, you dust the table after for your mother?"

"Sure, no problem."

---

[1] KJV.

CHAPTER FOUR

At dawn the following day, I wake to the tantalizing scent of pancakes, bacon, eggs, and hashbrowns wafting into the bedroom. My stomach grumbles as I hear the clank of pots, the clatter of dishes, and my dad singing. He makes the best pancakes in the world. They're thick yet fluffy and filled with fruit, usually blueberries or apples, with maple syrup and bacon, crispy the way I love it. I can eat three slices of bacon and four pancakes. That's my record to date.

I catapult out of bed, dress fast, and head to the bathroom to beat Nat, who's stirring.

"Good morning, tiger," Dad says, smiling and flipping a pancake at the same time. "How'd you sleep?"

"Great."

"Good. Are Nat and Quinn up?"

"Yes, Mom's helping Quinn get ready and Nat's just gone in the bathroom." I roll my eyes. "She'll take forever."

Dad only smiles at that and I'm reminded again that he and my mom seem to find everything Nat does charming, and everything I do unsettling.

"Are you hungry?" he asks.

"Starving. I'm going for five pancakes today. I want to set a new personal best."

He laughs. "Good, you'll need five. It's going to be a gorgeous day and I just got off the phone with Deacon Taylor. He apologized for not being here when we arrived. He was called out of town last minute. However, we're invited to his house tonight for a meet-and-greet dinner with the other deacons. We have the day to ourselves, so I'd like to get some hiking in before it gets too hot. They advise that no one hikes past 11:00 a.m. around here. I thought we'd drive down to Pekoes National Park and hike one of their less strenuous trails. What do you think? Sound good?"

"Sounds great, Dad."

I go to the cupboard to get dishes to set the table. I find five dusty plates and equally dusty glasses, as well as two dirty ceramic mugs. I give them all a wipe with a tea towel and place them on the table.

He juts his chin toward a drawer at the end of the counter. "Silverware's in that drawer."

I slide open the drawer and grab forks, knives, and spoons. "How far are we hiking?"

"Maybe four kilometres. That will be far enough for your brother. He's too young for anything more arduous. We'll follow a bushwalking trail northeast two and a half kilometres to some Aboriginal ruins and sacred burial grounds. There's also a national historic preservation site and an Indigenous Peoples' memorial of significance that I'd like us to see. I hear there's a shady picnic area with washrooms so we can have a quick lunch there before hiking back."

I nod, thinking that Mom and Natalie may only be able to manage a four-kilometre hike, too, considering searing temperatures.

"Tiger, this country is calling us to explore it, and I want us to see as much of it as possible whenever we have the opportunity," Dad says, his eyes full of anticipation.

I bob my head enthusiastically. "Me too, Dad."

He steps closer, ruffles my hair. "After you're done eating, see if you can find the boxes with all our hiking gear. I think they're the ones against the wall in the back porch. Find our boots, water canteens, and backpacks. Fill the canteens and put them in the pack along with a compass, binoculars, first aid kit, and matches."

"Sure."

"And when your mom comes down, help her make a good lunch and some snacks for the hike. There's some leftover chicken from supper. She can pack that, along with extra water and whatever else she decides."

I nod, but I'm a bit annoyed. Natalie is still in the bathroom and hasn't lifted a finger yet. Can't he see that I'm already helping him with breakfast?

"I think I know how to pack a picnic lunch for my own family, Rye," Mom says, entering the room. But she smiles when she says it.

He grins back, hands her a mug, and holds out the coffee pot. "I don't know what I was thinking. Coffee's ready. Want a cup?"

She laughs. "Yes, but don't think I don't know you're just trying to get back on my good side."

He pours her coffee and leans in for a quick kiss on the cheek.

"After we eat, I want to finish painting my name on the church sign out by the road," he tells her. "It won't take me long. I'll be right back to give you a hand."

"All right," she says.

After breakfast, I finish gathering our hiking gear and go outside to load it into the back of the SUV. The sun is already so bright and hot that it scalds my eyeballs. I put my hand over my eyes to shield them from the sun's rays and look around for my dad. He's standing on a tall ladder in front of the church sign, painting the last letter in his name. A shimmering wall of heat rises from the ground below the ladder. He's taken off his blue T-shirt and stuffed it into the back pocket of his shorts.

I shut the back door of the SUV and walk over to join him. He's climbed down off the ladder by now, eyeing his handiwork. His bare back glistens with sweat that rolls down and pools at the beltline of his shorts, leaving a dark wet spot.

BLUE ROCK RIVER CHURCH
Pastor Rye E. Hunter
<u>SERVICES</u>
Sunday School: 10 a.m.–11 a.m.
Sunday Services: 11 a.m.–12 a.m.
Wednesday Evening Prayer: 6:30 p.m.–7:30 p.m.

"Looks great, Dad."

"It does, doesn't it." He takes the T-shirt from his pocket and uses it to wipe the sweat from his face and chest.

"G'day, folks," a man's voice says from behind us.

Dad and I turn to see a man standing nearby in jeans, a pale blue T-shirt, and black boots. He's short and bony with leathery skin and deep lines around his eyes and the corners of his mouth. He has a thick bushy black moustache with grey in it.

"Hot as the fires of Hades, isn't it?" the man says.

"It sure is." Dad frowns as he peers over the man's shoulder to a dusty green Jeep parked about fifty feet away. "I never heard you drive in."

"Get's windy out here sometimes. Drowns out every little noise." He holds out his hand. "I'm Boyd Riggs, one of your deacons. Welcome to Desolation Creek and our little church."

Dad breaks out in a big smile and pumps the man's hand vigorously. "Nice to meet you, Boyd. I'm Rye Hunter and this is my daughter, Raine."

The man eyes me and nods, his greyish blue eyes gleaming in the sunlight.

Right then, Mom, Nat and Quinn come out of the house and join us in the driveway.

"This is my wife, Vivian, my daughter, Natalie, and my son, Quinn," says Did.

The man smiles at all three of them. "Nice to meet you, folks." Then he turns back to my dad. "So are you all moved in?"

"Pretty much."

Mr. Riggs lifts his black Crocodile Dundee hat and swipes the sweat from his brow before setting it back on his head. "Glad to hear it. I'm certainly looking forward to hearing your sermon on Sunday."

Dad grins. "Not as much as I'm looking forward to preaching it."

"Poor Cecil couldn't seem to get a handle on running a church out here, but maybe you'll do better."

"I plan to do just that."

"You're full of zeal, I see that. I like that. But listen… I came out to say hello, and also to talk to about a few things." Dad lifts a brow, waits. "This is the Outback and we've lost a few tourists and newbies in the past years."

Mom's eyes widen. "A few?"

Mr. Riggs smiles. "Well, okay… maybe three, four… something like that."

Mom gasps. Nat, who has taken to wearing thick-soled hiking boots, in and out of the house, looks down in fear, like she's surrounded by poisonous vipers and spiders. She seems afraid to take her eyes off the ground even for a minute.

Mr. Riggs nods at our house. "I'm just pulling your leg. We've only lost the one, and that was Pastor Cecil's mother who lived in the parsonage with him and Stella. The old woman walked around the property wearing open-toed sandals all the time. Had arthritis bad in her feet and they were too swollen to fit in a shoe. I warned her at least a hundred times, told her to buy a bigger shoe, but she wouldn't. Naturally, she got bit by a redback and that was that. Happened on a Sunday during services so it upset a lot of people."

"Goodness," says Mom shakily.

Mr. Riggs waves a hand in the air. "I'm sure it was a once-in-a-lifetime thing. Still, wear shoes all the time, inside or outside, in church or even in the parsonage. Wear them right until you jump into bed. Too many spiders about to take a chance. And don't forget to turn them upside-down at night and shake them out in the morning before you put them on again."

"We will," Dad assures him.

Without taking his eyes off Mom, he warns, "You kids keep an eye out for snakes and spiders when you're running around here." He lifts a hand and whirls it around. "Take a good look around. The ground's nothing but dirt and weeds, and that's a good thing. Can any of you tell me why?"

"So you can see the snakes good," I say.

Nat and Mom simultaneously draw in quick breaths. Quinn studies the ground with a hopeful expression, still intent on catching something for a pet.

Mr. Riggs scratches his chin, his eyes on me now. "Exactly. You're a clever girl. The lack of grass is a good thing out here because bare grounds makes it easier to spot snakes coming from a long way off. But the lack of grass doesn't help with the nasty little buggers called cut snakes... you can't see them. They bury themselves in the sand, and if you walk or run by they'll poke right up and bite you in the ankle before you know what hit you. Their venom's lethal if you don't get help in time. And there are copses of brush, rocks, and dead tree branches even in the desert. You watch when you're stepping close to brush or over rocks or dead branches, because snakes and insects like to rest in the cool shade of them. And same goes for when you're playing around the creeks or rivers here, especially Curillin Creek and the Blue Rock River. Keep a sharp eye out for crocodiles. They love to eat anything small... dogs, cats, but especially little kids."

The man studies us with a strange smile, and I see my parents exchanging displeased glances.

"Hey, now," Dad says.

"Just yanking your chains a little." Mr. Riggs tilts his head in an apologetic gesture. "I'm exaggerating the danger a little, but it's because I do have to warn you. I can't stress enough how important it is for all of you to be alert. I'm not saying venomous snakes are everywhere you look, or that all our waterways are crocodile-infested, but they are here. This is snake and gator country. It's a hostile environment. You're in the Outback, after all."

Dad nods. Mom shudders, and I'm not sure if it's because she's scared or she finds the man repulsive.

"Keep in mind that we've only had that one spider bite fatality, and only one crocodile fatality in the past twenty years," Mr. Riggs continues. "And the young man who died went swimming late at night in Curillin Creek, which is a known crocodile habitat. He was a local and knew better, so folks think he must have had a death wish."

Dad puts his arm around Mom. "We'll be careful. I've already spoken to my family about all that."

Mr. Riggs turns his peculiar smile on Dad. "Good on ya then." Dad nods but a bit stiffly. "So I'll see you all tonight over at Deacon Taylor's for the welcoming dinner?"

"Yes, you will," Dad says. "We'll be back from our hike in plenty of time."

"Good. Did Deacon Taylor say we'll be having a quick deacons' meeting with you after the meal to talk things over? Christmas is just around the corner and we have our upcoming program and service. We also go carolling around town to try to reach out to the lost."

"I understand, and yes, Deacon Taylor mentioned all that," Dad says. "Should we bring anything to dinner?"

"Did Deacon Taylor ask you to bring anything?"

"No."

He smiles. "Then I'd say just bring yourselves. And remember, Sunday will be the real welcoming service when you can meet the rest of the congregation."

Dad smiles back. "We're looking forward to both events."

"All right, we'll see you later today then. Enjoy your hike." He gives a little wave as he turns and strolls back toward his vehicle. "Cheers."

As we all walk to the SUV, I hear Mom say to Dad, "That man is a deacon of this church?"

"He is."

"He certainly has an odd sense of humour. I didn't find his comment about crocodiles eating children one bit funny."

Dad lifts his shoulder in a slight shrug. "I guess a rough country takes rough characters to live in it."

"Mmmm."

CHAPTER FIVE

I'm hiking along the trail behind my parents and Quinn, keeping a sharp eye out for snakes and spiders. All I've seen so far are harmless insects and one tiny green lizard. The air smells of dust, dead weeds, and brush. The blazing sun, despite Mom slathering suntan lotion on me, beats down and burns my face, ears, and neck. Despite the insect repellent she's sprayed on me from head to toe, I'm bitten relentlessly by tiny flies.

Nat walks grudgingly behind me because she doesn't like hiking. She isn't an outdoors person. She prefers to curl up in her room with a book or play the piano for hours. I love the outdoors. I'm passionate about books, too, but I prefer to read on rainy days or at night in bed.

I glance back and see that Nat is falling farther behind with each step we take. "Come on, Nat, hurry up!"

She heaves out an annoyed sigh but starts walking faster.

We walk on for another ten yards, and then I see a blur of movement to my right. A huge snake is slithering across the ground toward me, its pale fawn skin rippling. It emits a faint rustling sound as it glides over the dry weeds.

I stop dead. My heart seizes. My throat closes.

It's a deadly Taipan, Australia's most dangerous species of snake and the world's most venomous. A single drop of its venom can kill one hundred men. It's as thick as my dad's arm and at least six feet long. Its body is dark and its head and neck black as tar.

It stops a few feet from me, then slides into a tight S-shaped curve. It lifts its rectangular-shaped head and flicks its red tongue in the air.

Natalie comes up behind me but doesn't notice that I've stopped and nearly collides into me.

"Why'd you stop?" she says, annoyed.

"Snake," I whisper, nodding my head almost imperceptibly to the right. Nat makes a terrified gurgling sound in her throat.

"Dad," I call out in a shaky low voice. I can barely hear myself over the thundering of my heart in my ears.

Mercifully he hears. He stops, turns around, and frowns. "What's wrong?"

"Snake. Taipan."

I hope my whisper will carry to him, because I'm terrified to speak any louder and startle the snake into striking at me. I recall reading that the Taipan sometimes strikes its prey eight times. I'd never be able to move out of the way in time to save myself—and I don't know if Dad can get me to the park warden's office in time for the shots of antivenom I'll need.

If it strikes, I'm dead. It may go for Natalie, too.

Dad nods and Mom, who has moved up beside him, opens her mouth to scream, but only a peculiar tiny squeak comes out. She reaches behind her and holds Quinn firmly against the back of her legs.

Behind me, Nat's breath is fast and jagged, like she has the hiccups. She's standing so close to me and shaking so badly that I can hear the whisper of her clothing moving against me.

"No one move," Dad says in a voice almost too soft to be heard. He bends over slowly and picks up a thick tree branch from the ground.

I stand stone still. Ice fills my stomach. Nausea rises in my throat.

The snake sits motionless, its head held high, its cold, dark eyes locked on me.

Dad motions with a finger over his lips for us all to be quiet. He steps softly down the trail toward Nat and me, the branch clutched in his hands. He sees the snake and halts, eyes fixed intensely on it. Silent terror falls like a shadow over us.

"Girls," he whispers, "start stepping backwards. Slowly, though… Baby steps."

Nat and I take one step back, gingerly.

The snake lifts its head and body, revealing its yellowish and orange blotched underside. It lets out a low hiss that nearly stops my heart cold. Then its head sways back and forth, ready to strike.

"Keep going," Dad says softly.

We take another step, pause, and then a third.

Dad inches closer, then slowly lifts the branch high over his head to bring it down on the viper. But the snake abruptly slithers into the brush, vanishing in a dizzying blur.

We stand there, staring in stunned silence at the spot where the snake had been.

Dad recovers first. "Don't move yet, anyone." He steps cautiously toward the brush, the branch still held out in front of him.

He peers into the brush and pokes around a little with the tree limb. After a moment, he straightens up and blows out a breath.

"Well, that was a little hairy. But it's gone now." He looks up. "Lord, thank you for your protection."

"A little hairy?" snaps Mom, horror in her eyes. "That was more than a little hairy, Rye. We're turning around and going back to the car right now."

"That wasn't as close a call as it seemed, pet. That was a Taipan, but it was an inland Taipan, commonly called a 'fierce snake.' Unlike its bad-tempered cousin, the coastal Taipan, fierce snakes can be timid. This one clearly was more afraid of us than we were of it. I think we should push on. We'll be fine, really."

"I think it's called a fierce snake for good reason," Mom counters.

Dad shakes his head. "The word fierce describes its powerful venom. I've read that many reptile keepers regard it a docile snake to work with."

Mom casts a dark look at him. "Oh, my mistake. Taipan snakes aren't dangerous, they're just our shy friends."

Dad sighs. "Sarcasm doesn't become you, Viv."

Her expression suggests that she wants to wrap her hands around his neck and choke him to death. "Doesn't it? Well, that's just too bad. If we're going to live in this snake-filled country, it's something *we'll all have to get used to,*" she says, imitating my dad's voice.

Dad puts his hands on his hips. "Now, Viv, I think you're overreacting."

She points to the blistering red orb of the sun. "And another thing. It's much too hot for a long hike for Quinn. He's too young and he's getting badly sunburnt. The sun is broiling all of us."

The sun is so hot that it feels like it's burning my eyeballs, even though I'm wearing sunglasses. It scorches my lungs when I inhale.

I think Mom has a good point. Even though we're hiking during the recommended time of day, it does seem awfully hot for young children.

"But we're almost at the preservation site, pet. We've less than a kilometre to go." Dad gives her a pleading look. "There's a shaded picnic area there. Washrooms and a water tap. We can rest, cool off, and have a relaxing lunch. We've come this far. Just one dry riverbed to cross and then we'll be there. We might as well continue on."

Mom shakes her head. "No, Rye."

"Yes, we'll be fine. Come on now."

Mom is livid, but Dad only averts his gaze from her to us kids. "All set, gang?" Without waiting for our reply, he starts off down the trail again.

Quinn glances uncertainly at Mom, but she's staring at Dad's back like there's a bullseye on it. As Quinn starts after Dad, Nat and I stand behind Mom, waiting to see what she'll do. She just watches him for a minute before reluctantly following. Her hiking shoes kick up clouds of powdery sand as she steps furiously along the path.

We walk along in silence for a while. Mom hangs back, keeping an eye on us.

"That snake was enormous and it was staring right at you," Nat says quietly. "Yet you looked as cool as a cucumber, Raine. Weren't you scared?"

"Petrified."

"Me too. I've never been so scared before in all my life. But you know, Dad may be right. It did seem more afraid of us than we were," she says, trying to be brave.

I smile, admiring her sudden spunk.

"Not that I ever want to see another snake in my life," she says, her voice quavering.

"No," I say, chuckling.

CHAPTER SIX

F ace burning, my dad clears his throat. "Yes, I suppose we should have taken the guided tour, but as you said, the odds of encountering a Taipan are low to zero."

Deacon Taylor smiles, sits back in his chair, and folds his hands over his large belly. He seems to sweat more than anyone else in the room. His hair is damp and his white dress shirt is covered in sweat patches. Throughout the meal, he's been repeatedly dabbing at the sweat on his face with a white handkerchief.

"True," Mr. Taylor says. "But you're new here and you have young children. It's not just the snakes or venomous spiders, you have to be careful of the heat."

Mr. Riggs scowls. "It's not his fault. It's the Outback. Heat and snakes come with the territory. He can't keep them locked up in the house every day. Nothing wrong with taking your family on that hike, Rye. I'd have done the same."

My dad gives him an appreciative nod, then sees my mom glaring at him. He turns his head and studies a spot on the wall.

"You can't avoid the snakes," Mr. Riggs says. "We've had more than one come right into the house in broad daylight. Last year, a nasty brown snake came into our living room one evening and crawled right over the toe of my boot. Scared poor Miriam so bad she took off out of the house like a scalded cat." He slaps his hand on his thigh and laughs hard.

Nat loses colour, drops her head, and pokes at her food with her fork. My mom seems to chew the food in her mouth for a long time before she finally swallows.

Mrs. Riggs shakes her head at her husband, but not like she minds his laughter. She's the complete opposite of him, tall and sturdily built with warm green eyes and a cheery disposition.

Mr. Taylor pats his mouth with a napkin. "I think all I'm trying to say is to be very careful until you all get used to living here. Until then, when heading into the bushland, hike when it's cooler and take the guided tours."

"I'll remember that the next time," my dad says, his tone clipped. He's smarting from being rebuked in front of everyone gathered around the table.

Mrs. Taylor gives her husband a look, then lifts a white oval platter of barbequed chicken pieces from the centre of the table. "Who wants more chicken?" she asks, rescuing my dad.

"I do, please," I say. "It's delicious."

"Me too, please." Quinn holds up his plate. "Mrs. Taylor, you're a good cooker."

She smiles at us with her kind walnut-coloured eyes. "Thank you. I'm so happy you both like it. Natalie, what about you?"

Natalie shakes her head morosely.

Mrs. Riggs, sitting next to Quinn, reaches out and tousles his hair. "That's what I like to see. A hungry boy. Reminds me of my own son when he was little."

"Where is your son?" my mom asks her. "Does he live here in Desolation Creek with you?"

"Yes, he does. Tyler's seventeen and will be in Grade Twelve come March," she replies. "He's at his grandparents' house right now, but he'll be home tomorrow. You'll all meet him at church on Sunday."

Nat instantly looks up from her plate.

"And you'll meet our two," Mrs. Taylor adds, smiling at Natalie. "Our Charlotte is fourteen and our Ethan is thirteen. You and Ethan will be in the same Sunday school class. They're at youth camp this week but will be home after that. I'm sure you'll become fast friends. This might be a small church, but our youth group is very active. They go bowling, mini-golfing, and swimming at the river."

Natalie's face brightens considerably.

Mrs. Riggs pulls the collar of her rose-coloured cotton dress away from her neck. "Her Ethan is a good-looking young man, too, if I do say so myself." She nudges Natalie gently with her elbow.

"Miriam…" Mr. Riggs says.

"What? I may be old, but I'm not blind, Boyd." She throws her head back and laughs. "Ethan takes after his mom."

Mrs. Taylor's face flushes.

I believe it, for I find Mrs. Taylor so pretty with her shapely face, striking brown eyes and hair, and naturally bronzed skin.

"Miriam," Mr. Riggs says again, allowing a small smile. Though he seems harsh, I notice that his face softens when he looks at Mrs. Riggs.

Mr. Taylor looks at his bare arm and makes a face. "Yes, mercifully for them both Ethan and Charlotte look like their mother, and not me with my dull hazel eyes and pasty skin."

We all laugh, Natalie the happiest and loudest. Appetite renewed, she forks up a piece of chicken and pops it hungrily into her mouth.

The sun is descending when we leave the Taylors' and head home. The heat is still blistering, though, and the whine of night insects rises like a buzzsaw. Heatwaves undulate over the hot blacktop of the two-lane. On both sides of the road, the land is flat, treeless, and parched. The air smells of melted asphalt and baked earth.

In the car, my parents aren't speaking. We drive home in bone-chilling silence.

Later, the atmosphere in the house is strained, the tension unbearable. When Quinn goes up to bed, Nat and I go up, too, even though it's still early. I lay in bed, unable to sleep as I hear them arguing in the kitchen. I slip out of the bedroom and stand listening at the top of the staircase.

"Oh, you," Mom says, still smouldering. "You always get these crazy ideas in your head without thinking them through. You're too impulsive and careless. We have young children and neither of us are seasoned hikers. You heard Deacon Taylor. We should have taken the guided hike, not gone out on our own. It wasn't only unwise, it was dangerous. Raine could have easily been bitten by that snake."

"Yes, I did hear Deacon Taylor, and I also heard him say it was extremely rare to encounter a Taipan like we did," Dad responds. "He said the odds of that happening again are likely zero to none."

"I don't care about the odds. I care about my children. You have dragged us into some foolish escapades before, but nothing like this. Nothing this perilous."

"Now, pet," Dad says soothingly, "if we—"

"Don't you understand that we could lose a child here, Rye?" Mom shouts, cutting him off.

"And don't you understand that this is God's will for us?" Dad counters, his own temper rising.

"Are you sure about that, Rye? Or is bringing your young family to live in this wild dangerous country all your own will?"

"Of course it isn't! Have a little faith, Vivian."

The room goes silent. The friction in the kitchen is electric, so intense that I can feel it from the top of the stairway.

"Have a little faith?" Mom says finally, with ice in her voice.

"Yes, pet, please…" Dad is trying to erase the sting, but it's too late. I hear a chair scrape back and Mom's footsteps head out of the kitchen toward their bedroom.

"Viv, come on now, don't go to bed angry. Let's finish this!" Dad calls out to her, but Mom footsteps just thud harder on the floorboards. "Pet, please, come back."

I hurry back into my room, keeping the door open a crack so I can peer down the stairs to the hall.

Dad scrapes his chair back and stalks out of the kitchen to the front door. "Fine, be unreasonable then."

I watch Mom stop in front of their bedroom door. "If one more thing happens, one more little thing, Rye, I promise you I'll take the kids and go back to Nova Scotia."

She turns and goes into their bedroom, slamming the door shut so hard behind her that it sounds like a gunshot.

CHAPTER SEVEN

TWO MONTHS LATER

My parents are visiting an elderly church member who's ill, and Nat, who just turned fourteen, is in charge of me and Quinn. Nat and I are reading books while Quinn plays with toy cars. It's stifling out and I'm sweating like a pig. The ceiling fan does nothing but push hot air down into our faces, its ancient motor releasing a steady buzz that sounds like a cloud of cicadas swarming around my head.

"Nat, can we please go outside?" Quinn asks for what must be the twentieth time since our parents left. "I want to look for a Daly Waters frog."

"No, it's too hot out." Nat doesn't even look up from her book. "And Dad said to stay inside until they get home."

He looks at me with pleading eyes. "Raine, please."

"No, Quinn. You heard Nat."

"But it rained earlier. I think I could find one in a puddle in the yard," he says. "If we wait, the puddles will be all dried up."

I shake my head. "I'll take you out when Mom and Dad get home. We'll find one, don't worry."

He frowns at me but goes back to playing with his cars.

I begin reading again and get swept away in the book, which is about lethal snakes in Australia. It's so interesting.

"Where's Quinn?" Nat says later, yawning as she closes her book and sits up on the couch.

I reluctantly pull my eyes from the book and see that Quinn's cars are spread all over the floor but he isn't in the room.

"Quinn!" I call out, but there's no answer.

Nat swings her legs over the couch down to the floor. "Quinn?"

The house is silent. The only sound is the ticking of the clock on the kitchen wall.

"Quinn! Where are you?" Nat shouts, but he doesn't answer.

"I bet he went outside to look for that frog." I close my book and set it on the floor beside me. "You look upstairs and I'll look down here. If he's not up there, meet me outside."

Nat goes upstairs and I check all the rooms downstairs. I still can't find him.

I go out the kitchen door and stop on the back step, placing a hand over my eyes to shield them from the harsh sunlight. "Quinn!" I yell as I scan the backyard.

But there's no reply and I can't see him anywhere.

I shout louder, annoyed now. "Quinn, where are you? Answer me!"

The back door opens and shuts with a bang as Nat comes up beside me. "He's not upstairs."

"He's not back here, either. And he's not answering."

"He's in big trouble," Nat says. "Just wait till I tell Mom and Dad."

"You check in front of the house and I'll check over by the church. He can't have gone far."

"He better not have," Nat says, nervously looking around. Though Quinn and I have explored all over the property, Nat never has. She's too afraid.

He's not in front of the house or around the church, which is locked up tight, so we walk across the backyard toward the path that leads down to the river. I'm growing nervous because the land is flat and other than for some brush we can see a long way. He's nowhere in sight.

We reach an area of thicker brush and a copse of thin trees where the path to the river begins.

I let out a worried breath. "He's not anywhere around. He must have gone down to the river to look for that stupid frog."

"He better not have. He knows Mom and Dad said to never go down to the river alone," Nat says. "It's too close to Curillan Creek and there's crocodiles there."

I eye the path, deeply troubled. "Yeah, but he's only six and he's nuts about frogs. He's too young to truly understand the danger. And I didn't tell anyone, but I caught him right here yesterday. He told me he saw a frog on the path. If I didn't stop him, I think he might have kept going."

"Oh no… Quinn…" Nat moans. "We need to go back to the house and call Mom and Dad."

"And just leave Quinn here? It could take at least forty minutes for them to get here, plus the time it takes for us to go back and make the call…"

Nat looks back at the house. "Still, we have to call them."

"Okay, you go phone them and I'll wait here and keep shouting for Quinn. Maybe he'll turn up first."

Nat nods, then turns and races toward the house.

I keep yelling out Quinn's name and then listening intently for his voice, but I don't hear him.

A few minutes later, Nat comes running back, breathless.

"Mrs. Daye said Mom and Dad left ten minutes ago and told her they were going to stop in town for groceries and then at the post office. She doesn't drive, so she can't go look for them. She's phoning the Taylors now to ask them to drive into town and find Mom and Dad to let them know what's happened."

"Oh no," I cry out, my blood turning to ice in my veins. "What if they aren't home? Even if they are, what if it takes too long for them to find Mom and Dad?" I look down the path desperately. "That might be too late for Quinn. We have to go look for him now."

Nat looks down the path in fear. "No."

"We have no choice. It's going to take Mom and Dad too long to get here, even if the Taylors find them. We have to find Quinn before a snake or a crocodile finds him first."

Nat's face loses all colour and she sways.

I reach out and grab her arm to steady her. "Look, you wait here or go back to the house. I'll go look for Quinn. He's likely just somewhere between here and the river."

Nat gives a sharp shake of her head. "No. I'm responsible for you, too. I'm already going to be in trouble for not watching Quinn better. I can't let you go down there alone."

"Then we both have to go now. Nat, we're losing precious time standing here talking if he's down there. He could die."

She closes her eyes briefly and draws in a shaky breath. "Okay… but if we don't see him, we come back home and wait for Mom and Dad."

"Yes. Now, let's go!"

I take off at a jog down the narrow path as Nat follows me. I keep a sharp eye out for snakes, and we slow to walk at times to call out his name and listen for his voice calling back.

We follow the path through the brush for about a half-kilometre down to the riverbank. We emerge from the path onto the sand and look up and down the beach.

I swipe my forehead with the back of my hand. It's a brutally hot day. Even though it's nearly four o'clock, the temperature hasn't dropped. Our flesh is sticky, our faces slick with sweat.

"Quinn! Quinn!" we both scream, panic-stricken.

But all we hear is the sound of the cool water whispering over smaller stones and roaring over large rocks.

Tears flood Nat's eyes and her chin quivers. "Oh no, Raine, where is he?"

"Let's look further down the beach. Maybe he's in the brush along the bank."

We walk about a hundred metres down the beach searching the brush. We soon reach a secluded sandy area and stop there. Near the bank the water is slow and calm, slipping over the glossy bluish-black river stones with hardly a murmur. Not far from shore, the water is higher, the current stronger.

We step into the brush, calling out for Quinn. I keep a nervous eye out for snakes and Nat stays close to me. But all we hear is the murmur of the water and the whirr of insects in the bushes.

We come out of the brush and face the water. The air is hot and thick and I can see dark clouds and heat lightning on the horizon. I hear the low rumble of thunder and feel sick to my stomach with worry and fear.

We're farther down the beach from where our parents take us swimming, closer to where the creek empties into the river. There are danger signs posted everywhere here. I'm terrified that Quinn might have been bitten by a snake and is lying somewhere nearby, dying. Or maybe he chased a frog to close to the river and went in over his head. I'm even more frightened that he went to the creek where there's a lot more frogs.

"We need to go check the creek, Nat. He may have gone there."

"What! No!"

"We can't just leave without checking," I say, but the very thought of going to the creek sends an icy chill through me. I take in a deep breath to calm myself. "Come on, Nat."

I walk along the river's edge, surreptitiously scanning the water so Nat won't see that I'm looking for Quinn there. I'm so scared for him that I can feel my pulse thudding in my throat.

Nat hurries up beside me. She crosses her arms over her chest as we walk. Her entire body is trembling violently.

"If we don't see him right away and he doesn't answer our calls, we leave," she says.

"Yes," I agree. From the corner of my eye I catch dark movement in the water to my left. My blood runs cold.

Oh no, I think. *Quinn...*

And then Natalie screams—a scream so full of terror that it chills my blood. I watch in horror as a huge crocodile lunges up out of the water, jaws wide, and seizes Nat around the waist, pulling her down into the river.

Razor-sharp shock slices up my spine and freezes me to the spot.

The water thrashes all around and Nat surfaces right in front of me. She's on her back, floating parallel to me, head submerged, the croc's jaws clamped securely around her hips.

Strangely, the crocodile goes still, its cold eyes observing me over Natalie's body, as if it's considering attacking me, too.

Then Natalie's head breaks the surface. "Help, Raine, help!"

Her screams echo up and down the quiet shore. The terror in her screams hits me like a slap, snaps me out of my shocked paralysis. My heart throbs in my chest as I bend down and grab her right arm with both my hands, dig my toes deep into the sand and try to pull her out of the crocodile's mouth.

The croc stamps its tail hard on the water like a war cry, splashing water into my face and eyes. I clutch Nat's arm more tightly and the croc and I fight a deadly tug-of-war for Natalie's life. The croc whips up sprays of water and sand from the river's floor into the air. In the water I notice something dark pooling around Natalie's waist, something with a metallic smell. With rising horror, I recognize it as blood. I force the realization from my mind. It's too terrible to accept.

"Oh, God, help me," Natalie cries out as she punches and claws at the croc's snout in a desperate battle to free herself.

I yank on Nat's arm with all my might, but the crocodile is huge, at least six feet and more than five hundred pounds. I'm five feet and weigh a hundred pounds. My toes begin to slip in the sand and the croc pulls us farther out.

"Raine, help me, I don't want to die," Natalie pleads, her eyes staring up at me, burning with terror.

"Fight, Nat! Punch it!" I shout with mounting horror.

The croc continues to drag us out until I'm nearly chest-deep. The current is stronger and my toes lose what little power had been anchoring them in the sand. I can't keep my balance. I'm coughing and choking on the river water pouring into my mouth. My fingers cramp as my hands slip on Nat's arm. I kick my legs furiously, trying to pull us back to shore, but it's futile.

Weakened, sliding further into shock, Natalie whimpers and goes still.

"Oh Lord, please help us," I cry, begging God.

Then Nat lets out a low moan and her head drops beneath the surface. Her long auburn hair fans out atop the water.

In an act of desperation, for I can no longer keep a tight grip on her arm, I let go with my left hand and snatch a handful of her hair. Still grasping her arm with my right hand, I dig my toes deeper into the sand and pull with all my strength.

And then the crocodile decides it's had enough. Its tail flicks up out of the water, slashing my face as it flips over and rips Natalie out of my hands and drags her under.

The roiling water settles and I stand there, my head whipping left and right, left and right, frantically searching for Natalie.

"Nat! Nat!" I shout at the top of my lungs, the screams reverberating across the river and bouncing back off the bank on the other side.

But my beloved sister, my beloved Nat, is gone.

I turn and wade furiously through the water and back to shore. Chest heaving, exhausted, I stumble onto the beach.

I turn around and face the river. The surface glitters brightly under the sunlight. I'm in shock, shivering violently, staring at the spot where Natalie vanished. Blood gushes from the gash on my face. Thick strands of her hair are still tangled in my fingers.

Up on the highway, a car screeches its tires. There's the distant, mournful cry of a bird. Then black storm clouds slide over the sun and a hush falls over the suddenly darkened beach.

I hear some young people's voices calling out, asking what's wrong. It's teenagers on the beach and they've heard my cries for help. I take off running as fast as I can toward them, screaming at the top of my lungs for help.

CHAPTER EIGHT

"Oh no, no!" Mom cries out. "Oh, please Lord, no!"

Her face collapses as she crumples into a kitchen chair. Shoulders slumped, hands covering her face, she wails uncontrollably.

Dad staggers back against the kitchen wall like he's been kicked in the chest by a horse. He turns, leans his forehead against the wall, and weeps, his back heaving with great gulping sobs.

I stand in the middle of the room, a blanket from the trunk of the police constables' patrol car still draped around my shoulders. My trembling body is so heavy with shock and grief that I'm breathing irregularly and can barely stay on my feet.

The constables, a man and a woman, stand behind me, their expressions sad. They clear their throats and murmur about how they'll keep my parents posted with any news of the search for Natalie's body. They tell them once again how sorry they are, then quietly leave the room, walk down the hall, and let themselves out.

"Dad, I'm sorry," I sob once I hear the door shut behind them.

But he won't even look at me.

The wound on my face throbs with pain that nearly makes me throw up. "Dad…"

He stops crying and turns to face me, his eyes swollen, puffy, and red-rimmed.

"You're sorry?" he repeats with spite.

I nod, too frightened by his fury to say anything more.

He points a finger at me. "It was your idea, wasn't it? It was your idea to go down to the river and look for Quinn, wasn't it?"

I remain silent.

"Yes, it was your idea. I know you." He nods, glaring at me. "Nat wouldn't have gone there if you hadn't pushed her to do it. This is your fault."

"Rye, no," Mom says without raising her head.

Though he's always tried hard to conceal it, despite how alike he and I are, I've always suspected that Natalie was his favourite. Now, as he glares accusingly at me, I know I was right.

"Dad…"

As quick as lightning, he leaps forward and grabs me by my upper arms, lifts me, and presses me against the wall, his fingers digging into the flesh of my arms.

"Are you happy now?" he says, holding me there, his face only an inch from mine, seething. "Nat's death is all your doing."

His rage petrifies me. I see the potential for violence in his eyes.

Mom lifts her head and leaps to her feet. "Rye! Put her down at once."

Dad releases me and I slide to the floor, able to stand again but only very shakily.

Mom slumps back into her chair. "Stop it, Rye. That's enough. You don't know what you're doing or saying."

"Oh, I know exactly what I'm saying," he shouts, standing only a foot from me, his stare hardening.

"Rye, stop! You're going to traumatize her more than she already is," Mom says. "And you're going to wake Quinn."

She looks up toward the stairway where I know now that Quinn is sleeping in bed. When my parents arrived home, Quinn had told them that he'd been angry with Nat and me for not taking him outside. To get back at us, he'd hidden under some clothes at the back of his closet and ignored our shouting. He had just wanted to scare us.

Then he fell asleep in the closet and didn't wake up until our parents got home.

Mom looks at me, tears pouring down her face. "Come here, Raine."

The accusation and recrimination in my dad's eyes are too much. I run to Mom, tears pouring down my face. She opens her arms and embraces me. She kisses me above my right cheek, careful to avoid the thick bandage covering my wound, a deep gash that took more than fifty stiches to close.

"Rye, no more, I mean it." Mom strokes my head, her voice cracking with grief. "She's just a child."

Dad releases an ugly, bitter snort. "That may be so, but we've lost our oldest child. We've lost our beautiful Natalie because of her recklessness."

"No," Mom says. "This is no one's fault. You heard what the constables said. It's the first time a crocodile attack has occurred in that area so far from the creek—and they only went there because they were worried Quinn was lost or hurt."

"Doesn't matter, Viv! We forbade her to go there. She shouldn't have disobeyed us in the first place. And Quinn wasn't even down there. If she'd just waited for us, this wouldn't have happened. And you know as well as I do that Nat wouldn't have gone down there to look for Quinn without Raine badgering her."

Mom closes her eyes. "Rye, please," she murmurs in anguish.

Dad goes quiet and stares at me for a long moment, his blue eyes as shiny and cold as river stones. Then he nods slowly. When he speaks next, his condemnation ricochets off the kitchen walls and through the rooms of the house. "You are responsible for your sister's death."

"Rye, no," Mom says, holding her hands up to stop him. "That's not true. It's ugly talk."

"It… is… true."

He steps toward me again, and I flinch involuntarily.

Mom moves between us. She looks Dad in the eye, and says quietly but firmly, "I want you to stop this. I mean it. Stop, now."

"Fine. I'm going down to the river to help look for Natalie." He casts one last terrible glare at me, then turns and stalks out of the room. A moment later, the front door opens and slams shut. The SUV starts up and roars down the driveway.

Mom looks at me, her soft brown eyes streaming with tears. "Pay no mind to what he says. He's out of his mind with grief."

"But Mom, he's right. Dad hates me."

She shakes her head, fiercely, then reaches out for me and presses me so tight against her chest that I can hear her broken heart beating fast and erratically. "No, he doesn't. Don't listen to him. He didn't mean what he said. It's just his sorrow talking."

But the reproach in my dad's eyes, his harsh words, have sliced me like razors, shredding my heart, scarring me much more deeply than the horrid wound on my face.

An immense wave of sorrow washes through me. Broken inside and out, I slip out of Mom's embrace and stumble out of the room.

"Raine, come back. Stay here with me…"

"I can't, Mom."

I climb the stairs and go into my bedroom. Sitting on the edge of my bed in the darkness, I look across the room to Natalie's bed. My heart burns with shame and guilt. The blankets are still thrown back from when she climbed out of bed this morning.

"Oh, Nat, I'm so sorry," I whisper, my voice choking.

I hang my head and weep in the horrible hollow silence.

Later, Dad returns from the river and I hear my parents talk in the kitchen. I slip out of my room and stand at the top of the stairs.

"We can't stay here," Dad says. "I can't stay here. I'll hand in my resignation to the board of deacons tomorrow."

"Where will we go?" Mom asks in a quavering voice.

"Home, pet. We'll take Nat home to Nova Scotia. I want her buried in Blackheart Bay."

I slip down a few steps and peer through the railing into the kitchen. My parents are sitting at the table, facing each other, holding each other's hands.

"But how?" Mom sobs. "They said her body may never be recovered. I can't go home without her, Rye. We can't."

"They'll find her, pet. I know they will. We'll wait however long it takes."

"Yes, but how can we take her home if it takes a long time?"

"We may have to have her cremated," Dad says sorrowfully.

"No!"

"I understand, pet. I don't like the idea either, but we may have no other choice. I don't want to bury her here. We can't leave our Nat behind."

Mom releases Dad's hands, slides off the chair, and drops to her knees on the floor and wails. Dad drops down beside her, gently putting an arm around her and murmuring something low to comfort her.

I slink back to my room and shut the door softly behind me. My chest feels so crushed that I can hardly draw a breath. We're going home. Because of me, Nat's dead and everything my dad has hoped and wanted here in Australia is over. I've destroyed everyone, everything.

Two days later, they find human remains inside the six-foot crocodile believed to have killed Natalie. The crocodile is found by wildlife officers glutted and sunbathing on the banks of Curillin Creek. A specialist from Alice Springs examines the animal and then euthanizes it.

My parents, devastated, make arrangements to have the remains cremated. Four days later, with a ceramic vase containing Nat's ashes packed in my dad's suitcase, we fly home to Nova Scotia. My parents and Quinn, shattered and silent, occupy a row of three seats. I sit two rows behind them with strangers on my left, staring mournfully out the window of the plane.

CHAPTER NINE

On a frigid, gusty February morning, my dad turns in off the highway onto Lighthouse Road and drives up the icy, narrow lane. Tall pines, spruce, and firs block our view. I hear the sound of the ocean before I see the lighthouse. Dad steers around a curve in the road and the lighthouse appears. I gasp aloud in wonder, for it looms so formidably high in front of us. At the same time, I feel a pang in my heart. It looks lonely in its isolated location outside of town.

Dad pulls up in front of the lighthouse and kills the engine. I open my window and instantly feel the freezing, salt-laden wind. Despite being winter, there's no snow on the ground. The branches of the evergreens hang heavily with ice; the rocks are so cloaked with it that they glitter like diamonds under the bright winter sun.

We four climb out, Mom is last, and stand facing the red and white seventy-seven-year-old lighthouse and attached cottage. The roof of the cottage is painted a bright red that can be seen a long way off at sea.

The wind shrieks off the open Atlantic like a train slamming into me. It pushes me back against the car, wets my face, and freezes my eyelids as it holds me in place. I shield my eyes from the brilliant sunlight and survey the property. A dense forest of pine, fir, and spruce grows on either side of the lighthouse. The branches creak and sway in the wind, ice breaking off them and shattering on the frozen ground. Behind the lighthouse, leafless wild rose bushes line the edge of the cliff.

There wasn't a pastoral opening in our home church, so my dad, who'd worked as a lighthouse keeper when he was a young man, took a temporary job to fill in for the permanent keeper; he'd slipped on the ice and broken his leg. It provided us an income and home for the time being.

Mom leans sideways and looks past the rose bushes on the cliff's edge. "That cliff is too dangerous for Raine and Quinn. They could easily fall over."

"I'll build a fence along it first thing tomorrow," Dad replies, his voice dull and listless. Both he and Mom's voices have been like that since Nat's death.

"Promise me, please, Rye," Mom says, tears threatening. She reaches out with trembling fingers to touch his upper arm. "I can't lose another child."

"I promise, pet," he says solemnly. He then takes her hand and leads her down the drive toward the cottage. Quinn and I follow.

Just as we near the front door, a man and three boys step out from the side of the cottage, startling us.

"How's it going, Rye?" the man calls as they approach. He's about my dad's height but stocky with a hard round belly and bushy blond hair.

"Hello, Karl," Dad says without a smile, then nods at the boys. "Jarrod, Aubrie, Cormac."

Karl Skinner snorts. "You weren't gone long. Too bad about what happened. With your daughter."

My mom's face blanches.

"Yes." And that's all Dad says, in a cold voice that states clearly he doesn't want to talk about it.

"So you're taking over for Blaise?" Karl asks.

"Yes, until his leg heals."

"Broke it bad," Karl says. "How long you think he'll be laid up?"

"They told me six months."

"You're a pastor. How'd you get this job? Don't you have to be certified?"

Aubrie and Jarrod snort in laughter at that.

"I am certified, Karl. Worked in lighthouses before I went to Bible school."

Karl's eyes narrow. "Is that right?"

"Yes."

The man observes us coldly. When his eyes fall on me, I feel an ominous chill. His grey-green eyes bulge. Though I'm only eleven, I sense an aura of evil that raises the hair on the back of my neck.

The youngest of his sons, Cormac, is about my age. He has brown hair and aqua-blue eyes, like a tropical sea. Unlike his older brothers, this one watches us darkly and gives me a shy smile. The oldest, Jarrod, looks to be in his early twenties. He has a goatee and the same short husky build as his father. The second son, Aubrie, is already bald despite being in his late teens. His eyes bulge like his father's and flit back and forth constantly.

Jarrod has been eyeing Mom the whole time and I find his gaze disturbing. He slides his eyes briefly to Quinn and me, then back to linger on Mom. My parents seem too distraught to notice. They just stand there waiting for the Skinners to leave so we can go inside the cottage.

A gust of wind rises off the ocean and we shiver uncontrollably.

"We really need to get inside, Karl," Dad says.

As Karl and his sons turn to leave, Jarrod winks lewdly at Mom and steps past her so close his body brushes against hers. Mom flinches.

Jarrod glances back over his shoulder, laughter in his eyes, as he saunters after his father and brothers.

Dad's face is stiff, like he can't believe what just happened. Then he takes a step after Jarrod, but Mom puts a hand on his arm to stop him.

"No, Rye," she says quietly.

Dad makes an odd, choking sound deep in his throat. I can see by his facial expression that he's really struggling to stay put. Mom reaches out and covers his clenched hand with hers. Calmed by this, he nods.

But as we four walk up the front steps of the cottage, I glance at Dad and notice that although he lovingly holds Mom's hand, his furious eyes still follow Karl Skinner and his sons as they stroll across our property and vanish into the treeline.

CHAPTER TEN

Spring arrives early and is unusually warm. Tired of hitting my handball against the side of the boat shed, I head into the woods.

It's not only boredom that sends me into the forest. I've found that the heady scent of pine and the birdsong brings me a trace of comfort I can't find anywhere else.

It's been nearly six weeks to the day Natalie died, and I miss her so much that the pain in my chest is excruciating. It feels like someone is slicing my heart to shreds with a razor. And almost every night I dream of the crocodile attacking Natalie. I awake gasping for air, my pyjamas soaked with sweat, my heart pounding in my chest so powerfully that I'm afraid it's going to explode.

Before I get too far, I hear a woman's muted cries coming from the direction of the Skinners' house. I hold my breath, listening as the woman's cries grow sharper.

I set off at a run down the path until I reach the edge of the treeline facing their house. I hide behind a thick pine and peer onto the property. Mr. and Mrs. Skinner are on the ground next to their pickup truck in the driveway. He's straddling her chest and slapping her face over and over. Tears pour down her cheeks and she screams.

The sight terrifies me and I can't move. At last, I draw a breath and race back to lighthouse. I sprint past Mom and Quinn, who are bent over his bicycle, putting the chain back on the sprocket.

"What is it?" Mom asks, frowning at me as I huff by.

"Need Dad."

I vault up the steps and into the lighthouse, yelling up the tall stairway for Dad. I know he's cleaning the light room windows.

"What's wrong, Raine?" he shouts down to me.

"Mr. Skinner is hurting Mrs. Skinner. Please, come and help her."

I whirl around and run back outside to wait at the edge of the woods for him. Once he catches up with me, we run together along the path that leads to the Skinners' house.

They're still there, on the ground adjacent to the driveway. Karl Skinner is sitting atop his poor wife Loretta.

"Karl, stop that!" Dad shouts. "Get off her!"

Karl glances at my dad, then raises his hand to slap his wife again. Dad rushes over and shoves him hard in the chest, causing Karl to fly backwards and hit the back of his head on the ground. He sits up heavily, glaring at Dad while rubbing the back of his skull. Then he makes a move as if he's going to go after Loretta, who's dazed but has managed to sit up.

Dad stands between them and holds up a hand. "Don't you lay a hand on her again," he tells Karl in a voice laced with disgust.

Loretta looks up at me, her cheeks fiery red from his blows. Tears run down her face, soaking the collar of her green blouse.

I help her stand. She clutches her face between her hands, shoulders shaking with sobs. My heart hurts for her.

Karl rises slowly to his feet, too, and gives Dad a slow, ominous smile. "You shouldn't have done that, Rye."

"I'm not going to allow you to hit your wife, Karl."

"Oh, you're not, are you? Well, you can't talk. You're the biggest hypocrite in this town. When you're not pounding on your Bible, I know you're pounding on your own wife."

Dad shakes his head, dismissing that. "You touch her again and I'm going to call the police."

Karl barks a loud laugh. "Go ahead. You forget my brother's a town cop and my uncle's the chief of police."

The three Skinner boys come bursting out of the house and stand alongside their father. Jarrod and Aubrie clench and unclench their fists, glaring murder at my dad. Cormac looks lost and sad. His eyes dart from his mom to his dad, then to his brothers. He doesn't seem to know what to do or think.

Aubrie emits a laugh… a disturbing laugh that sends a chill rippling up my spine. I also notice that he walks with a limp. I've overheard my parents say that he was born missing two toes on his right foot and that some people in town call him Three-Toed Aubrie, but only out of his earshot.

I look at Cormac, who lowers his gaze and kicks at the dirt. He seems so different than his brothers. He's quiet and moves slower, in a watchful kind of way. He seems nice, too. But he's a Skinner, so I can't be sure.

"None of you boys could hear what was happening?" Dad says to them. "You couldn't come out and help your mom?"

Jarrod's eyes darken with malevolence. "Hey, don't you talk to us like that. You need to mind your own business."

Aubrie points a finger at my dad and then over to the woods. "Get out of here while you can still walk, old man."

Cormac steps over to his mom, puts an arm around her waist, and helps her up the steps and into the house. After threatening my dad some more, Karl, Aubrie, and Jarrod turn and go inside, too.

Dad and I walk home in sombre silence.

"I'm sorry you had to see that, Raine," Dad says once we reach home.

"It's okay," I say, though in truth it has truly upset me.

"No, it's not okay. What you saw was awful and something no eleven-year-old should ever witness. A man who hits a woman is a coward. Pure and simple. There's no excuse for hitting a woman, none at all. You understand?"

"Yes. But what about what Jarrod and Aubrie said? They're going to break into our house some night and kill you."

Dad shakes his head with disdain. "No, they won't. They're as much cowards as their father. Besides, God is watching over us. He'll protect us. Remember that."

Like he protected Natalie, Dad?

But I don't say it, don't want to remind him of it. Too often, I catch him staring at me with the same angry, blaming expression as the night when Natalie died.

Our relationship hasn't been the same since the crocodile attack. Frequently I feel he's cooler and more distant toward me. His angry expression hurts, as though he's stabbing me in the heart with an icepick. I already miss Natalie so much and blame myself every minute of every day for her death. Can't my dad see that I'm guilt-stricken and impossibly sad?

So I only nod, but as we climb the steps to the parsonage I stop and look up at him. "The boy my age, Cormac... he seems nice."

Dad meets my eyes. "Maybe. Let's hope so, but with Karl for a father and those two brothers for examples, it's hard to say how he'll turn out."

That night, after everyone else is asleep, I lie awake for hours worrying and listening for the sound of footfalls on the back porch.

CHAPTER ELEVEN

I hike along the dirt path towards the Skinners' place under a hot June sun, still piqued about that time back in April when Karl called my dad a hypocrite. I know that if anyone is a hypocrite, it's Karl. My knowledge isn't just because I saw him hitting his wife; it's because I've often spied on the Skinners since that day.

Yesterday, after supper, I slipped over to watch the Skinners' place. I climbed a big oak at the edge of their yard and sat on a limb in the shadowy branches, peering into their lit kitchen window. Loretta was at the sink washing dishes when Karl came up alongside her, leaned over, and snapped his thumb and index finger repeatedly against her cheek until tears filled her eyes.

Since April, I've seen him do this to her at least ten times. Yet whenever I see them in town he calls her "Sweetie," puts his arm around her, and pulls her into him in a hug so everyone can see.

I decide to go over to spy on them after supper again today. After supper, I again cut across our yard and hike through the woods until I reach their property. I climb up my usual tree and sit on a branch, arms looped around the trunk, legs dangling.

The Skinner house faces the Atlantic, like ours, and the ocean sparkles under the early evening sunlight. I watch a blue-and-white fishing boat head back into town, then shift my attention to the backyard where Loretta is on her knees working in her garden. She's wearing yellow garden gloves and a wide-brimmed hat. She's humming a hymn, and I think it's *Fare Thee Well, Lord*, one of my favourites. She seems so happy and at peace. Then I recall hearing my mom say that Loretta is a Christian, but Karl won't let her attend church. Sympathy for her fills my heart.

The back door quietly opens and Karl appears. I inch myself further around the tree trunk, watching as he slips out of the house and across the yard to a white plastic lawn chair set under the trees. He pulls the chair back at an angle so Loretta can't see him and sits. He folds his arms over his belly, stretches his legs out in front of him, and locks his eyes on her.

I've just completed a science project at school on Komodo dragons, and it strikes me that with his bulging, hooded eyes, pock-marked face, and bowed legs, Karl looks like one. Like a dragon, he sits hidden, lounging calmly in the hot sunlight and watching his prey with dead, lizard-like eyes.

After a few minutes, I hear him say something to Loretta. She jumps and stops humming, startled by his voice. Without turning around, she answers him—and suddenly he leaps out of the chair, darting across the lawn. He boots her hard in the backside and she yelps, tumbling head over heels and landing on her back.

He yells down at her, spittle flying in her face. "You look at me when you speak to me, woman!"

She rises to her hands and knees and starts crawling toward the house. He follows her across the lawn, then lifts his foot and gives her another boot in the backside. She screams in pain.

I can't help it—I cry out, and Karl's head whips up to the tree and our eyes meet. His eyes narrow.

"Get down out of there and get home," he says in a quiet, lethal voice that makes the blood roar in my ears. I feel suddenly dizzy and have to grasp the trunk tight so I won't fall from the tree.

He then turns his unflinching stare back to Loretta, who's still crawling across the lawn. He casually follows her up the back steps and into the house. The door bangs shut.

As the wind rises off the sea in front of the Skinners' house, hissing through the trees, I climb down and stare at the home, frozen, my eyes full of tears. I don't know what to do. I want to run home and get Dad, but I can't move. It feels like my legs are stuck in concrete.

Under the slowly sinking sun of a gorgeous June day, I decide to keep what I've seen to myself. Unlike my dad, I believe the Skinners will hurt him if he confronts them about this.

I make my way home, weeping, my heart torn and filled with deep sorrow for Loretta.

CHAPTER TWELVE

At midnight, my friend Malin and I sneak out of my house. She's staying over because it's a Friday night and we have no school tomorrow.

Malin and I sneak out to catch June bugs for a school science project, which counts for forty percent of our final grade. Carrying empty jam jars, we make our way across the lawn and into the woods where the June bugs are so plentiful that we can easily fill our jars.

As we near a narrow dirt road in the woods that leads from the highway to a former lookout on the cliff's edge, I hear the low thump of music and the growl of a car's engine.

"Someone's coming," I say.

"Who is it?" Malin asks.

I hear a car but can only see its headlights as it approaches. Low male voices and rock music carry through its open windows.

The lane is barely wide enough for a car and has potholes the size of craters, with tree branches stretching across the road like ghoul's arms. It was a logging road at one time, but now only partying teenagers ever use it, and even that's rare.

As the car draws near, a bottle flies from a window, sails through the air, and smashes against a tree trunk. A man's voice rises above the engine—and he doesn't sound like a young person. Mean laughter follows.

Alarmed, I grab Malin's hand and try to pull her down with me behind the trunk of a big spruce. She yanks her hand free and stands staring at the approaching headlights.

"Mal, get down!"

She scowls at me. "Why? It's just teenagers, I bet."

"Maybe not." I seize her hand again and yank her down. This time, she falls to her knees beside me and opens her mouth to say something. I place my hand over her mouth. "Ssssh, quiet."

The rumble of the engine gets louder as it drives past us. The driver's shadowed face is partially visible in the fingers of moonlight slashing through the canopy of trees. I make out a face with a goatee. The man's wearing a dark ballcap. I catch the silhouette of a passenger in front, and two more in the back.

The car proceeds on, snaking around the potholes and ruts, and then stops. It sits there, its engine idling over the forest floor, its brake lights illuminating the trees in a garish shade of red. Deep bass thumps from the car, vibrating the ground beneath us.

The driver kills the engine and the music dies. He leaves the headlights on, lighting up a thick copse of bushes in front of the car. Over the tick-tick-tick of the cooling engine, the driver speaks again, menacingly. Then his door clicks open and a dome light illuminates the interior.

I hear a woman's frightened sobs come from the back seat. She sounds young!

Mal gasps, and I feel my own stomach lurch. A young blond girl is slumped over in the back seat, her head drooping against the window. Her face is pale, her eyes fluttering open, then closing. I think I recognize her, too. It's a girl from high school who works weekends at the town grocery store. Her name is Chloe Reynolds and she's always been nice to me and Quinn when we go in there.

The driver gets out, opens the rear passenger door, and reaches in for the young woman. He pushes her out and lifts her arms like a baby, pressing her against his chest and carrying her into the bushes. When they passed in front of the headlights, I made out her long, honey blond hair swaying as she struggled to free herself. Now I hear her cry out, notice her legs kicking. She tries to free herself but the man holds her tight against his chest.

One of other men slides out of the back seat and follows the driver. He's younger and walks with a limp. I recognize them both. It's Jarrod and Aubrie Skinner!

Left alone, the man in the front passenger seat opens his door and climbs out. He drains a bottle of beer and tosses it into the trees. It slides down the branches and hits the ground with a dull thump. He burps loudly, hitches up his jeans, and walks around to the front of the car. He crosses in front of the headlights and stops to light a cigarette. He has bushy blond hair and a hard round belly.

I recognize him too, and the shock of it sends a fiery rush of blood to my head. I feel sick and dizzy. I have to place a hand on the ground to steady myself.

Malin looks at me, her frightened eyes huge in the moonlight. "That's… that's…"

But she's too terrified to finish. I reach over and squeeze her hand to settle her. Cold panic drives her to her feet, though, and she takes a step to bolt. Her hands, slick with sweat, are slippery and she drops her jar. It hits a rock and shatters. The sound is like a chandelier crashing onto ceramic tile, the shards of glass exploding in the quiet night air.

"What the—?" Karl Skinner shouts. He looks in our direction just as the clouds slide away from the moon and light up the woods.

Jarrod and Aubrie stop at the edge of the bushes and whirl around to face us. Jarrod carries Chloe back to where his dad stands in front of the car's headlights.

I see Karl's face clearly and understand, with horror, that he sees ours.

"Who is it?" Aubrie snarls.

Chloe suddenly lifts her arm and punches Jarrod in the face. He jerks back and releases her. She hits the ground running and takes off, passing Malin and me as she tears into the woods.

I jump to my feet and take Malin's hand, trying to haul her along with me as I chase Chloe. But Malin's feet are like cement; her mouth gapes, her eyes are glazed. She won't, can't budge. I grasp her hand tightly and yank her as hard as I can until her feet move. I drag her along with me as I race through the dark woods, the Skinners' footsteps on the forest floor loud behind us.

Somehow we catch up to Chloe.

"Follow us," I tell her as we run in the direction of the lighthouse.

We make it back to my house, but the men's footsteps are so close behind us that I'm not sure we'll make it inside. I lead Malin and Chloe over to the garden shed and hurry inside. We push a metal table holding my dad's table saw in front of the door.

Hearts thrashing, lungs afire, heaving for air, we watch the woods from the small back window. As we watch, the Skinners step out from the woods at the far side of the lawn and stand in the shadow of the treeline. Aubrie lights a cigarette and smokes it while they silently eye the cottage.

Malin and I clasp our hands tightly to fight the icy, shuddering panic that screams at us. I want to run into the house and get my dad, but I waver. If I tell my parents that Malin and I snuck out to go into the woods in the middle of the night, I'll be in deep trouble.

Suddenly, a light turns on in the master bedroom window. A moment later, the bathroom window light goes on. At least one of my parents is up.

The Skinners see the light and Aubrie drops the cigarette, grinding it out with the heel of his shoe. Then they turn and walk swiftly back towards the woods, disappearing into the shadows.

The lights go out in my house and all is dark again.

"Thank you so much," Chloe says in a hushed voice. "Please don't tell your parents what happened tonight. They'll tell mine and I'll be in huge trouble for drinking underage. Please promise me you won't tell them or anyone else."

I look at Malin, and she nods.

"We won't tell anyone, don't worry," I say. "We snuck out of the house and we'll be in big trouble, too, if they find out."

Chloe lets out a relieved breath. "Thank you."

"What were the Skinners going to do to you?" Malin asks, the whites of her eyes visible in the glow of the moonlight.

Chloe shakes her head. "You don't want to know, and you're too young for me to tell you anyway. I think I'm going to go home now. You two should go in the house. Will you be okay if I leave?"

"We'll wait out here for a bit. Don't worry, we'll be fine," I assure her. "But what about the Skinners? What if they're driving around looking for us and see you?"

"I'll stay off the highway and walk in the woods next to the ditch all the way to town. They won't see me."

After Chloe leaves, Malin and I clasp sweat-slicked hands and huddle together in shivering silence, afraid to move even an inch. We stay there, wide awake, until the first pinkish-grey hues of the sun rise in the eastern sky. Then we creep out of the shed, hurry across the yard, and slip quietly into the cottage. Malin and I crawl into bed together.

She falls asleep at once, but I lie trembling under my blankets until I hear my parents get up and move around in the kitchen.

CHAPTER THIRTEEN

After lunch, our family go with Malin into town. While Mom shops for groceries at Munro's, and Dad and Quinn go to the barbershop, Malin and I head towards the library.

It's a gorgeous morning, the sun sparkling on the water in the harbour, the breeze soft and briny. Still shaken, we walk along the sidewalk with our heads bent together, discussing what happened the night before.

Suddenly we hear the sound of an engine approaching. A shiny black car slides up to the curb beside us, and I see that it's the Skinners.

We freeze, paralyzed with fear.

Karl climbs out of the front passenger seat and walks over to us. He squats down to our eye level.

"Well, hello there, girls," he says, smiling. It's a chilling smile.

Mal makes a dry rasping sound, half-gasp, half-squeal. I take her hand and hold it, giving it a calming squeeze.

The car idles at the curb, the low throb of bass coming from its windows, its thick exhaust spoiling the fresh morning air.

"What's wrong with your friend?" Karl asks.

I fight to keep my voice steady. "She's upset."

"Is that right?" He fixes his gaze on Malin. "What's wrong, sweetheart?"

I feel Malin sway, her pulse throbbing in her wrist. I'm sure she will collapse if I let go of her hand.

I garner all my courage and give him a defiant gaze. "It's nothing. She's just worried about a math test we have on Monday morning."

He narrows his eyes at Mal. "Is that right? Surprising, since I've heard your mom telling everyone at work how smart you are."

His eyes are a granite grey, cold and unnerving. His breath smells like a dank and mouldy grave. My courage flees and I begin to shake. Malin and I stand so close together that I feel our bodies quaking against each other.

He scratches at his chin, then looks around before returning his eyes to us. "Did you girls tell anyone what you saw last night in the woods?"

Petrified, I glance behind me to the car. The driver, Jarrod, watches us through the windshield, rubbing his goatee with his fingertips, his cherry-red lips twisted in a snarl. Aubrie's in the back. He has the window down and leans out, staring at us. Every few seconds he giggles under his breath.

I find Karl repulsive, Jarrod frightening, but Aubrie petrifying, for he laughs constantly, like there's something wrong in his head.

Karl reaches out and pokes me in the chest. "I asked you girls a question."

We both shake our heads. It's all either of us can manage.

"Good. Now you two listen to me. What we were doing with that young lady was our own business. She's a good friend of ours and she had too much to drink. We were simply giving her a drive, making sure she got home safely. But on the way to her house she said she felt sick, so we had to stop and help her into the bushes so she could throw up. We couldn't let her be sick in the car, understand?"

His unflinching gaze is too frightening to look at, so I lower my gaze to the ground and swallow. It hurts because my throat is so dry.

"Are you girls listening?"

We both nod.

"Look at me then."

We both raise our eyes to meet his.

"Good girls," he says. "Because if you were to tell anyone"—he nods towards the car—"then I would have to tell your parents you were out in the woods in the middle of the night. You don't want that, do you?"

"Nooo…"

"Didn't think so. And if you don't keep your mouths shut, there could be dire consequences for your parents, me owning the fish plant and my uncle being the mayor. You don't want your mom to lose her job at the plant, do you, Malin? Her being a single parent and all? How would she pay her bills, put food on the table? And think of the hardship for your parents if the mayor were to order the town council to fire your dad, Raine?"

"He can't do that," I shoot back, my anger overcoming the terror.

Karl grabs my arm and pinches my flesh, bringing tears to my eyes. "He'd be out of work and you'd have to move out of the lighthouse keeper's cottage. No job or place to live. You'd have to move away. How would that affect your parents so soon after losing your sister? Is that what you want?"

I feel a twist of raw pain in my stomach. "No," I murmur.

He smiles cruelly. "Have I made myself clear, girls?"

Mal and I both nod vigorously, our petrified hearts thudding in our throats.

"Good." He gives us a long, cold look and then stands to his full height again. He walks back to the car and climbs in.

Jarrod puts the car in gear, pulls away from the curb with a squeal, and speeds away. The roar of the engine diminishes as it rounds a curve in the road and vanishes.

Mal and I stand on the sidewalk shaking for a long time after the car is gone, too numb to speak or move.

"You believe him?" I ask Malin once my fear eases and my breathing has normalized. "You really think they were just driving Chloe home? That she was just sick?"

"I g–guess," she stutters. "I mean, I don't even know what they were doing, do you? And Chloe wouldn't tell us. Maybe she was just too embarrassed to say she drank so much that she threw up."

I nod, but uncertainly. I'm not sure what they were going to do to Chloe either, but it still didn't seem like anything good.

"But Mal, why then would he threaten us not to tell anyone?"

She gives me an anguished look. "I don't know, but Raine, please don't say anything. You heard what he said. He owns the fish plant. He can fire my mom if he wants and she needs the job bad. And Karl's brother can easily get your dad fired, too."

Malin is right. I overheard my parents once say that Karl's family ran the town and that he and his sons were never held accountable for their crimes. I just can't risk anything bad happening right now.

"Okay, I won't tell anyone," I say.

"Swear?"

"I swear."

We sprint across the road and go into the library, staying there until my parents come to get us.

PART
TWO

CHAPTER FOURTEEN

Since the day my fiancé dumped me for a skinny young blonde, I've liked to start my mornings off on a bright note. I get out of bed, make a coffee, and take it and the newspaper out to the deck to enjoy while I read the obituaries.

The *Chronicle Herald* is available online, but I'm old school and prefer to read the physical paper. It has mostly local news, which is always my first priority when starting a new day. It keeps me from feeling overwhelmed with everything that's going on around the world. Once I'm done, I'll go online and read the world news.

Not only do I love the local paper, I also work there, writing the very obituaries I always flip to first thing in the morning.

To others my age, this ritual may seem strange, but to me there's no more enjoyable way to start my day than with a cup of coffee and the city newspaper in my hands. Today is no different, other than that I wake to a cold, drenching rain. It's been a full week of fog and raw winds, but then, that's typical spring weather in Halifax.

I groan, toss back the covers, and totter out to the kitchen in my shabby flannel pyjamas, something my ex-fiancé would have reminded me were the least sexy nightclothes a woman could wear. I put on a pot of coffee and smile as I remember telling him that was a crying shame because I didn't have the slightest desire to wear anything else.

While the coffee brews, I go out to the front porch and retrieve the daily edition of the *Chronicle Herald*. I pull it from its plastic wrapper and go back into the kitchen. I make two pieces of toast and slather them with peanut butter and slice some banana on top. When the coffee's ready, I pour a cup and take it and the toast out to the screened-in back deck.

I have no one else to blame but myself for the breakup. Lots of people warned me about Hudson, but I ignored them. He owns a busy travel agency and I'd heard rumours he flirted with his female clients, even the married ones. He wasn't choosy.

Malin, after meeting him, gripped my arm and whispered into my ear, "Raine, don't go rushing into anything with this guy all willy-nilly. I don't like him. I think he'll hurt you."

Did I listen to her? No. Instead I yanked my arm free from her grasp, told her, to my later mortification, that she was just jealous.

My brother also cautioned me and said he thought there was something slippery about Hudson, that he was hiding a mean side.

Did I listen to my brother, a kind-hearted pastor who had never criticized another human being before? Who always saw the good, even in the worst of people? No. I decided he was being judgemental and overprotective. I told him to leave my place and not come back.

I should have listened. After a year of dating and only two months of engagement, Hudson showed up at my condo on a mild March day to tell me he was breaking up with me. He told me he had met someone, said he couldn't take one more nanosecond of being with me.

I wish I could say I told him to get out of my house. Instead I pushed the couch up against the front door and stood on it, begging him not to leave, creating a pitiful blockade. He told me to stop the drama and move the couch out of the way. To my deep humiliation, I dropped to my knees, wailed, and pleaded with him to stay.

Apparently the melodrama was just one of the many things he couldn't stand about me. And apparently I also wasn't feminine enough for him. Too reserved. Socially inept. Apparently I came off to his family and friends as standoffish and cold.

Apparently I embarrassed him!

The next thing he said was soul-crushing, each word feeling like a punch to the face: "I… don't… love… you."

Unable to stand under the pain and cruelty, I collapsed on the couch in a sobbing heap. He cast me a cold, scornful look before shoving the couch, with me on it, out of the way. And without a backward glance, he went out the door.

I felt like I'd been bludgeoned over the head by a steel pipe. I lurched around the apartment that day, shattered.

Why didn't I listen to anyone? How could I have not seen this coming? How had I let that blindness I called love lead me into such a mess?

And then, thankfully, anger replaced heartbreak. I straightened my back, lifted my chin, and vowed to never shed another tear over Hudson, or any other man, ever again.

I found an empty cardboard box and went through the house collecting anything he'd unwittingly left behind. In went his fancy hiking boots. I found his windbreaker hanging from the doorknob on the foyer closet and heaved it into the box. Next I tossed in two of his cherished DVDs. And last of all, I slid my engagement ring off my finger. I drove to the nearest thrift store and cheerfully handed the box to the young female clerk who answered the bell at the donations door.

My cell phone abruptly chirps and vibrates across the patio table, returning me to the present. I ignore it as I turn to the obituary pages. Despite the rain, birdsong rises from the trees in the backyard, nearly drowning out the faint hissing of traffic on the wet city street as commuters head downtown to work.

The phone again chirps, and I again ignore it.

Finally, it goes silent.

I finish the obits, my mood lightened, and turn to the front page. A story in the bottom corner sends my breath whooshing out of me:

NOVA SCOTIA WOMAN DIES IN AUSTRALIAN CROC ATTACK

Brisbane, Australia—A man from Truro struggled in vain to drag his wife from a crocodile's jaws during a late-night swim off a northwest Australian beach, police said on Monday.

The pair were swimming in the Isola River near the town of Thornton in Queensland State on Sunday when the 27-year-old woman was snatched by the crocodile, according to Constable Oliver Parker.

"Her husband tried to grab her and drag her to safety but he just wasn't able to do that," Parker told the Australian Broadcasting Corp.

Police said the husband told them the couple were swimming in chest-deep water when the crocodile struck, attacking his wife and dragging her away.

A rescue helicopter fitted with thermal imaging equipment failed to find any trace of the woman Sunday night, Parker said. The search will resume Monday with a helicopter, boat, and land-based search teams.

The husband was taken to hospital suffering from shock, an ambulance service spokeswoman said.

"There were plenty of crocodile warning signs in the area," Parker said. "I can't understand why they went swimming there. They were tourists from Canada. I guess they didn't fully understand the danger."

I drop the paper on the table.

My sister's grisly death still haunts me, and my memories of that night are sparked by stories like this, or even a sudden scream or the faint odour of blood.

I get up and go into the living room, pulling my childhood Bible from the bottom drawer of the bookcase. Inside, tucked between pages twenty-one and twenty-two, is an old newspaper clipping. It's from the *Desolation Ridge Bugle* and it's dated three days after Natalie was killed. I skim it quickly, a lump forming in my throat. I've read it so often I can quote it verbatim:

GIRL KILLED IN CROCODILE ATTACK

Desolation Ridge, Australia—The body of a 14-year-old girl was recovered by Australian wildlife officers Tuesday following a reported crocodile attack near the town of Desolation Ridge.

Police said the girl had been walking along the Blue Rock River with her sister when she was taken.

Wildlife officers found the six-foot crocodile sunbathing on the banks of Curillin Creek. The young girl's remains were found inside the crocodile.

The crocodile was euthanized.

I swallow hard, refold the clipping, and slip it back into its hiding spot. I go back into the kitchen and stare out the window without seeing anything, lost in the nightmare of that night. My guilt is enormous. It's with me always. The memory of my parents' grief, my father's anger and accusations, still scalds me. I know his accusations were true.

Since that terrible night, I've lived with a constant dull ache in my chest. But now, with the horror film of her death playing in my mind, my chest throbs with acute pain. I pick up my cup to drink some coffee, but my hand shakes and coffee spills over the rim onto the newspaper. I set the cup down, staring sickly at the circle of dark coffee spreading across the paper.

Without thinking, I trace the familiar ridges of the jagged scar that begins at the righthand corner of my mouth and trails crookedly down to my chin—the laceration from where the crocodile's tail flicked me, requiring fifty stiches and three rounds of antibiotics to kill the festering infection that refused to heal even weeks later.

For months after our return to Blackheart Bay, whether at school, in church, or in town I faced whispers, gossip, and unashamed stares at my scar. Even now

I still catch people casting furtive glances at the wound. The scar only intensifies my naturally harsh countenance.

Once, when I wore ratty grey gym pants, a black T-shirt, and cheap flip-flops, I'd smiled at Hudson's father, and he'd flinched, telling me I looked like an escaped felon. I pretend to be impervious to such stares and comments, but in truth they feel like a needle probing a festering wound. It's something I'll never get used to.

My cell phone chirps again, vibrates across the tabletop, and pulls me from my dark memories. I drop my hand from my face, grab it.

"Hello?" I nearly bark.

"May I speak with Raine Hunter, please?"

"Depends on who's calling."

"This is Sergeant Baily Flynn of the RCMP. I'm calling from Blackheart Bay."

I frown, taken aback by the seriousness in her voice. "This is Raine."

"Ms. Hunter, I'm calling about your brother, Quinn. I need to ask if you've seen or spoken to him in the past twenty-four hours."

"No, I haven't seen Quinn in almost a year. Why are you asking?"

"And you haven't spoken to him?"

"No, not for a few months. Why, what's going on?"

"I'm afraid I have some bad news. Your brother is missing."

"What? Missing... what do you mean?"

"He vanished from his house sometime last evening," the sergeant answers gravely. "We're searching for him now, but so far we haven't found him."

"Vanished from his house?" I repeat. "What happened?"

"No one knows for sure. Your nieces, Brie and Pella, told us that after supper he made them a snack and then put them to bed. They heard Quinn downstairs in the kitchen, cleaning up, but when they woke up in the morning the lights were still on and no one was there. They checked his bedroom and his bed hadn't been slept in. The whole house has been checked, but he's nowhere to be found."

"What about his vehicle?"

"Still parked and locked in the driveway. His cell phone, wallet, and car keys are all still in the house. Brie called your dad and the two searched the whole property right away. That's when your dad called the police." She pauses. "And your dad is the other reason I'm calling. He suffered a heart attack this morning and is in the hospital."

"How is he?" I ask.

"It was a mild heart attack. He's in the ICU."

I don't say anything for minute. My mind is reeling from the shocking news.

"I have to hang up now," Flynn says. "I'll keep you posted on any new developments in the search."

After we hang up, my phone rings again, and this time I quickly answer.

"Hello?" I say.

"Hi, is this Raine Hunter?"

"Yes, speaking."

"Hi, Raine. This is Phil Henderson… Pastor Phil Henderson."

"Oh, right." I suddenly remember that he's the pastor of the church my dad and Quinn attend back home.

"I'm calling about your brother. I'm sure you've spoken to the police by now—"

"Yes, I have," I say quickly. "You know Quinn well. He would never leave the girls alone. This doesn't sound like Quinn."

"You're right, it doesn't. He wouldn't voluntarily vanish." The pastor pauses. "There's something else, though. I don't know if Quinn has told you, but he's been having problems with his neighbours."

"No," I say, closing my eyes briefly as panic rises in my chest. "I left Blackheart Bay when I was eighteen, and I've only been back a few times: for Quinn's wedding and his wife Holly's funeral. She died along with six other missionaries when their bus was swept away by the raging water and mud of a flash flood."

"Yes, Quinn told me," the pastor murmurs.

"Quinn and the girls usually come to the city to visit me, but the last visit was over a year ago. We exchange emails once every few months, pictures of the girls mostly. I haven't actually spoken to Quinn for a few months now, and I don't keep in contact with my dad at all."

"It was actually your father who gave me your number. That's the other reason I'm calling."

My heart plunges, but only briefly before a burning sensation fills my throat. "The police already told me about the heart attack. Has his condition worsened?"

"Sorry, I didn't mean to scare you. The good news is that, yes, the heart attack was very mild… the doctors don't think there's any lasting damage. He'll hopefully make a full recovery, meaning he could be released in a few days."

"Where did this happen?"

"He collapsed on the Skinners' front yard," Phil says, then pauses. "He went there looking for Quinn."

"Why would Quinn have gone over there?"

"They're the neighbours Quinn's been having problems with. They've been harassing him, trespassing on his property, vandalizing… things like that."

My mind flashes back to our former neighbours in Blackheart Bay, and in particular the clan's patriarch, Karl Skinner.

"Yes, I remember them well," I say grimly. "When I lived there, my parents had problems with Karl and his sons coming on the property whenever they felt like it. Tools used to disappear from the tool shed, and there was often damage to the rescue boat in the boathouse. It was stolen once and Dad found it washed up on the beach not far from the Skinners' place. He figured it was the Skinner boys. They were always up to no good."

"They're still up to no good, I'm afraid."

"Quinn never said a word to me about this. Karl Skinner? He must be in his seventies by now."

"Yes, and the older sons are in their forties. The youngest's his mid-thirties, I'd guess."

"Thirty-three, same as me," I say. "I went to school with him from kindergarten up until he dropped out in senior year."

"I hear he's quite intelligent."

"For a while it seemed he'd take a different path than his brothers, but three months from graduation he started getting into trouble with them. Stopped coming to school."

I thought back to an afternoon in Grade Twelve math. A boy who had liked to tease me snatched my notebook from my desk and refused to give it back, so I'd stood up and tried to take it from him. The boy just laughed and held it up high over his head, but then Cormac had lunged to his feet, stepped over, and grabbed my notebook. He'd stared into the boy's eyes and told him in a quiet voice to leave me alone.

Without a word, but with a shy smile, Cormac had handed me my notebook and sat back down.

"His older brother Jarrod is smart, too, but he was always more cunning and dangerous," I continue. "He's sly, in an unnerving kind of way. He'd do something malicious to someone and you'd just never predict it at all. Even if you suspected it was him, you could never prove it."

"I see," says the pastor. "Anyway, your dad thought the Skinners might have something to do with Quinn's disappearance. That's why he went over to talk to them."

"But why is Quinn having problems with them?" I ask with mounting panic.

"Quinn once told me he thinks it's because a prominent real estate developer wants to build a seaside resort out there," Phil says. "I tend to agree. This developer, some guy named Laramount, plans to demolish the lighthouse and build a luxury hotel with swimming pools, tennis courts, the whole deal. Quinn's a member of the Historical Society, so naturally he's horrified at the idea."

"Yeah, he wouldn't like that," I murmur.

"Karl's told people he and the Malones have both been offered more than a half-million, and they've accepted. Laramount made Quinn a substantial offer, too, a little more than a million, but Quinn refused. Told the guy flatly that he'd never sell. Karl's furious because if Quinn doesn't sell, then the whole deal is off. Apparently there's another potential site down around Digby."

"I had no idea this was going on," I murmur. "You said the Skinners and Malones have agreed to sell, but what about Gloria Jean Vance?"

Gloria Jean was our neighbour to the north. When I lived there, she weas a loner who detested people. She'd always dressed in men's jeans, long-sleeved plaid flannel shirts, and knee-high rubber boots, having no compunction at all about running people off whether they were mail carriers, delivery drivers, or lost tourists. She ran them out of her yard with a rifle.

I can't imagine she would ever sell.

Phil laughs softly. "I heard Gloria Jean chased the developers off a few times before they even had a chance to speak with her. The Mounties seized her rifle, but in the end the developer decided—wisely, I think—to proceed with the resort without her land."

"I see."

But now Quinn was missing, after deciding not to sell. His vehicle was still in the driveway, and no one had taken his cell phone or wallet...

An icy chill slivers through me from my head to my toes. "Well, what about Brie and Pella? They didn't hear or see anything?"

"I guess not. Ms. Hunter, hopefully you see that you need to come home as soon as possible."

"W–well... um..." I sputter, mind reeling. Other than the wedding and the funeral, I haven't been home in fifteen years.

"Ms. Hunter?"

"It's Raine."

"Okay, Raine. Will you come home?"

"Yes of course. I just need to arrange a couple of things, but I'll leave as soon as possible. Likely first thing tomorrow morning. I want to help in the search."

"My wife and I are caring for Brie and Pella right now, but we can't continue much longer. Our daughter's getting married next Saturday in Vancouver and we're flying out late tomorrow evening."

A bolt of panic rushes through me. "You want me to take care of them?"

"As does your father. He asked me to speak to you about this."

"Oh... sorry, that's impossible," I blurt. "I'm a writer. I work for the *Chronicle Herald*. Who would look after them when I'm at work? And my condo's too small... and it's an adult-only building."

"I understand," he says, his voice gentle. "Let me be clearer. I'm actually asking you to come here to Blackheart Bay to care for your nieces. This is a family emergency. You must have emergency leave or some vacation time? Besides, your father mentioned you're the obituary writer..."

"Obit writer, yes."

"And you work out of your home? Couldn't you still work and send your obituaries from Quinn's home?"

"I just can't do that. You'll have to find someone else."

"But you did just tell me that you would come home to help in the search for Quinn. Now you're telling me you can't come home to care for your nieces?"

I feel my neck grow warm. "Can't you take them with you?"

There's a teensy, appalled pause. "Take Brie and Pella to Vancouver?"

"I'm sure they wouldn't be any trouble. And what little girls don't love a wedding, right?"

"No, that's not possible."

"You sure?"

"Very sure."

"And the wedding can't be rebooked? It's over a week away." I can't keep myself from blurting this out, even though I know it's a terrible joke.

There is another appalled pause. Bigger. Longer.

"No, it cannot," he says, his tone a tad cool. "That's entirely out of the question."

"I'm really, truly sorry, pastor, but you'll have to find someone else. I wouldn't be any good with them. I don't like kids and they don't like me. And the last time I saw my nieces was, as I said, over a year ago. I'm afraid I'm a lousy sister, a terrible daughter, and a worse aunt."

"Yes, your fa..."

I scowl into the receiver, bristling, wondering why it is that a person can criticize themselves but if someone agrees they'll want to choke them.

"Look, I understand this is difficult for you," Phil says. "But there's no other option. Quinn has vanished and Brie and Pella are extremely distressed. The fact is, they need you. Your father is their only relative here in town, and he's too ill to care for them."

"What about Holly's sister, Piper?"

"Her last known address was in Ontario. It doesn't matter. Your father stated firmly that Quinn wouldn't want her to look after them."

My pulse throbs behind my eyes. "There are some cousins out west. Alberta or British Columbia, I think."

No shocked pause this time. There's a period of icy silence.

"I'm not about to put two traumatized little girls on a plane and send them out west to some distant relative they've never met," he says finally.

I frown, about to argue, but then think better of it. "No, of course not."

"So you'll do it?"

"There's no possibility at all that my father can do it?"

He exhales heavily. "Not from his bed in the cardiac care ward, no."

"And there's no one else in your church who can take them? What about my friend, Malin Winter? She's a member of your congregation. Everybody loves Malin. She's warm and outgoing and wonderful with kids to boot. Let me give her a call and get back to you."

"Actually, it wasn't only your father who recommended you. Malin suggested you, too. She mentioned you had gone through a hard time recently, a breakup or something, and that you might look forward to coming home."

"She told you that? What a blabbermouth," I say.

He stays silent for a moment. "I truly believe that at a distressing time like this, people need to be with family."

"Won't being in their house traumatize them even more? I mean, with Quinn gone and law enforcement around?"

The shocking truth of what I've just said sends a shiver through me. My hands begin to tremble and I nearly drop the phone.

"I've spoken to the police and they say they'll be gone by mid-afternoon. They've set up a command centre in the woods between Quinn's place and the Skinners'."

I turn my mouth away from the phone, take a long and deep breath. "Fine, yes, I'll come. But only until Quinn is found."

"Yes, just until Quinn is found," he says, but his tone lacks confidence. "Call me when you arrive at Quinn's place and I'll meet you there. And of course I'll keep in touch with you and your dad while I'm away, to find out how the search is going. My wife and I, and our entire congregation, will be praying for all of you."

"Great," I say flatly. But my tone implies otherwise.

CHAPTER FIFTEEN

At 6:00 a.m. with my stomach churning, I climb into my car, leave Halifax, and head southwest through a cold drizzling rain and early morning mist. Three hours later I arrive in Blackheart Bay. The sky is cloudy, but the sun peeks out occasionally, diminishing the low-lying fog over the water.

I drive slowly along the main drag, Harbourview Street. It's early, just after nine, and the downtown area is starting to get busy. Businesses are open and townspeople are making their way along the street and sidewalks.

Little has changed in the fifteen years since I left. On the coastal side of Harbourview are the same red-bricked town hall, library, two banks, and post office. On the left side I see Munro's Grocery, Driscoll's Pharmacy, Burke's Hardware, and Molly's Diner, all of which have been there since I was a child. Next to Molly's is a seafood restaurant that's been there for years, and some local gift shops that cater to the tourists who visit in the summer months.

A few new businesses do surprise me, including a craft and gift store called Lena's. That one belongs to my dad's girlfriend. Then there's a vegan café, a health food store, and a chic designer clothing store. I figure they're the result of newbies coming to town. I silently wish them good luck.

I keep driving, past the road that leads to the wharf and encounter a new mini-mall with a grocery store, bank, gym, and pizza place. Down the street is The Sleepy-Tyme Inn, which has been there forever. Its vacancy sign is lit up.

Soon the businesses give way to houses, most with slate-blue or brown cedar shingles—many have been there for more than a century. I pass the large Presbyterian church on my right; and on my left, a Catholic church. Not far from up a street, I come to New Hope, my family's church.

Three kilometres outside of town, I pull over at the sign that reads *Blackheart Bay Lighthouse*. I'm surprised the province hasn't changed the sign, since the lighthouse was deactivated in 2007, my dad retiring on the same day. The automated light was moved to a tower down the road where it's maintained by the Coast Guard. The government put the lighthouse and attached cottage up for sale, and that's when Quinn and Dad purchased it and began renovations. The cottage itself was too rundown, though, so they demolished it and began work on the lighthouse. When Quinn and Holly married a couple of years later, Dad moved into a house on Harbourview.

I drive up the narrow, tree-lined dirt lane, hearing the sea crash into rocks. Before I even see the lighthouse, I smell the ocean.

When I finally reach the end of the lane, my heart flutters. The last time I was here was the day of my worst fight with Dad. We'd shouted ugly, bitter words to each other, and then I packed my bags and caught the next bus to Halifax. I'd been saving up money since I was twelve, and Mom had left me some money, too.

I'd found an apartment to rent, and in September I began classes at King's College where I studied journalism and creative writing. I'd published six books since then before falling into a slump. Now I couldn't seem to write another.

I pull up next to Quinn's cobalt blue Chevy and shut off the engine. I peer through the windshield and take in the property. There's a new garage to the left and next to it a big garden shed. I turn my eyes to the lighthouse.

When my parents lived there, the lighthouse and attached cottage had been one unit, with a door leading from the kitchen to the lower level of the lighthouse. Now the lighthouse's faded red and white shingles have been painted periwinkle blue, with white around the windowsills. It sits on a cliff facing east, bathed by early morning sunlight. The view of the ocean from here is spectacular, something I've always loved about the place.

The sound of another car approaching snaps me back to the present. I turn to look behind me as a white Chevrolet sedan comes down the lane.

Dolores and Harold Shaw, old friends of my parents and members of Quinn's church. They climb out and walk over to join me on the lawn, their faces sombre.

"Hello Raine," says Dolores—although I've always known her as Dolly.

Harold nods and smiles at me. He's bald and his face is as white as a corpse. He has a prominent mole on the ridge of his nose and stiff white hairs sprout from it. I find it revolting and have to look away.

Dolly, on the other hand, is a large woman and wears denim capris, sandals, and a red T-shirt with the words 'Git 'er done!' printed on the front. Harold's pole-thin and wearing baggy khaki shorts, a white T-shirt, and black hiking sandals. I smile, remembering that the locals here have never been bothered by cool temperatures; they wear shorts nine months of the year.

"It's nice to see you again, although Harold and I are both sorry about the dreadful circumstances," Dolly says. "But I'm sure they'll find Quinn soon. And your dad is doing much better. We're all praying for the whole family at church. We've the prayer chain going all the way across Canada and even into the States."

I look away, feeling a sharp wrench of pain in my heart at the mention of Quinn's name. Although I haven't seen him in over a year, he's my younger sibling and I've always felt protective of him.

Dolly notices and pats my hand. "Don't worry, dear. Trust God. He'll bring Quinn home safe."

I look away and draw in a breath. *Give me a break.*

"It's been a while," she says. "Think it was at your mom's funeral the last time I spoke to you."

She's wrong. The last time we spoke was at Quinn's wedding, but I don't care enough to correct her. As if Quinn's disappearance isn't horrible enough, I have to swallow against the sudden lump in my throat over the mention of my mom. She never got over losing Nat. The shock proved too great. Only five years after Nat's death, Mom's health took a turn for the worse and she was diagnosed with acute myelogenous leukaemia, a fast-progressing cancer . She was given only six months to live, but Mom hung on and outlived the doctors' prognosis for two more years.

I favour my dad in looks and personality, and we were close when I was a child, but later I became closer with my mom. The memory of her suffering strikes me down at times. I remember her crying out, then doubling over in pain just from walking across the kitchen floor.

"Your hubby not with you, dear?" asks Dolly, her nosy eyes looking past me to my car.

I pause, remembering that she's a long-time member of the town's ardent chinwaggers. When I was growing up, Dolly and a group of about seven men and women with nothing better to do used to meet at Molly's Café. They all sat at a long table facing the big plate-glass window that looked out onto the street. From there, they wouldn't miss a thing. The talk that went around that table would have turned the ears red on half the people who lived in Blackheart Bay.

I meet her gaze but keep my face benign. "I'm not married."

She widens her eyes. "Oh, I thought Quinn said something about you being engaged."

"I was." I feign a yawn. "Now I'm not."

She runs a hand through her straight white hair. "I'm sorry to hear that."

I shrug nonchalantly. "Nothing to be sorry about I dodged a bullet there, for sure."

"I see." She's unable to hold back a smile, revealing small even teeth. She glances at Harold, clearly thrilled with the new gossip they can spread around town.

I could kick myself for giving them fuel for the fire.

"Well, come on," Dolly says, leading the way at a brisk pace. "Hope you don't mind us letting you in, but Pastor Henderson was called to the hospital. There's an emergency with a member of our congregation, Lonnie Calloway. You remember him?"

I nod, remembering that Lonnie was a good friend of my dad's. He was a lobster fisherman, and when I was a child he often took us kids out on his boat. He was a kind, gentle man.

"He's eighty-two now and had a stroke last night."

"Oh, that's too bad," I say—and I mean it.

"He's going to pull through, thank the Lord for answered prayer." She casts her eyes to the sky. "Pastor Henderson asked me to tell you that he'll bring the girls over tonight before he and Denise fly out. That will give you time to get settled in."

"I appreciate you letting me in," I say, following her to the front door with Harold beside me.

"Not a problem," she says. "Some of the women from church will be bringing some food over for you, and the girls are coming later today."

I don't reply to that. Maybe I just won't answer the door when they come. Along with those ladies' food will come a pile of nosy questions and an invitation for me to join them in a prayer session for Quinn.

"Don't worry. Like Dolly said, God will protect Quinn," Harold says as he reaches out to pat my shoulder. I move away, finding the gesture too intimate. I'm irritated to death by both of them. "I bet the Skinner boys are responsible for this. They've been trespassing and damaging Quinn's property for almost a year now and the cops haven't done much to help. It's all to try to force him to sell to Laramount. You don't have to be Sherlock Holmes to figure that out."

Despite my attempt to stop it from happening in front of the Shaws, my eyes well up. I turn my head sideways to hide it. Being here, seeing Quinn's vehicle sitting in the driveway, seeing the lighthouse... and knowing Quinn is gone… it's so frightening that I feel sick. I hope for the best but expect the worst.

More distressing than the fact Quinn left without his wallet and cell phone is the fact that he left Brie and Pell all alone. Quinn is an excellent father and he loves his daughters deeply. After Holly's death, he became both mother and father to them and they share a strong father-daughter bond. He would never voluntarily leave them on their own like that.

Though my mind won't accept it, my heart screams that something terrible has happened to my brother.

"So where exactly is the search and rescue command centre?" I ask shakily.

Harold points to his right. "They've set up in a clear area between here and the Skinners' place."

I look towards the woods, and think about the Skinners' two-story house, out of sight at the moment.

"Quinn has done a nice job renovating the lighthouse," I say to change the subject.

Harold nods. "Yes, wait until you see the inside. Quinn and your dad have done a marvellous job. Your dad told me their next project was to build a decorative stone wall on the right side of the lighthouse to shield it from the wind."

"That's a good idea," I say.

Dolly bends down to pick up a newspaper encased in a pink plastic sleeve that's lying on the front step. She opens the door and looks back over her shoulder. "Are you two coming?"

"Hang on," Harold says. He looks at me and juts his chin toward the cliff's edge behind the lighthouse where the land disappears into the sea. "This is no place for two little girls to run around. I don't know what your dad was thinking even bringing you and Quinn out here to live years ago." He shakes his head. "We lost a young newlywed couple from Maine two years ago. He was taking a picture of her, and she stepped back and fell over. He must have tried to help her because they found his body on the rocks next to hers, along with their camera. The last picture taken on it was the one of her standing right at the edge. I don't know what it is about human nature, but we seem to find a cliff's edge seductive. Well, I'm preaching to the choir, aren't I? You know that. You grew up here."

I give him a small smile.

"Still, you've been living away for a long time now, Raine," he says kindly. "The fence your father put up along the cliff is long gone, so be careful and watch the girls closely. And keep a sharp eye when you're out walking. The high grass along the edge can hide a hole. If you step in one, you'll fall over. And the wind is constant and powerful. Wicked gusts can come off the sea and blow you right over the side. It's a two-hundred foot drop down to the rocky beach."

"I remember," I tell him. Besides, my nieces have been living her since they were born. "I'll be careful and I'll watch the girls."

"Good," he says with a warm smile.

"Get the lead out, will you, Harold!" Dolly shouts from the doorway of the lighthouse.

Harold and I enter, brushing past her. I stop inside the hallway and let Harold shuffle on into the kitchen alone.

Dolly closes the door and nods towards her husband. "Oh that man. He walks so slow, don't he? Lord forgive me, I know it sounds unchristian, but I just want to push him sometimes. And I did once. On the steps at home. Oh, don't look so shocked. It was just two little bitty steps. It's not like he was in any danger of falling down and breaking his neck. And we were running late for our son's wedding. Who could blame me? You'd think for that one special occasion he'd move those legs of his…"

She hustles away and disappears around a corner into the kitchen. Harold gives me a look of misery, then draws a finger like a razor across his throat.

CHAPTER SIXTEEN

After the Shaws finally leave, I inspect the place. The lighthouse has been extensively renovated and it's amazing. Beautiful really. Quinn has knocked down two walls to open up the kitchen, dining room, and living room. He's retained many of its original features, from the oak hardwood flooring and ceiling beams to the antique staircase.

The kitchen has been completely redone with ash cupboards, matching island, stainless steel appliances, and a wooden dining room table and chair set. The living room has a white leather couch set and oil paintings of the sea. I wonder if the furniture and paintings were Holly's touch before she'd died.

What takes my breath away is the same thing that always takes my breath away—the circular wall of oversized windows. Sunlight angles in from them, brightening the first level with its warm rays and affording a heart-stopping view of the Atlantic. Quinn has added two sets of French patio doors and I step over to look out into the backyard. The deck is new, with steps that descend onto a lush lawn. To the left is the path that leads to the cliff's edge, where rose bushes grow. A tilled section of ground betrays the presence of a large garden. A row of cedar bushes line the far edge of the property. I figure Quinn is responsible for all this. He takes after my mom and her love of gardening.

A strong breeze rushes in as I open the door. It fills the house with the fragrant scent of rose and the sea. And the noise is deafening—the shriek of wind and the boom of the sea exploding against the rocks below. On blustery days, our family had to raise our voices to be heard over it.

I ascend the stairs to the second level where I find two bedrooms on one side that are clearly the girls'. On the other side is a guest bedroom and bathroom. One of the girls' bedrooms is painted pink, and by the toys on the floor and teddy bears on the bed I guess that it's Pella's. The other bedroom is painted a tropical blue, and it's clear from the books scattered everywhere that this is Brie's room.

The master bedroom is up on the top level and has an en suite bathroom. It also has a circular wall of windows, but its most stunning feature is the wraparound widows walk deck. I open the French doors and step outside, gasping aloud at the majestic view. I can truly appreciate why Quinn tore down the cottage and moved into the lighthouse.

And then I spot the RCMP and police rescue boats in the water, gliding quietly and up and down in a grid over the water as they search for Quinn. My throat tightens and I quickly go back inside to compose myself.

I look around the room and see an open Bible on Quinn's night table, the breeze puffing the curtains and ruffling the pages. My gaze falls on 2 Timothy 4:17: *"But the Lord stood at my side and gave me strength, so that through me the message might be fully proclaimed and all the Gentiles might hear it. And I was delivered from the lion's mouth."*

I certainly hope so, Quinn, I think to myself. *For your sake.*

I don't share my brother's deep faith. There's something about begging God to save your sister from being killed by a crocodile and Him saying no that pretty much killed it. I still attended services after Nat's death, but only because my parents made me. I stopped once I moved to Halifax.

Still, I can't seem to let go entirely. I can't seem to grab hold of it again, either.

I enter the guest bedroom on the second level and put my things in the closet. When they're put away, I head outside and cross to the cliff's edge, looking down at the search boats. The sea slams into the rocks below, the water roiling and frothing. It's a dizzying drop and I step back.

I follow a path that runs along the cliff's edge for a few hundred yards, and then slopes sharply downhill, leading towards a private white sand beach. It's the same path my dad always used to pull the rescue boat down to the beach. It seems wider now.

The beach is gorgeous and stretches along the shoreline for a quarter-kilometre. Quinn and I practically lived on this beach during the summers. Being back here floods my mind with happy memories.

But the respite is short-lived. It's no surprise this Laramount fellow wants such a prized piece of property.

I take off my sandals and sink my toes into soft sand. Closer to the water, it becomes hard-packed and cold. The breeze smells of salt, seaweed, and shells. I run my tongue over my lips, tasting the salt, then I draw in a deep breath and release it. The sea air revitalizes the body, soothing the soul. It hits me that although I've never missed this town, I have missed living by the ocean. I've always had a profound love of the sea.

I go back inside and see the weekly town newspaper, *The Blackheart Bay Leader*, still in its plastic wrap on the kitchen counter. I pull it free and spread it out. The headline on the front page makes my heart sick:

LOCAL MAN MISSING

Digby County RCMP are searching for a Blackheart Bay man who vanished from his Lighthouse Road home after accusing his neighbours of trespassing and harassment.

Quinn Hunter, 29, a father of two little girls, was reported missing by his father on Tuesday evening.

RCMP Sergeant Baily Flynn said Mr. Hunter's Chevy Tahoe is still parked in his driveway and his wallet and cell phone are in the home. The police said no trace of the young father has been found.

Hunter's pastor, Phil Henderson, said Hunter, who works with him as a youth pastor and choir director at New Hope Church in Blackheart Bay, has had multiple problems in the past year with his neighbours.

"Quinn has been in a battle with this neighbour, who he's accused of trespassing and vandalizing an outbuilding on the property," said Henderson. "Quinn was last seen by his daughters at his home on Tuesday evening. He didn't show up for work the next day, nor did he call in. That's out of character for him. He has two little girls and he's a wonderful, caring father. He wouldn't leave them all alone in the house."

Police and search and rescue teams launched a massive search for the missing man on Wednesday morning. More than one hundred law enforcement and land-based search-and-rescue personnel are searching the forest and waterways within a 25-mile radius of Mr. Hunter's home. Police have deployed scent-sniffing dogs. Boats, planes, and a helicopter with thermal imaging equipment are scouring the waterways and terrain, but so far Mr. Hunter hasn't been found.

Police said it is unlike Mr. Hunter to fall out of touch with his friends and family. While they won't call his disappearance suspicious, they do admit that due to recent events concerning Mr. Hunter and his neighbours, it is troubling. They haven't named any suspects.

Police, working in co-ordination with the search-and-rescue teams, have set up a command centre near Hunter's home. They continue to follow leads and information received from the public.

"There have been several tips received from the public, and they're very much appreciated. They've all been followed up and acted upon," said Constable Flynn. "Unfortunately, so far the tips have led nowhere."

Hunter is described as five-feet, eleven inches tall and weighing about 170 pounds.

He was last seen at his home on the evening of April 11, wearing black jogging pants, a long-sleeved dark green T-shirt under a red hoodie, and black running shoes.

Anyone who may have seen Hunter is asked to call the local RCMP.

My stomach turns to ice. I set the paper down with shaky hands, looking around the quiet, empty lighthouse.

"Oh Quinn, no," I whisper, fighting back tears. "Where are you?"

CHAPTER SEVENTEEN

"Raine, I can't tell you how unbiblical that was," Malin says, her voice betraying her shock.

"What was?" I ask.

"Throwing Hudson's things away."

We're in the lighthouse waiting for Pastor Henderson to bring Brie and Pella over. While waiting for the coffee to finish brewing, I push the kitchen curtain aside and look out. Dark shadows fill the backyard.

I turn and give my friend an evil grin. "It felt so good, though."

Malin shakes her head. "But you threw your engagement ring away? Aren't you supposed to return it if the engagement is called off?"

"I don't know and I don't care. Anyway, I didn't throw it away. Not exactly. I donated all his things to the thrift store."

I pick up the coffee pot, fill two mugs, and carry them over to the table. I set one down in front of her and take the seat on her right.

"Thanks," Malin says, picking up a spoon. "Still, it's the same thing. How much did Hudson pay for that ring? Must have been a couple thousand at least."

My heart flares with hurt and anger at the mention of my ex-fiancé. "I don't know. I never wanted it anyway. I wanted two sterling silver rings handcrafted by a local artist. Hudson didn't like that idea. He wanted a huge diamond on my finger so he'd look like a big spender in front of everyone."

I watch Malin lace her coffee with cocoa and coconut sugar. She sips it and then is quiet for a time, her gaze locked on something on the counter.

"What? Just say it, Mal."

"I know what Hudson did was terrible, but you threw away the ring. I mean, wow."

I frown. "Why does that bother you so much? I thought you didn't like him."

"Couldn't stand him." She shudders. "I found him as slimy as a fat snail on a damp summer morning." We both laugh. "Who knows? Let's hope some young guy who can't afford to buy a ring will find it and will ask his true love to marry him."

That's Malin for you, always the romantic.

"Yeah, well, if she has even half a brain she'll say no," I say, always the cynic. "Let's drop it. I don't want to talk about him ever again. Anyway, he's not important, not with what's going on right now with Quinn."

She nods sombrely. "Agreed."

I blow out my breath. "Oh, Mal, I'm worried sick. I find myself waiting every second for the phone to ring. At the same time, I don't want it to ring, because I'm terrified it will be bad news."

She gives my arm a tender squeeze. "I know. But it will be good news. Think on that only."

I nod, but uncertainly.

We fall silent as we sip our coffees. The fridge hums, the butter-yellow curtains over the window puffing out in the light sea breeze.

"So you're all moved in and ready for the girls?" says Malin.

"I'm all moved in, but I'm definitely not ready for kids. They can be little terrors. I don't like them, even if they are my own nieces."

"Oh, you'll be fine," she says with a dismissive air.

I give a disgruntled moan. "Easy for you to say. Tell me how I'm supposed to write with two little kids around my feet all day long."

Malin looks surprised. "You're writing again? That's wonderful, Raine. What are you working on?"

"At the moment? Nothing."

"So you're not writing."

I frown at her. "I am writing."

"I'm not talking about your obits for the newspaper."

"Well, I also write them freelance, for people whose families find it too hard to do it themselves. Either they're too grief-stricken or they don't feel like they'll do a decent job."

"How do they find out about you?"

"I advertise online. You'd be surprised how many people are looking for that."

"Wow. And you make a living from it?"

"I make a decent living from my book royalties. The obit job adds to it."

Malin sets her cup down. "I can't tell you how depressing I find that."

"Really? I find it entirely enjoyable."

She props her chin on one hand and eyes me despairingly. "No surprise there. Anyway, what I meant is that you're not working on a new novel."

"For the moment. I could start anytime. Like, say, tonight."

She smiles. "All right. So you start a new novel tonight as soon as your nieces arrive. Well, then you'll deal with it. Try not to worry. It will all work out."

"Don't be so sure of that. Besides, I should be helping in the search for Quinn, not babysitting."

She shakes her head. "No, they don't need you. There are almost a hundred searchers out there now. Police, a helicopter, and the local ground search-and-rescue team, volunteers from church. I heard the RCMP may send home some of the volunteers. They're worried about someone accidentally contaminating a... well..."

"A crime scene," I finish for her.

"Um...maybe," she says quietly, sadly.

"Yeah," I say, all I can manage against the sudden lump in my throat.

She covers my hand with hers. "But I bet they're wrong and they'll find Quinn alive and well."

"Mal, they've been looking for Quinn for two days now. If he was conscious, out in the woods somewhere, he would've heard the helicopter and tried to signal it in some way. Doesn't that mean he's either badly injured and can't... or that he's...dead?" As I say it, my fear and anxiety escalates.

"Don't even think that. Maybe they haven't searched the right area yet."

"If he's on foot, they should have found him by now." My voice shakes from the horror of what I've just said. "But whatever has happened to Quinn, I know the Skinners are responsible. They're the only people in town who are capable of something like this."

"You don't know that for sure, Raine. Try not to think the worst."

"I'm not the only one who thinks that. Harold Shaw told me as much, and my dad thinks so, too, or why else would he go storming over there? Pastor Henderson told me Karl was offered more than half a million for his place and he accepted, as did the Malones. By refusing to sell, Quinn was stopping this development from happening... and the Skinners are a bad bunch to get in the way of."

Mal nods. "I know, but still, it's always been petty crimes with them. Theft, vandalism, things like that. I can't believe they'd go so far as to hurt Quinn. Maybe they are responsible for this, but if so I think Quinn is alive. I don't believe Karl would let his sons hurt Quinn. Give him a good scare? Sure. But kill him? No way. And," she adds pointedly, "all the Skinners have alibis. Loretta swears they were all home that night. She told police she couldn't sleep and was awake from midnight until six. She swears Karl was in bed with her, and her three sons were all asleep in their rooms."

"All three still live with their parents?" I asked, shocked. "They're adults now."

"None have married or moved out. Karl has quite a grip on them."

"Incredible. Still, I don't believe Loretta—and I think they've done something horrible to Quinn. I think somehow they got Quinn to open the door, after which they grabbed him and drove him away somewhere."

"No, Raine. His running shoes and hoodie are gone, too. He went out, maybe for a walk."

I roll my eyes. "And then didn't come home? No. The Skinners likely just let him put on his shoes and a hoodie before taking him away."

"All right, say this did happen," Malin concedes. "They probably just drove him into the woods and left him there to walk back. To scare him. There are lots of old logging roads around here. That's the worst they'd do."

I look at her in surprise. "The worst they'd do? I don't know about that. Are you forgetting what we saw in the woods when we were kids? I may not have understood back then, but I certainly do now. You know we stopped them from doing something bad to Chloe."

She goes silent for a few seconds. "I hadn't thought of that in a long time. Yes, I agree."

"So they *are* capable of hurting Quinn. Mal, if all they did was take Quinn into the woods to scare him, he'd be back home by now."

"I just don't think Karl would hurt him, or let his sons hurt him. Not in the way you're thinking. And the Malones certainly wouldn't. Fred and Joan Malone are in their seventies and they're good people. You know that."

"Then what about this developer, Laramount? Is he capable of doing something to Quinn, or maybe hiring someone to get rid of Quinn?"

She gives me a small, sad smile. "No, Raine. From what I've heard, Colin Laramount is a decent guy. He's told many people that if Quinn doesn't sell, he'll simply build his resort over by Digby. Anyway, none of it matters because Quinn is fine. He'll be home soon. Either he'll walk home or the searchers will find him."

I finish my coffee. "I hope you're right," I say, but my doubt and fear leave a dry, charred taste in my throat that not even the coffee can remove. "Want more coffee?"

"Sure."

I get up, refill our cups, and sit down again.

Malin arches her eyebrows. "Speaking of your dad, are you going to go over to the hospital and see him?"

My shoulders tense. "No," I say firmly.

"Why not?"

"You know why."

"Raine, why can't you forgive him?"

I shrug, knowing that it's because I still feel hurt, sad, guilty, defensive. And now, added to that mix, being dumped by Hudson had made me feel ugly and unlovable.

"It's not healthy to hold on to a grudge the way you do," Malin said. "It's like a newborn puppy or something, the way you stroke and pamper it."

"I do not."

"Yes you do. It's been fifteen years. It's time to forgive and forget."

"Tell him that. He blames me for Nat's death and always has. He's supposed to be a strong Christian." I blow out a scornful breath. "He's such a hypocrite."

"Log, meet splinter."

"Whatever."

"We're all hypocrites at times, Raine. I think you're too hard on him." She smiles gently. "Besides, I've never heard him say he blames you for your sister's death. He's not going to live forever. You should go see him, and meet his girlfriend, too. I think they're planning on marrying soon. In the fall sometime."

I look at her, incredulous. "What? He's sixty-five… and she's what, eighty? Why bother getting married now?"

Malin laughs. "Lena's not eighty. In fact, she's a couple years younger than your dad. And I imagine they want to marry because they've been seeing each other for two years now and are in love. I think they're good for each other. She's outgoing and your dad is, well… like you. Kind of reserved."

"I'm not reserved."

She sets her elbows on the table, peering at me over the rim of her mug. "Well, you're not exactly outgoing. But really, Lena's a nice person. Remember me telling you that she owns a craft store on Harbourview? She opened the store not long after she moved here from B.C."

"Yes, I remember. I saw it when I drove through town this morning."

"I think she does pretty well with it. People in town like her. She's nice, Raine. You should meet her."

I shake my head. "Look, I'm not going to see him, so I'll never meet her."

"Go see him," she says tenderly.

I fold my arms. *No way.*

"Raine..." Malin sighs. "You're being unre—"

I hold up a hand. "I don't need a lecture, thanks."

She huffs out a breath. "Fine."

We fall into silence again.

It's a clear, windless evening, unusual out on the coast. We hear the clang of a bell buoy far out at sea. Outside, long streaks of crimson and orange fill the sky as the sun continues its descent. The fading light falls across Malin's face, accentuating the fine lines around her mouth and eyes. It's a reminder that we're both getting older. We've been friends since childhood, and we've stayed close despite the fact that she's remained in Blackheart Bay—other than for her four years at university in Fredericton. She's a kind, caring, and loyal friend. She's visited me in the city at least twice a month for the past fifteen years, even though I never return to Blackheart Bay to visit her.

Suddenly, we also hear a car pull up on the gravel driveway. Malin and I exchange looks.

"They're here," she says.

I groan and set my cup down. "Terrific."

"Now, Raine..."

There's a knock at the door, and I don't move. Malin tilts her head sideways to the door, but I don't budge.

We hear another knock, louder this time.

"Raine," says Malin. "Answer the door."

I let out a breath and push my chair back noisily. I pull open the inner door, leaving the screen shut so I can peer through it. A thin, bespectacled man in his late fifties stands on the steps, my nieces standing on either side of him.

"Hi there, I'm Phil Henderson. You must be Raine?" He smiles, and I nod. "It's nice to meet you. How are you holding up?"

"Not good." I scowl down at Brie and Pell, and they drop their eyes to the ground.

I haven't seen the girls in a year, other than in photographs. They look the same as they did in the last photos Quinn emailed me, just a little taller. Brie has dark brown hair and her eyes, like mine, are the deep moody blue of a winter sea. Pella favours Quinn with her fair skin and long legs. The thing that makes my heart hurt is how much she looks like Natalie with her aqua green eyes and long auburn hair. The resemblance is getting stronger as she grows up.

Both girls are willow thin with a pile of freckles on their faces. They look so fragile, so needy. Panic rises in my chest and I feel a sudden desperate urge to grab my car keys and bolt.

"That's certainly understandable," Phil says.

"What?" I say.

"You said you weren't good," he says, his tone kind. "That's understandable, with what's happened to Quinn."

I lean in closer and whisper in his ear. "It's not that, no. You see, I've changed my mind. I can't do it."

He looks perplexed. "Can't do it? What?"

"I can't take care of them."

The girls hear anyway despite my low voice. Pella looks scared. Her chin quivers and she starts to cry. Brie looks defiant and glowers at me; her eyes have shifted from deep blue to a stormy grey. It strikes me that we share that trait.

Phil looks at me for a long time without blinking. "I understand this is difficult, and an unusual situation, but please understand that there's no one else to care for them right now."

"Mm–mmm, you mentioned that."

The pastor looks down at the girls, his gaze lingering on little Pella whose glasses have fogged up with tears. I find her silent weeping unsettling.

Phil places his hand on Pella's shoulder, gently pats it, and turns to me. "But you are *here*, and you agreed to care for them."

"Did I?"

"Yes, you did."

You cold, selfish woman, I add silently for him. His eyes go cool. His posture stiffens. *He doesn't like me and I don't blame him.*

Blood rushes to my face. I feel my cheeks burn.

"Raine," he says. "I wish you would re—"

Malin comes up beside me, bumps me out of the way with her hip, and pushes open the screen door. She holds it open so our guests can come inside.

"She'll take good care of them, don't you worry, Pastor," she says. "Come on in, girls."

I push her just a little out of the way, but she regains her balance and gives me a look that freezes me on the spot.

"Hi, Malin," Phil says with a relieved smile. "Thank you. Yes, let's go inside, girls."

He leads Brie and Pella past us and down the hall toward the kitchen,

"They've been through a terribly distressing time," he whispers in my ear as he passes me. "Try to be gentle with them, please."

I glare a bullet at the centre of his back. When have I ever been not gentle?

Malin shuts the doors and turns to face me.

"Judas Iscariot," I accuse her.

She stares hard at me for a few seconds. "You need to smarten up."

"Me, why? What did I do?"

"You can be so insensitive, Raine. Now, you listen to me. Brie and Pella have no one else. They're traumatized by this, and they're your nieces, your family. They need you. And by the way, you—"

"Don't you dare say it, Mal."

"I will too say it. *You* have no one else, either. Despite how you pretend that what happened with Hudson doesn't bother you, I can see right through you. You practically flinch when I say his name."

I snort. "I do not."

She only continues: "You are hurting and your nieces are hurting. I think this could be good for all three of you."

"Oh, is that right, Dr. Winter? I didn't realize you were a therapist as well as a bank manager."

She allows a small smile and softens her tone. "Look, Raine, I know you're afraid, but—"

"I am not afraid."

"Yes you are. When you're afraid, you get angry. You've been like that since we were kids. But there's nothing to fear. You won't be alone. I'll come over and help as much as I can."

"Sure, Mal," I scoff. "You have a busy life of your own. You have Tanner. You work full-time."

She shrugs. "Tanner travels to Calgary a lot for work. He's sometimes gone two months at a time. You know that. And I have lots of vacation time saved up. And I *am* the boss."

I study her face. "You promise you'll help?"

"I promise," she says, putting her arm around my waist as we walk down the hall to the kitchen. I let out a breath. "Thanks, Mal."

"You're welcome. And it wouldn't hurt you to be nicer to Pastor Henderson," she chides, shaking her head. "I can't believe that glare you gave him. If looks could kill, he'd be laid out on the floor right now."

I laugh quietly in delight.

"You're shameless." She frowns. "Listen, he's a good man, a good pastor."

"Sure he is," I huff sceptically. "They all have skeletons rattling in the closet."

She arches a brow. "Even Quinn, then?"

I feel my ears burn a little and give her a sheepish smile. "No, of course not Quinn."

Malin looks pointedly at me. "Not Pastor Henderson, either. He's a good pastor and a kind man. When my aunt was dying at home, he stayed with us for thirty-six hours straight until she passed. And he didn't just pray! He helped with everything—meds, making meals, even cleaning the house. Mom and I held one of Aunt Alexa's hands, and Pastor Henderson held the other."

I don't say anything. What can I say to that?

"And you be nicer to those sweet little girls," she adds, elbowing me in the side none too gently. "Maybe try smiling instead of scowling at them. That'd be a good start."

"Like this?" I say as I give her a big smile, one I know will make my scar twist up. It would frighten away a starving cougar.

"For pity's sake." She sighs and shakes her head in exasperation. "What is wrong with you? Oh, never mind."

Later that evening, as I go upstairs early to get ready for bed, I hear the patter of small steps on the floor. Seeing a light come on in Brie's bedroom, I duck back around the corner and peer into the hall. Pella comes out of her room and dashes into Brie's bedroom.

I pad softly over to the doorway and listen.

"There's a redback spider in my room," Pella says worriedly.

"No, Pell," Brie tells her. "Redback spiders live in Australia, not here. Come on, scoot down so I can pull the blanket up over you."

I hear the bed creak as Pella snuggles down under the covers.

"There are no venomous spiders in Nova Scotia," Brie says. "None in all of Canada."

"I saw it, though."

"You saw a spider, sure. But it's not a redback, trust me."

I peer around the edge of the open doorway and see Brie put her arm around little Pell and pull her in close.

"Are you sure, Brie?"

"Yes, I'm positive. You're safe. Now, close your eyes and try to sleep."

"I can't. Aunt Raine's grouchy and she tells scary stories. I miss Daddy. I want him to come home."

"Me too, but he'll be home soon. Close your eyes, try to sleep, and I'll sing you a song."

Pella shuts her eyes. Brie rubs her back and begins singing softly until the younger sister falls asleep. Then Brie turns out the light and lays back with a sigh.

I walk softly to my bedroom, wishing I understood children better.

Earlier, I'd looked up from my laptop and told the girls to get their butts to bed. Pella, who'd been sitting on the floor playing with her dolls, jumped about a foot in the air. Maybe my voice had been too gruff?

When I'd gone up later to shut off the lights and say good night, Pella had asked me to read them a bedtime story—and then a Bible story, like Quinn did. I looked at them for a long time, then told them they were both old enough to read on their own.

But then I had a good idea: "You know what? I don't read books to kids old enough to read them themselves, and pigs will fly before I ever read you a Bible story, but... I'd be happy to tell you a good story."

I sat down on the edge of Pella's bed and told them about the time a venomous redback spider had crawled across my bare foot in my bedroom in Australia. I'd even gone into great detail about the gruesome way I would have died if I'd been bitten. By the time I'd finished, Pella's face had been as pale as wax. She looked scared half to death, so I gave her a big smile. That seemed to frighten her worse than my story, so I just gave up and told Brie to go to her own room and go to sleep.

I know my smile can look more like a snarl, and it seems even more hair-raising because of the crooked white scar at the corner of my mouth. Tiny little pinpoint scars line each side of the wound, scars from the stitches I got. The scar twists up when I smile and looks like a fat white caterpillar with tiny legs. And I guess I can look pretty grumpy. And my voice can be sharp. With all that and my stormy blue eyes, it's been said that I seem to stare right through a person.

I suppose the whole thing is a tad frightening for Pella.

I go into my bedroom and shut the door quietly, thinking that Pella will probably be jumping in bed with her older sister a lot at night until Quinn gets home.

CHAPTER EIGHTEEN

I wake to the warm caress of sunlight on my face and turn on my side to face the windows. The impenetrable fog that had shrouded the property last night has been burned away, giving way to a flawless sapphire blue. It's warm and the breeze carries the scent of salt, seaweed, and seashells into the room. A gull glides past the window, the light wind carrying it gracefully out over the water. I inhale deeply of the revitalising sea air, then toss back the covers and get up.

I pad into Pella's bedroom to wake her and my heart gives a start. Her bed is empty.

I walk down the hall to Brie's room and find Pella in Brie's bed, her thin arm thrown over her older sister. They look so young and vulnerable, like two little lost waifs.

My heart twists with fear and doubt again. I shouldn't have agreed to this. I'm lousy with kids. For the tenth time since they arrived last night, it takes everything in me to keep from grabbing my things and driving back to Halifax. The only thing that stops me is Quinn. I have to wait until Quinn is found.

When I look back at the girls, they both stir and open their eyes. Pella eyes me a bit worriedly and Brie watches me with a serious expression that seems to pierce right through me. Her look says that she knows what I'm thinking, that she understands I want to abandon them.

I redden.

"Let's go, girls. Hit the deck. It's almost chow time," I shout, and then flash them a smile.

Pella's eyes go wide and she pulls the blanket up over her nose, peering over its blanket's edge fearfully. Brie just stares at me.

I flee downstairs to the kitchen, where I put on coffee and look in the fridge. I find a two-litre carton of milk, margarine, a carton of orange juice, a bag of apples, some yogurt, and a jar of grape jelly. I make a mental note to pick up some groceries.

There's a loaf of bread and a box of granola in the cupboard and I take them out. I pour the granola into three bowls and drop some bread in the toaster. I cut up some apples and put them on a plate in the centre of the table, then place butter and jelly on the table along with silverware, the yogurt, and three glasses of juice.

"Breakfast is ready!" I roar up the stairway. "Get a move on, girls, or you're going to miss your bus."

Seconds later, Brie walks into the kitchen wearing an avocado green T-shirt and blue jeans. She's got a neon pink sock on one foot and a lemon yellow sock on the other. She sits at the table and pours granola into a bowl.

"Couldn't find a mate?" I say.

She frowns. "What?"

"Your socks. They don't match."

"Oh, right." She shrugs. "That's the style now. It's sick."

"What's sick?"

"My socks. They're sick; that means cool."

"Sick is cool?"

She beams. "Exactly."

I nod quietly, thinking to myself that I'm getting old.

The toast pops up and I place the four slices on a plate and set it down in the middle of the table.

"Thanks." She picks up a container of blueberry yogurt and studies the label. "Oh, it's expired. I remember now. Dad was going to throw it out, but he must have forgotten."

"Throw it out? Why?"

"It's way past the expiry date. Like, over a month."

"A month?" I wave that away. "Poof, that's nothing."

"It might be sour."

"No, it's not. Go ahead, eat it. It won't kill you."

She makes a face. "But it might make me throw up."

I snort. "Trust me, it's just a freshness date. That only means it would taste fresher up to that date. It doesn't mean it will be bad after the date. Well, not too long after."

She lifts a brow, then sets the yogurt down next to her bowl.

I pour myself some coffee and sit. I butter some toast, put grape jelly on it, and take a bite, chewing in awkward silence. Every time I make eye contact with Brie, she holds my gaze with unsettling intensity. Quinn always said how much he thought Brie took after me—not only in looks, but also because she loved to write stories. She'd even submitted some to children's magazines in the hope of being published. And though only ten, she'd told Quinn she wanted to be a writer when she grew up.

"Where's your sister?" I ask after I finished the toast. "She's taking forever."

"I think I know."

Brie stands and heads out of the room. I stand too and follow her up the stairs and into Pella's bedroom.

Brie stops in the middle of the room, goes quiet, and motions for me to do the same. I hear someone talking in a low, muffled voice. My heart plunges. It's Pella, whispering to herself in the closet.

I look at Brie. "What is she doing in there?"

"She hides in there sometimes when she's scared."

"Did I say something to upset her?"

Brie thinks for a minute, then her gaze slides over my scar. "Mm, maybe it was the spider story last night before bed."

"Spider story?" I echo, puzzled. "The little tale about the redbox spider? Really? Did it upset you?"

"No, but I'm almost eleven and I like spiders."

I'm impressed. "You do?"

She nods. "But not Pell. She's only six and she's scared of them."

"Oh, all right then. Good to know. I'd better stick to snake or shark stories from now on." Brie's eyes widen and she looks at me like she isn't sure if I'm joking or serious. "Never mind. I'll think of something else."

I cross the floor and open the closet door. Little Pella is cowering in the corner, legs drawn up, hugging her knees. She stares at me with wide eyes, trembling all over.

I squat down to her eye level. "Why are you in here, Pella?"

"I heard a noise outside," she says in a faint, choked whisper. "I think the bad men are outside."

"What men?"

"The men who took Daddy," she says, her eyes full of fear.

"Oh, Pella, no. There are no men outside." I reach out my hand for her. "Everything's fine. Take my hand and come on out."

She stares at my hand uncertainly. "But I heard something."

"I think what you heard was just the television. I had it on earlier to hear the news."

Brie nods encouragingly. "Yeah, I heard it, too. That's all it was, Pell. No one's here but me and Aunt Raine."

Pella still won't move.

"It's okay, Pell, really," Brie says. "No one is here—and I won't let anything happen to you." She pauses and looks at me. "And neither will Aunt Raine."

"Yes, you're safe. Come on out now," I say, taking her hand and lifting her out.

She nearly jumps on me in her rush to wrap her arms tightly around my neck. She lays her head on my shoulder. I feel her small heart thumping like a frightened bird. Carrying her in my arms, I walk down to the kitchen, with Brie following.

"You must be hungry," I say. "How about some breakfast?"

"Okay," Pell murmurs.

I feel her sweet breath against my neck, which sends a wave of panic through me. I have no clue how to comfort this child.

"Good. You can't go to school on an empty stomach. I did that once in Australia and my stomach growled so loudly my teacher told the class she was sure there was an angry kangaroo in the school."

Pell lifts her head. "Really?"

Brie narrows her eyes and watches my face steadily.

"Really, it's a true story. Kangaroos are mostly docile, but if they feel threatened they can be aggressive and attack. When they're getting ready to attack they make a scary growling or clucking noise, like this." I make a fierce growling noise and Pella's face relaxes. A giggle escapes her lips.

I see that Brie thinks I'm making the story up, but since it worked to cheer up Pell she seems to decide to let it go.

Pella starts eating cereal. After a moment, she looks up from her bowl. "Aunt Raine, you can call me Pell. That's what Brie and Daddy call me."

"All right," I say.

"Aunt Raine?"

"Yes?"

"Is Daddy going to come home today?" she asks, her voice a whisper.

Now Brie looks apprehensively at me, and I know she's having the same thought.

"Sure he will," I tell them, hiding my own doubt, not wanting to crush their hopes. "If not today, then tomorrow."

They give me small smiles.

I summon all my courage. "You know, you don't have to go to school today. It might be hard. Some kids might talk about what's happened with your dad."

"We missed Wednesday and Thursday already," Brie says. "We want to go."

"You sure?" I wonder if they're going just to avoid staying in the house with me all day.

Brie nods, and then so does Pell. "Yes, let them talk."

"All right, then," I say, greatly relieved.

After they finish eating, they hurry down the lane to the highway. They throw me a wave before disappearing around the curve.

Once they're gone, I wonder if I should have walked them to the bus. But then I remember that Quinn and I walked down that very same lane to catch the bus out on the highway when we lived here, so why should I treat Brie and Pell any differently?

And yet, an ominous, unsettling sense still lingers that I need to watch them more carefully.

As I walk back to the kitchen, I'm struck by the realization that, like me, Brie and Pell have experienced their own sorrow and terror after losing their mom, and now their dad. Both tragic events will stay with them forever. Brie is close to the same age I was when Nat died and Pell is close to Quinn's age. Though Brie rarely lacks in bravery or confidence for someone so young, Pell is clearly more traumatized. I understand that I need to be gentler with them.

I close my eyes and rub my lids, uncertainty overcoming me. I feel incapable of caring for these girls, of helping them overcome the trauma they're going through. And I don't know when, or even if, Quinn is ever coming home.

CHAPTER NINETEEN

While putting the dishes in the dishwasher, my cell phone rings.

"Hello," I say.

"Hi, Raine. It's Nellie Armstrong—from church?"

"Oh, right." I remember her as being a good friend of Mom's years ago, and a long-time member of the Ladies' Auxiliary. My mom liked her a lot, so I tell myself to be gracious and not hang up in her ear.

"How are you?" she asks.

"I'm fine, Nellie. Thanks."

"I'm so sorry about Quinn. It's terrible what has happened. I hope it helps to know that we're all praying for him… your dad, for all of you. We have the prayer chain going at church 24/7. Members are taking turns coming in to pray, and we've got it going all across Canada and into the States. Quinn will be found soon, Raine."

"I hope so."

"Some of the ladies from church have prepared some meals to help you out with the girls. We'd like to bring them over this morning if you're going to be home."

"Um…"

"Is ten a good time?"

"That's fine," I tell her, though I already know I'm not going to be here. I'll just leave a note on the door saying I've run out for a minute. They can leave the food on the step.

"Good," she says. "It will wonderful to see you again, Raine. It's been years."

"Yes," I mumble with a trace of guilt, knowing she'll be disappointed.

After I hang up, I go into the living room and turn on the television just in time to see an RCMP sergeant holding a press conference at the command centre. It's Sergeant Flynn, who I spoke to on Wednesday morning—and then again last night when she called to give me an update on the search. I'm expecting her here later this morning so we can meet in person and talk.

"We've searched the area extensively for the past few days without finding Mr. Hunter or any evidence of his whereabouts, so we've made the difficult decision to descale the search-and-rescue operations," she says. "Some local volunteers will be sent home late today. However, the helicopter will remain in the air searching the land and waterways. And search-and-rescue teams will continue searching for Mr. Hunter. I stress that this remains an active investigation by the RCMP. We are continuing to act upon any tips from the public. I encourage anyone who thinks he or she has seen Mr. Hunter, or knows anything at all about Mr. Hunter's disappearance, to please contact us immediately."

I shut off the television and fight back tears. Though this wasn't a complete shock—after all, Sergeant Flynn warned me last night they were considering descaling the search—hearing her say it on television is devastating.

A rush of anger surges through me. Furious, I decide not to wait for her. I leave the house and walk through the thick trees over to the RCMP command centre. That same sergeant is standing outside a large white tent, speaking to a dark-haired man wearing an orange vest with a yellow horizontal strip over a long-sleeved flannel shirt—obviously a member of a search-and-rescue team.

I approach them, my stride quick, but they turn and go inside before I get there.

I follow them inside, where they stand behind a wooden fold-out table, studying a map. The dark-haired man talks while running the tip of his index finger around an area at the bottom of the map.

They both notice me and look up.

The sergeant approaches me, lifting her brows. "Can I help you?"

"Yes, I'm Raine Hunter, Quinn's sister."

She nods once and holds out her hand. "Hi, Raine. It's nice to finally meet you in person."

I shake her hand. "Yes, I just saw you on television, giving the reporters a briefing."

"Then you heard me say that we've scaled back the search?"

"Yes, I'm surprised. It's only been, what... two days?"

"Today's the third day. But as I explained last night, so far there's been no sign of your brother. But it's not as bad as it sounds. We're not stopping the search by any means, only descaling it. We just don't need so many searchers anymore. However, we've only sent home the civilian volunteers, not the trained SAR techs. Your father was here asking the same questions and I told him the same thing."

"He was?"

"Yes. You just missed him, in fact."

Good, I think to myself.

"What we know at this point is that your brother gave the girls a snack and put them to bed around seven o'clock. Some time after that, he put on a red hoodie and his running shoes and left the house. Your nieces woke up the next morning to find the lights were still on, your brother's cell phone still in the house, and his vehicle still parked in the driveway, locked and untouched. The keys were in his bedroom."

"I'm surprised he left the girls alone in the house."

"His daughter Brie says he had been going for walks alone in the early evenings for the past few months. He told her he thought she was responsible enough to watch Pella."

"So you think he went for a walk and got lost? Or maybe he fell and is hurt somewhere in the woods?"

"That's one scenario we are investigating. But as I explained to your father, we do have to consider other possibilities."

"Like the Skinners abducting him?"

Flynn cants her head. "We have no physical evidence of anything criminal. Your nieces heard him downstairs in the kitchen before they fell asleep and the house shows no signs of a break-in, no signs of a struggle, nothing to indicate he was taken away by force. The dogs picked up his scent on the back deck, and from there along the path toward the cliff, but then they lost it. It appears your brother left the house of his own accord."

"What are the other scenarios then?"

"It was extremely windy Tuesday night. A gust may have caused him to lose his balance and fall from the cliff. It rained very heavily Tuesday evening, so he wouldn't have been able to see clearly. Or it's possible your brother may have walked into the deep woods and gotten lost."

I shake my head adamantly. "No. Quinn has lived here since he was a boy. He knows every inch of this place like the back of his hand. He'd never fall from the cliff top and he'd never get lost."

She nods. "Then we also have to consider that your brother may have vanished of his own accord, or even intentionally stepped off the cliff."

I release an incredulous laugh. "What? No way."

"Brie told us that his phone battery was dead after supper and he left it charging on the kitchen counter. His wallet and keys were on his dresser. It appears he changed into gym pants and a T-shirt after supper, and then later put on a hoodie and left the house."

"And no other clothing is missing?"

"Not that we can tell."

"Well, that sounds like he wasn't planning to be gone long. Not like someone who was running away from his family."

Flynn lets out a dismal breath. "It's been my experience that people intent on committing suicide don't care if they're dressed too lightly for the weather. And they nearly always leave their personal items at home or at the scene of the suicide."

"Suicide!" I shout. "That's crazy. Quinn would never kill himself."

"As I said, that's just one scenario we have to consider. We have your brother's cell phone, tablet, laptop, and office computer and are checking his internet searches to see if anything there might help us understand what happened."

I frown. "Help you with what?"

She bites her bottom lip. "People are surprisingly good at hiding their true emotions from their loved ones. We have found that if they want to disappear, they often plan it out to the last detail. Sometimes we find things on their cell phone records—calls to taxies, airports, bus or train stations, or hotels, often in foreign countries. Or they research methods of committing suicide ahead of committing the act."

My pulse quickens. "Quinn would not abandon his daughters or commit suicide!"

The dark-haired man has been taking notes up until now, but he finally lifts his eyes from his laptop screen and looks at me. Our gazes meet and my breath catches. He is slender, looks to be in his late thirties—and is impossibly good-looking. He gives me a small, kind smile.

My face flushes. I look away fast, slightly flustered.

"I know that's hard to hear," Flynn goes on to say. "But we've been told that after your brother's wife died, he was inconsolable and not in a good mental state."

I shake my head impatiently. "That doesn't mean what you're thinking."

"I'm sorry, but given what we've been told, and what he was wearing when he left the house, we have no choice but to also consider that he may simply have walked away—or jumped from the cliff…"

My stomach drops as though *I* have just stepped off a cliff. Anger bubbles up hotly in my throat.

"And where did you get that ludicrous idea from?" I snap in irritation. "From the town chinwaggers when you were having coffee and donuts at Molly's?"

Flynn's jaw tightens a little, but she keeps her voice even. "Of course not. In fact, our information comes from sources very close to your brother."

I give her a hard look. "What sources? Who?"

"I'd rather not say at this point."

"Suicide is the easy answer, but that doesn't make it the right one," I say angrily.

"I understand, but we have to take it seriously."

I scowl. "It's not true. Quinn would never abandon Brie and Pella. He loved his girls more than life itself. He would never do that to them, send that message to them. Whoever told you that is wrong. What about the big development that's planned for this area, the one Quinn stalled by deciding not to sell? And what about the problems he's been having with the Skinners? They've been offered a lot more than their house is worth and Karl's agreed to sell. But he can't until Quinn does. That's motive for sure. Have you even talked to Karl or his sons?"

She nods seriously. "We have spoken to Mr. Skinner and his sons, but they all have solid alibis to prove they were home from six in the evening until eight the next morning."

I shut my eyes, seething with anger and disgust. "Come on. This is beyond ridiculous. You think Karl isn't smart enough to make sure he and his sons have a solid alibi for the night? Who gave his alibi, his wife Loretta? No surprise, since she's terrified of him."

The sergeant rubs her chin. "It's also been my experience that if someone is planning to abduct another person, they don't do it in the early evening when they might be seen. Odds are they'd do it in the middle of the night. That's the time of day when people are most vulnerable. And as I said, there's no evidence to prove anyone broke into the house. There aren't any signs of a struggle along the edge of the cliff. Or anywhere else on the property, for that matter."

"No footprints? It was raining. The ground would have been muddy."

"It rained heavily that night," Flynn says. "Unfortunately, it was a real downpour and it washed away footprints. We can't tell which way your brother walked when he left the house other than for a few steps along the path toward the cliff's edge. The dog picked up his scent there and followed it into the woods and along a trial he liked to hike through the forest. We have learned that he hiked down this trail many times, usually for thirty minutes before turning around and coming home."

"But this time he vanished," I say, badly shaken. "It has to be the Skinners. Maybe they knew his routine and they grabbed him in the woods."

Flynn lifts a shoulder in a shrug. "Until we find some proof of that, their alibi prevents us from taking them into custody. As I've stated, we've found no evidence of foul play."

I blow my breath out in frustration. "What happens if you don't find Quinn?"

"If we don't find your brother or any sign of him by the middle of next week, we will bring in the cadaver dog."

My stomach rolls. I open my mouth but can't speak, and only close it again. I had expected this, but to hear her say it makes the reality that Quinn might be dead more real. I drop my head and stare at the ground, ice forming in my stomach.

"But it hasn't come to that yet." Flynn hands me a card. "Feel free to call me anytime with questions you might have, or if you want an update on how the search is progressing. I'll call either you or your father immediately if I have any news."

I take the card and nod silently as she starts to walk out of the tent.

From where he stands at the end of the command centre, I feel the dark-haired man's eyes on me as I turn to follow her out.

"Sergeant Flynn," he calls out.

We both stop and turn to face him.

Flynn arches a brow. "Yes?"

The man steps over. "Why don't I show Ms. Hunter around and explain what we've done and what we're doing? It might help a little," he says in a low voice.

The sergeant considers this. "Sure, go ahead."

He looks at me and waits. His eyes are the warm blue of an autumn sky. They mesmerize me.

It takes me a few seconds to reply. "All right, thanks."

He walks me around the tent, pointing to the search equipment lined up on four long folding tables.

"There's the dispatcher radio, maps, laptops, and the GPS unit," he explains, his voice unexpectedly kind. "We've divided the search area up into quadrants. There are three search teams, and three of the four quadrants have been searched twice in a four-mile radius of your brother's house."

I nod and study the equipment, very aware of him. Under the vest, he's wearing a dark blue flannel shirt, a black windbreaker, jeans, and green knee-high rubber boots. His hands are calloused, his lips chapped, his face red from the wind and sun. And he smells nice, like the sea. It's a refreshing, wonderful scent.

He notices me staring at him and smiles. "All that's left is this fourth quadrant. As we speak, search-and-rescue teams are there meticulously searching for your brother. The fourth team is getting ready to join the search, and all four teams will continue until the area has been searched extensively."

"All on foot?" I ask.

"No. Some of the searchers are on ATVs and the RCMP helicopter is flying over the area, too." He tilts his head in regret. "I'm afraid they haven't found anything so far."

"Yes, Sergeant Flynn said that. She doesn't seem to have a lot of hope."

He eyes me, seeming to contemplate his words before speaking. "It's hilly here, and there are many ridges with deep crevices that are hidden by thick brush and trees. Lots of places he could have fallen into or simply got turned around if he was in the deep bush. Don't give up hope. We'll find him."

"She said that, too."

He gives a kind nod. "I hope this has helped a little."

"It has. Thank you."

"You're welcome." His voice is surprisingly warm, his manner gentle, and it stirs me. I watch him walk away, his step light and agile.

I turn and head for my car, face flushed. My heart tumbles strangely in my chest.

CHAPTER TWENTY

I push a cart down the aisle in Munro's Grocery Mart and spot Marty Munro at the back, talking to a store clerk. I graduated high school with him and we hung out together with Malin and a few other friends. We weren't really close, though.

Marty's family has owned the grocery store since our parents were children, and I'd heard he took over the store after his father retired. Other than for his eyeglasses and full petulant lips, he's changed a lot. He's bald with a fleshy hypertensive face, and at least forty pounds heavier.

He looks over the clerk's shoulder and sees me.

"Hi, Raine," he calls out, striding towards me.

I'm in no mood to talk, so I pretend I don't see or hear him. I turn my cart around and walk the other way. But I can hear his footsteps coming up behind me. And then he's there, next to me. He places one hand on my cart.

"Hey, hold on there, Raine."

"Hi, Marty." I try to keep pushing the cart, but he holds onto the side and walks alongside me down the aisle. His shoes make a scuffing sound on the floor as he drags his feet.

"Long time no see." He beams at me. "I never thought you'd come back to Blackheart Bay."

"Trust me, it's temporary."

"I'm sorry it's under such horrible circumstances, though."

Go away, Marty. I keep moving full steam ahead.

"Hey, slow down, Raine."

I groan inwardly, regretting my decision to shop here.

He presses his lips together in annoyance. "Whoa. Come on, stop, will you? If I didn't know better, I'd think you didn't want to talk to me."

I turn my head to the left to scan the rows of canned goods. "I'm in a hurry, that's all."

He smiles and scratches his cheek. "Sure, I understand. It's nice to see you again, Raine."

"Hmm."

"You look great, by the way."

"Thanks," I mumble, thinking that he doesn't look so great. He's freely sweating even though the air conditioning is on and the air in the store is quite cool.

He wiggles his eyebrows. "I just wanted to tell you how much I admire you for what you're doing."

"What do you mean?" I grab some cans of pasta and tomato sauce for the girls, then think they probably need a home-cooked meal. I set them back on the shelf. I make a mean spaghetti dish they may like.

I push the cart down the aisle a bit further and grab a box of spaghetti noodles, a can of diced tomatoes, and some tomato paste. I head toward the produce section to look for garlic, onions, and green peppers.

Marty is hanging onto the cart for dear life. As we walk, he glances around and then lowers his voice. "It can't be easy coming back here to look after your nieces, with Quinn abandoning them like he did."

I halt. "Pardon me?"

He lets go of the cart and tilts his head. "A lot of folks in town are wondering if he kind of cracked up and abandoned his girls. Not me, though. Or maybe, well... you know, living so close to the cliff. He's been really quiet, really down since Holly died. Anyway, whatever has happened, it's awful and I admire you for stepping in and parenting Brie and Pella now. They're sweet little girls."

I feel a rush of heat in my face. "Quinn didn't abandon Brie and Pella," I say, my tone blistering. "And he didn't commit suicide. Those are vicious lies. You need to watch what you say, Marty, especially since you used to complain all the time when we were teens about the gossipers in this town. I'd think you of all people would understand that this town has enough blabbermouths without you joining the club."

His ears turn bright red. "Oh, Raine, no, I didn't mean—"

"Yes, you did."

I whip my cart around, nearly hitting his hip, and stride away as his weak voice pleads for me to stop.

The day started out badly, and it's only getting worse. I'm putting the groceries in the trunk of my car when I hear a another familiar male voice call out. I recognize and despise it. Gritting my teeth, I straighten up slowly, shut the trunk lid, and turn to face him.

"Well, well, so the prodigal daughter has returned," says Karl Skinner.

He stands so close that his big hard belly almost touches me.

"Back up, Karl."

He smirks but steps back. "You haven't changed much."

I remain silent and think that he hasn't changed that much either. His hair is still thick, although it's now coral white. His bulging hooded eyes, pock-marked face, and bowed legs still reminds me of a Komodo dragon.

I walk past him to go around the back of the car.

He smiles. "I just wanted to say hello. What are you so afraid of?"

"I'm not afraid of you, Karl. I just don't want to talk to you." I step over to the driver's side door, but Karl darts around and blocks my way. "Get out of the way."

He watches me steadily, a half-sneer on his face.

"Move," I say angrily.

He moves out of the way and gives a dry, mirthless laugh. "Calm down. What are you so angry about?"

"Like you don't know why."

He blows out his breath. "What? You think me and my boys had something to do with Quinn's disappearance?"

"Me and everyone else in this town."

"Oh, don't be so foolish. None of us laid a hand on him. I think he took off. Probably sunning on a beach in Tahiti right now."

Heat rises in my face. "Liar. If you're so innocent, why did my dad go over to your place Wednesday morning?"

"Because he's a hothead and the biggest hypocrite in town," he says in a snide tone. "Christian or not, he always was, always will be."

"You're the hothead. You're the big hypocrite."

"Look, I told your dad this when he came storming over like a lunatic, and I'm telling you now." He holds his hands out in an innocent gesture. "I wasn't happy with Quinn for refusing to sell, but I wouldn't hurt him. Neither would my boys. So how about you try to be civil when you talk to me?"

"Are you serious? Why would I be civil to a liar and a wife-beater? And your sons are even worse. The worst cowards in town. They're very likely murderers now. And that makes you a murderer, too, because they do what you tell them to do."

His face darkens. "Don't you ever say anything like that about me or my boys again."

"I'll say it as often and as loudly as I want." I raise my voice for the whole town to hear. "You and your sons are cruel cowards who harassed my brother and likely killed him. But you're not going to get away with it. The truth always comes out. Whether now or in the future, you'll all pay for what you've done to Quinn."

He stares at me with predatory eyes. Then, as quick as cobra, he lunges and grabs my forearm, clenching it hard and twisting as he pulls me toward him. His hand is ice-cold and clammy. His fetid breath smells like a dank and mouldy grave.

"Let go!" I shout, trying to wrench my arm free. He won't let go.

He tightens his grip and I feel his pulse through his fingers. His nails cut into my flesh. "No, you listen to me," he says in a low, menacing whisper.

"Get away and get your hands off me, Karl!"

He pulls me in close so his face is only an inch from mine. "I'll put a hand on you and I'll talk to you any time I feel like it. You understand?"

The stench of his breath hits me and I see a big whitish sore with a bright red head on the tip of his tongue. An infected canker or boil. No wonder his breath smells like a grave. I clamp my teeth together, otherwise I might vomit.

I yank with all my power and break free.

"Hey, what's going on there?" says a man behind me.

I turn and see a bent, elderly gentleman walking with a cane. He's stopped on the sidewalk to watch us.

"Nothing's going on, Paul," says Karl. "Raine and I are just catching up."

I realize the old man is Paul Talbot, the former weigh station manager. He takes a shaky step toward us. "Are you all right, Raine? Did he put his hands on you?"

"I'm fine," I assure him. "Everything's fine, Paul."

The frail-looking man, a friend of my dad's and a member New Hope Church, eyes me with concern. "Are you sure? It didn't look or sound like everything is fine to me."

"You heard her. She's fine," snaps Karl. "Now take off, Paul. This is no concern of yours."

"I'll let her tell me that." Paul looks at me again.

"It's all good, really," I assure him. He's clearly too elderly and weak to help even if I needed it, which I don't.

He squints and studies me for a moment. Then he nods and walks away, his pace slow and careful.

Once he's gone, Karl swings his head back to me. "You watch yourself, Raine. Watch your big mouth. I own this town. Always have, always will. Remember that."

He spins around and saunters away, calling out to someone I don't recognize, though he's been watching all this with an open mouth.

Karl treats him to a black look. "You have a problem, too, buddy?"

The man shakes his head nervously, then continues on down the sidewalk.

I watch Karl go up the steps and into the hardware store. Then I get in my car and sit behind the wheel for a minute, trying to calm my breathing. My forearm burns and blood throbs in my ears. I vow to myself that Karl Skinner will never put a hand on me again.

CHAPTER TWENTY-ONE

I pull up the driveway, turn off the engine, and sit there. The ticking of the engine is quickly silenced by the wind and roar of the sea. I see a pile of ceramic casserole dishes and plastic food containers stacked on the front step beside the door, meaning the New Hope Church Ladies' Auxiliary, God's army, has been here.

Movement to the right catches my attention and I spot a tall woman with long, stringy white hair lurking at the side of the house. Our eyes meet and she dashes around to the back.

I climb out of the car just as a gust blows off the Atlantic, laden with brine, kelp, and the scent of pine from the trees on either side of the lighthouse. I draw in a deep breath, then walk around to the back.

There, Gloria Jean Vance crouches with her back pressed against the concrete wall. Her head is bent forward so her forehead rests on her knees, the hood of her green windbreaker pulled up over her ball cap—as though that will keep me from spotting her.

"Hi there, Gloria Jean," I say, searching around her for a shotgun. "How are you?"

She lifts her head. "Raine…"

She stands and shifts something in her hands, although the object is hidden behind her back.

"Is that a gun you're hiding?" I ask. "Because if it is, I'll remind you that this isn't your property, so there's no need to shoot me."

"I know that, Raine." She scowls. "No, it's not a gun. Mounties took my rifle last month after I chased a couple of Mormons off my property. They had no right to take my gun. I only shot it in the air to scare them. I didn't hit anyone."

"I see." It's all I can think to say.

She stares at me with her wildly unnerving crystal-blue eyes, eyes that look startled and frenzied at the same time. They seem to scream that she's suffered an acute shock at some point in her life, something she hasn't fully recovered from. I know from overhearing my parents' whispers that it had something to do with her young husband; I seem to recall that his chainsaw kicked back one day and cut his carotid artery. Gloria Jean, once outgoing and vibrant, had retreated to their home and become a recluse.

Despite being a loner, this woman liked my mom, and when I was a child she sometimes came over to talk to her. She even tolerated the occasional visit from my mom. As far as I know, Mom was the only person back then in all of Blackheart Bay to see the inside of Gloria Jean's house after her husband's death.

After returning from a visit with Gloria Jean, Mom once told my dad that she worried about the woman and felt sorry for her, living such a solitary life. As I study her now, I can't help feeling sorry for her, too. And I wonder if her condition has worsened.

Gloria Jean brings her hands from behind her back and holds out a plastic container of food. She lowers her eyes and drags the toe of her knee-high rubber boot into the dirt.

"I borrowed this beef stew," she says. "I didn't think you'd mind, since you have so much. Your brother always lets me help myself to the vegetables from his garden."

I don't think taking extra veggies from Quinn's garden is the same thing as taking food from containers sitting on the front porch, but I decide it doesn't matter. She must need it. And I'm glad to learn she's been talking to Quinn. At least he provides a little human company.

I smile. "Sure, that's fine."

"The food isn't for me, though," she says. "It's for my babies, Bella and Ben. My old age pension cheque is pretty thin. I can barely afford to feed them. I snare the odd squirrel or rabbit to add to the peas, carrots, and potato mash I make from what I grow in my own garden, and from what your brother gives me, but it's just never enough for them."

"Your babies?"

She allows a tiny smile. "My dogs. Bella's my watchdog, a murderous little Pomeranian. She's only twelve pounds, but she'll take the foot right off anyone before they even realize it's gone. Ben's pretty much useless that way. He's a big gentle Lab and would probably lick the skin right off you. But they're both big eaters!"

"I see."

Gloria Jean looks skinnier than I remember. Her hips are narrower, cheeks hollower, and nose more knife-like. She likely needs the food for herself but is too proud to admit it. Her hair hasn't been cut in years; it hangs loose around her waist, the cotton strands thick, frayed, and split.

She eyes me suspiciously. "You're not going to call the Mounties on me, are you?"

I shake my head. "No."

"Because you don't want to do that," she warns. She lifts a hand and pretends to point a pistol at me. "That wouldn't be a good idea at all."

I stare at her in quiet wonder. She's trespassing and stealing food, yet now she warns me not to call the cops? I can't tell if she's serious.

"No worries there, Gloria Jean. The church ladies have dropped off enough for an army. We'll never be able to eat it all."

She narrows her eyes until they look like cold blue stones. "You making fun of me?"

Great, she's a homicidal recluse and paranoid to boot.

Despite my mom's belief that Gloria Jean was unsociable but harmless, I have to wonder now if she's truly dangerous.

"No, not at all. We have too much food. If you need any more for Bella and Ben, let me know. I'm happy to share it."

She eyes me warily, then nods.

I look up at the sun. "It's getting hot. I should get my groceries and the food into the house before it all spoils. It was nice to see you, Gloria Jean."

Clutching the container of food in her hands, she whirls around and strides across the yard in the direction of her house, disappearing into the trees.

I walk over to the front step and look at all plastic storage containers of chili, chicken soup, Irish stew, and mac and cheese. Two ceramic casserole dishes contain ham and scalloped potatoes and a green bean casserole. There's an ice cream container with a piece of masking tape on the cover that says *Baked Beans and Molasses* in black ink. Next to that are a couple bottles of homemade pickles—one dill, the other bread and butter. There are four bottles of homemade jams in a cardboard box: strawberry, raspberry, strawberry-rhubarb, and blueberry. Next to the box is a chocolate cake with chocolate icing, and two bags of cookies, peanut butter with walnuts and chocolate chip.

I'm glad I missed the women, since they'd have wanted to haul me right down on my knees and have a mini prayer meeting. But I'm thankful for their generosity and kindness. I make a mental note to buy a thank-you card and get Malin to pass it along on Sunday.

I set the container of chocolate chip cookies in the cupboard and the mac and cheese in the fridge for supper. All the rest goes in the freezer. Once the groceries have been put away, I put the kettle on for a cup of tea.

That's when I hear the crunch of tires on the driveway. From the living room window, I see a woman climb out of the driver's seat of a glossy black sedan. My dad is getting out the passenger side.

I flinch and step away from the window, anger flaring up. What is he doing here?

I don't move when I hear the knock on the door. Then there's a second, more forceful knock and I heave out a breath.

Opening the door, I peer out at my dad. I haven't seen him since Holly's funeral, though we didn't speak at the time. He tried a few times, but I avoided him. He looks older now, thinner and greyer. His face is drawn and heavily lined. His frail appearance shocks me, but that's exactly what he is now.

His smoky blue eyes are almost hidden by puffy flesh, but they light up when he sees me. "Hi Raine. It's so wonderful to see you."

"They let you out of the hospital early?"

He breaks into a fragile smile. "Apparently I'm not going to die—yet."

I nod, unamused.

He rubs the grey stubble on his chin and clears his throat. "My doctor thought I was doing well enough to go home, but I have to go back for a stress test and bloodwork. After that I should be fine. I can't drive for a month."

I give him another quick, indifferent nod.

"I hope you're not angry I've come here without calling first," he says. "I was afraid if I called, you'd hang up on me.

"You thought right," I say coldly.

Sorrow passes over his face and I feel a twinge of guilt. I bury it fast.

"So how are you, Raine?"

I give a tepid shrug.

"May we come in?" he says. Hesitating, my eyes go from him to the woman beside him. That must be Lena. "Please, Raine. We haven't spoken in fifteen years. You're my daughter and I love you. I hate this awful bitterness between us. I want it to end, please."

I let out an irritated breath and look over his shoulder towards the trees. Although I'm annoyed, his words penetrate the wall of anger I've erected around my heart—at least, enough to let him in for a short time.

"Fine," I say flatly.

I stand back and he pushes open the screen door, holding it for Lena to enter first. He comes in next and turns around in the foyer to face me. We stare at each other, saying nothing. Then, before I can dodge out of the way, he pulls me into an embrace, abrupt and firm.

"I'm so glad you came, Raine," he says into my ear. I stand stiff, my arms at my sides. "This is Lena, my fiancée."

He smiles as he looks at her, his eyes full of love.

"Wonderful," I say and we fall into tense silence.

To break the tension, Lena steps forward. "It's nice to finally meet you."

She's tall, not fat but solidly built. Her hair is an unnatural shade of red with streaks of pink on one side. Her eyes are sage green, big and round. Her face is pale and she has freckles across her nose. She's wearing a turquoise ankle-length skirt, a white cotton top, and brown leather sandals—and a lot of sea glass jewellery. Earrings, necklace, and three bracelets on each wrist.

"Hi," I say without a smile.

"I've heard a lot about you." Her jangling voice sounds like waves rolling in over small pebbles.

I laugh bitterly. "I bet."

Her smile fades and we stand there awkwardly, staring at each other. She lifts her sea glass bracelets up and down repeatedly, the clinking noise filling the room.

I avert my gaze. The woman is so nervous to meet me that she's making me nervous. And her habit of widening her eyes creeps me out. In three months, she'll be my stepmother.

Terrific.

"Aren't you going to invite us inside?" Dad raises his eyebrows. "Or are we going to visit here in the foyer?"

I hesitate. "Come in," I say with enough reluctance in my tone that it's impossible for him to miss.

Lena follows me into the kitchen, but Dad takes longer, shuffling along at a glacial pace. Once we're all in the kitchen, I gesture for them to take a seat at the table.

"Want a tea or coffee?" I ask. It's clear that I'm just being polite and don't really want them to stay long enough to have one.

Dad picks up on my tone. "No, but thanks."

I lean back against the counter, fold my arms, and eye them like they're here to sell me pots and pans.

After an uncomfortable minute of silence, Dad pinches his lips together. "What's wrong? Are you okay?"

"I'm fine."

His thick grey eyebrows furrow. "You sure? You look a bit frazzled around the edges."

"Oh?" I almost laugh. I look frazzled around the edges? Maybe he should take a closer look at his girlfriend. But I keep my mouth shut and simply shake my head. "It's nothing. I bumped into Karl Skinner earlier when I was in town."

"Did he do something to you?"

I shrug it off. "No, he was just trying to rattle me. It's nothing to worry about."

His face tightens. "Tell me if he did something to you, Raine. I'll go over right now and talk to him."

I shake my head, since he doesn't look like he can walk from the house to his car without help.

"Dad, I can take care of myself. It's just been a frustrating morning. I spoke to Sergeant Flynn earlier and got the feeling she thinks Quinn either committed suicide or took off to Tahiti. It's ludicrous."

He nods grimly. "I know. She told me the same thing, that they have to take those possibilities into consideration."

"I just don't understand why they can't arrest Karl and his sons now," I grumble. "Alibi or not, they have the motive to want Quinn gone and they're the only ones in town who are capable of doing it."

He only shakes his head. "I know. I'm not sure about Cormac, though. He doesn't seem capable of the same violence as his brothers. Do you know that when I had my heart attack, Karl, Aubrie, and Jarrod just laughed and went back into the house? They left me lying on their lawn. But Cormac called 911 and stayed with me. He even took off his jacket and put it under my head. He talked to me, comforting me until the ambulance arrived."

"I'm glad to hear that, Dad. He wasn't a bad guy in high school. I really hope he didn't have anything to do with Quinn's disappearance."

"Quinn's been going for walks in the early evenings," Dad concedes. "Maybe he just got lost this time. Or stumbled and fell. The weather turned so quickly he may have lost his bearings. There are crevices in the woods he wouldn't have been able to see in the dark. If so, the searchers will find him. We have to keep hope."

"Yes," I agree.

We fall silent for a time.

"I want to tell you something else," Dad says guardedly. "Quinn had been depressed. It began after Holly died and worsened the first year after her death."

"Yeah, so? Holly's death hit him hard. He was crushed. That's natural. It's a wonder he didn't lose his faith. I mean, how ironic is it that a pastor's wife dies in a flash flood while on a mission's trip to Costa Rica? But he seemed better when he came up to Halifax last year."

"I know, but still—"

"What are you saying? That you think Quinn killed himself, too?"

He shakes his head. "I don't know. It's just that if the Skinners didn't do this, and he didn't get lost or fall accidentally, then…"

I blink, can't speak.

"It's not what I truly believe has happened," he clarifies. "I just wanted you to know, in case you heard some talk around town. People noticed how down he'd been."

"People can be cruel," says Lena, reaching out and squeezing my dad's arm. "Better to let it slide right over your shoulder. That's what I've always done."

I look at her, ready to agree, but she's smiling that jittery smile and blinking way too fast.

"I just think maybe we should be prepared," Dad says with a grave tone. I stare at him in shock. "You're shocked. I understand. But Raine, what if—"

"Dad, I can't believe you'd even consider that."

He sighs. "Raine…"

"Raine what? How can you even think this? I don't know why I even let you in here."

Dad tries again. "Come on now."

I glance at my wristwatch and head out of the kitchen. "I'm going to pick up the girls at school. You guys can let yourselves out."

"Raine, please," Dad says to my retreating back. "Don't leave angry."

I look back over my shoulder. "I'm not angry. Lock the door when you go. And there's no need for you two to come back here again."

"She's really fuming," Lena says to Dad, as if I'm not standing right there in earshot.

"I know, love." Dad pats her hand. "I know."

Angry as all get out, I leave the house and bang the door hard behind me.

CHAPTER TWENTY-TWO

"Pell, hurry up and finish getting dressed," Brie says to her sister. "Malin's going to be here soon."

"But Aunt Raine's still in bed. I don't think she's coming."

"Yes, she is. I heard her walking around her bedroom. She's just stalling. Come on, lift your arms."

I peer around the open doorway into Pell's room and see her lift her arms so Brie can pull her top on. I slip away and go back into my bedroom to change.

I agreed to take the girls to church today mostly because Quinn would have wanted me to, but also because Malin has been driving me nuts about it. Truth is, I hate the whole idea. But Malin loves going. She's a devout Christian and active member of New Hope, singing soprano in the choir and teaching Pella's Sunday school class.

Malin has said she'll pick us up. She's probably afraid I won't go if she doesn't drive. That means we'll get to ride in her gleaming red convertible. I know the girls will be happy about that.

I don't like people much. In particular, I don't like the people at New Hope much. I think half the members still blame me for my parents leaving the ministry back in 1996. When I attended with my family after we returned from Australia, it felt like I'd been dropped in a pit of Taipan snakes—and they were all watching me with a fierce, predatory intensity.

I hear a car door open and shut outside, followed by footsteps on the porch.

"I'm here," Malin shouts up the stairs. "You guys ready?"

"Yes!" the girls shout back in unison. They run down the stairs.

My phone rings and I see that it's Sergeant Flynn. She calls every morning with an update.

"I've got a phone call, Malin," I yell down. "I'll be a few minutes."

After a brief, discouraging update from Flynn, I hang up the phone. There's nothing new to report. Heartsick, I finish dressing, then head out of my room. Downstairs, the girls are talking to Malin and I stop and listen.

"In case you don't know, Malin, the Taipan snake is just one of the many lethal snakes that live in Australia."

Malin sighs loudly. "Please tell me you acquired this knowledge in school."

"No, Aunt Raine told us."

"Oh course she did."

"When she and Dad were children, they lived for a short time in Australia. Last night she told Pell and me a story about how once she and her family were hiking along a trail and came upon a fat Taipan slithering right toward them. She said it was as thick as a telephone pole and coiled not more than three feet from her, tongue darting in and out, head high and weaving, ready to attack her…"

Grinning, I peer down to the lower level and see Brie standing in the foyer. She's holding her arm up and moving it in the air like a snake. The blood drains from Pell's face. Malin must have seen it, too.

"That's enough, Brie," she says sharply. "No more snake stories. Anyway, listen: your aunt isn't married and has no children. Thus, she has no clue how to raise children, or especially how to put them to bed. What she should be doing is saying your prayers with you, then tucking you in and reading you a good wholesome children's story. Not telling you some horror story about close calls with venomous snakes."

"And spiders and jellyfish," Brie says, sounding like she enjoyed those stories. "I like when she says goodnight the best. She says, 'Well, okay then. Goodnight, sleep tight, and don't let the redback spiders bite."

Malin groans. "All right, that's enough. You girls go out and get in my car. Your aunt and I will be out in a minute."

Uh-oh, I think.

Once the girls are gone, I come down and join Malin in the foyer. She stands in the foyer with her hands on her hips.

"No more horror stories before bed," she barks. "You hear me?"

"Fine."

"And no more complaining about the members of New Hope. I'm sick of it. Sure, a few of them stare, but most are genuinely nice. Almost all ask how you, your dad, and the girls are doing and tell you they're praying for you all. Many of them brought food, and many others are helping in the search for Quinn. So you need to quit all this grumbling in front of the girls."

I close my eyes.

"Raine, I mean it."

"I said, fine."

"Was that Sergeant Flynn on the phone?" Malin asks.

"Yes, but I'll tell you about it later. I don't want the girls to hear us talking about it in the car."

"Okay. Now put a cheery smile on that face in front of those sweet little girls. The last thing we want is them turning out like you."

Malin goes out and walks towards the car, her steps brisk. I trudge behind her, grumbling under my breath the whole way.

After the service is over, we all gather downstairs for some light refreshments.

"Now how adorable is that?" Malin says, nudging me.

I follow her eyes to Marty Munroe, who's standing at the buffet table vacuuming up piles of food from a paper plate he's holding in one hand. Even from across the room a big blob of mayonnaise is visible at the corner of his mouth.

I frown. "Marty?"

"No, the guy walking toward Marty. Della Darling's nephew."

I see a dark-haired man join Marty at the table. He picks up a Styrofoam cup and pours coffee into it while greeting Marty. I recognize him as the man who showed me around the RCMP command centre tent.

"Ooh lala," says Malin. "I believe he's the one. Your soul mate, your true love."

I snort. "You forgot Mr. Right."

"Him, too." She adds, grinning.

Marty leans sideways and says something to the man, who still hasn't formally introduced himself to me. His eyes wander around the room. Our gazes meet and a corner of his mouth turns up in a shy smile, revealing even white teeth.

For some reason I can't begin to comprehend, I shoot back a nasty scowl.

He frowns, puzzled, and then turns his attention to Marty again.

Malin cringes. "Oh, no, no, no… did you just give that man a dirty look?"

"Don't think so."

"You did, too. I saw you." She smacks me hard on the arm. "What is wrong with you? Unbelievable. The hottest guy to ever live in this town smiles at you and you shoot him a glare that would scare away a bunch of starving coyotes."

"It's a pack or a band."

She makes a face. "What?"

"You said a bunch. A group of coyotes is called a pack or a band."

She stares at me for a minute. "Whatever. I just wish you hadn't looked at him like that."

"Why?"

"Because he'll think you're rude *and* crazy."

I laugh quietly.

"Where did he go?" she says, frantically searching the room. "I can't see him."

"Haven't a clue."

"Well, I'm going to find him and apologize for you. How are you ever going to meet someone if you—"

"Stop."

She shakes her head and walks toward the food tables. And once she's gone, I scan the room again. I don't see him anywhere. I sigh, uncertain why I even looked for him and appalled that I felt disappointed.

"Hi, Raine," Marty calls towards me with a big wave and a concerned look. He's walking right at me, perspiring so heavily that when he lifts his arm to wave, I see a circle of sweat under his armpit. "How are things going?"

"Fine, Marty," I blurt, throwing him a small wave back as I stride quickly away. "Sorry, have to run."

He halts in the middle of the room, looking baffled. A blob of mayonnaise still hangs at the corner of his mouth.

"Raine, hold on," he calls again. "You're not still upset with me, are you?"

"Of course not," I say over my shoulder, and keep going. "Have to collect my nieces for their dental appointments."

He frowns. "On a Sunday?"

Oops. I walk faster, ears burning. Have I no shame? Lying right in church.

I lose him and step into the children's play room, but seconds later I leave again without the girls. They're too deeply engrossed in a game of Uno to drag them away.

Scanning the room for Marty, I'm relieved not to see him. I walk over to the refreshment table and pick up a fudge brownie. I open my mouth wide to take a big bite and—

"I read the obituary you wrote for my aunt," a man says behind me.

I spin around, brownie halfway to my wide open mouth. My heart flutters strangely again. It's him, that dark-haired member of the search-and-rescue team.

"Pardon?"

"I said I read the obituary you wrote for my aunt, Della Darling. She died last month. It was in the *Herald*. It was very interesting, to say the least."

"Do I know you?" I mumble around a mouthful of brownie, pretending I don't remember him.

"We met a few days ago at the command centre. I showed you around the tent?"

I shake my head, my expression blank. "Sorry."

He smiles. "That's understandable. This is an extremely difficult time for you." I stay silent. "I'm Landry Storm. You're the obituary writer for the *Herald*, aren't you?"

"Mm–mmm," I murmur, holding my hand in front of my mouth as I swallow.

"Anyway, I found Della's obituary enjoyable. It wasn't the typical cookie-cutter obituary!"

"Well, your uncle gave me some information about your aunt and he asked me to make it a bit humorous. Apparently your aunt didn't *want* a traditional obituary…"

"It was very funny. I laughed and I cried. You did a wonderful job."

A flash of warm blood surges to my face. I drop my eyes and nod vaguely, my back slick with sweat.

He's wearing a white dress shirt with a red tie. His shirtsleeves are turned up and his tie is loosened, but not because he's hot; he appears to be as cool as a cucumber. I stare at his forearms. They're tanned, lean but chiselled and covered with fine hair that's turned golden-brown from the sun. And he still smells good—sweet yet salty and tangy, like the sea.

I also notice that he's observing me with an expression of amusement.

My temper flares. "Is something funny?"

He seems to consider that before he replies. At last he says, "No. I enjoyed my aunt's obituary, actually."

I nod once. Slowly, doubtfully.

His eyes are a startling blue. His brown hair has receded at the temples and is greying at the sides. He has an unflappable confidence that reveals a quiet strength. I have to admit, he's attractive with his quick smile and easy laugh.

And he oozes honesty. Definitely out of my league, since I'm disfigured, rarely smile, laugh like a hyena, and the only thing quick about me is my temper.

I touch my scar and turn my face sideways to hide it from him.

He pours coffee into a Styrofoam cup and holds it out to me. "Why don't we call a truce?"

I narrow my right eye at him.

"Oops. No truce or… you don't like coffee?"

"In fact, I love coffee."

"Ah," he says. "Okay, no truce then."

"I didn't realize we were at war."

A corner of his mouth turns up in a smile. "Aha, so you don't like *this* coffee then." He studies the cup. "You might have a point. It does look strong. Why don't we grab a coffee somewhere else? There's a nice little café on the corner."

I eye him cynically. "We, meaning you and me?"

"Yes, of course we meaning you and me."

"What's going on?"

He shakes his head, perplexed. "What do you mean?"

"What are you up to?" I ask, gazing around the room. "Did someone put you up to this?"

"Up to? I'm not up to anything. And no one put me up to this. I just thought it would be nice to go have a cup of coffee with you. If you needed to talk or had any other questions about the search for your brother, I thought I could help."

Malin is standing against the wall to my right, watching us. She has gotten as close as she can without looking like she's snooping. She gives me a shameless smile and I look back murderously.

"So?" He lifts an eyebrow, waits.

"So what?"

"So would you like to have a coffee with me?"

"That will be the day."

He tilts his head to one side. "Pardon?"

I look him right in the eye. "Let me make this clear. To be honest, Mr. Storm, I'd rather be stung by a box jellyfish than go for coffee with you."

He blinks and steps back. I feel appalled with myself. Face hot as a forest fire, I abruptly stride away, feeling his eyes searing the back of my neck.

I walk speedily to the door and pass Malin, who knows me well enough not to look shocked. "Raine, why would you say something like that to him?"

I shake my head and reach for the door handle.

"You'd rather be stung by a box jellyfish?" Malin says to my fleeing back. "Now how cray-cray was that?"

"Mind your own business for a change."

123

"Raine… no, wait. That's the fire es—"

I go out and let the metal door slam hard behind me, setting off the fire alarm. The cacophony shrieks through the entire church and out into the quiet afternoon air. I ignore it and jog across the parking lot to Malin's car, but the doors are locked. Flustered, I run out of the parking lot and head down the sidewalk at a fast clip, the alarm not fading until I'm four streets away.

Five minutes later, a car pulls up alongside me.

"Raine, come on. Get in," Malin calls through the window of her convertible.

Brie and Pell are watching me from the backseat. They look at me like I'm a patient on the lam from an insane asylum.

I just keep walking. "No thanks."

"So you're mad at me? Hey, I'm not the one who told an exceptionally attractive guy who just asked me out on a date that I'd rather be stung by a jellyfish."

Brie and Pell erupt into giggles.

"He wasn't asking me out on a date," I say defensively. "He just asked me to go for a coffee."

Malin groans. "That *is* a date, you moron!"

"Doesn't matter. I don't want to go for a coffee with him."

"Why on earth not? You must be completely deranged to turn him down, and oh so politely, too!" she says with an exasperated roll of her eyes.

"I'm done with men. I've sworn off them."

She laughs. "You've sworn off men?"

"Yes, it's for the best. I don't get them, and they don't get me."

"Big surprise there."

I'm almost to the centre of town now, but Malin and the girls just keep following me in the car. Brie's and Pell's eyes are bright with glee. They're enjoying this far too much for my liking.

Malin softens her tone. "Raine, get in. It's a gorgeous day. The girls and I are starving. Let's get some fish and chips from Molly's and eat at the park."

"Yay!" Brie and Pella shout in delight, clapping their hands.

"You guys go ahead," I mutter.

"Not without you," Malin says. "Come on."

"Yeah, come on, Aunt Raine," Brie and Pella chime in.

I wave them off. "I wouldn't be good company. I'm in a bad mood."

"You're always in a bad mood, Aunt Raine," Brie says frankly. "Come with us anyway. We want you to."

I can see that they genuinely want me to join them, and instantly my bad mood fades.

"Fine," I say, then walk around the front of the car and climb in the passenger side.

Malin steers away from the curb. "Stung by a jellyfish? Really, Raine?"

"Oh, be quiet."

She grins. "All right."

CHAPTER TWENTY-THREE

We sit at a wooden picnic table under the shade of an oak tree eating our takeout fish and chips. The leaves on the trees shiver in the breeze coming off the harbour. A young female park employee steers her ride-on lawnmower across the lawn about fifty yards away, filling the air with the smell of freshly mown grass.

"How'd you find church?" Malin asks.

I shrug. "Not as bad as I expected. It was a nice service and most people were concerned about Quinn, the girls, and Dad."

"And you," she adds. "They're concerned and praying for you, too."

I shrug again, feeling indifferent.

"They're good people, Raine, and they're my friends. They love your dad, Quinn, and the girls. Give them a chance." I nod vaguely. "I noticed your dad and Lena weren't there. He knew they were having a special prayer service for Quinn and a gathering downstairs after. He must not be feeling well enough or he would have attended. I think you should go check on him after we're finished eating."

"Didn't we just have this discussion the other day?"

She takes a drink from her bottle of spring water. "Yes, we did. So what?"

"So I already saw him."

"I know he and Lena came to visit," she says pointedly. "I'm saying it's your turn to go visit him."

"I can just call him, Mal. I don't have to drive over there to check on him."

"Yes, you do. And bring the girls. It's not all about you. He's their grandfather. They've always been close to him and haven't seen him since he went in the hospital. He misses them and they miss him." She looks at Brie and Pell. "Don't you, girls?"

"Yes!" they say in unison.

Malin looks at me and smiles triumphantly.

I sigh through my nose, slightly irked. But she has a point, and clearly Brie and Pell want to see their grandfather.

"Fine," I say. "But we're only staying a half-hour, max."

"We'll give him a call after we're finished lunch and see if he's up for some company," Malin tells them.

I give her a dirty look, but she just grins at me.

This is when I notice a couple and their two young children coming our way. The dad carries a picnic cooler, the mom a canvas tote bag overflowing with food. They sit at the picnic table nearest ours, their voices and laughter clearly audible.

I glare over at the family. "Unbelievable."

"What's wrong?" Malin asks.

"I hate when people sit right next to you in a public park when there are other empty tables available. People do it in restaurants, too. There's plenty of empty tables, and they plop their butts down right beside you chattering away like a bunch of squirrels. Drives me nuts."

She glances over at the family. "You familiar with any of the symptoms of Asperger's Syndrome?"

I shake my head. "No, why?"

"Look it up. While we're on the topic of Asperger's, I still can't believe what you said to Landry Storm. That's always the way. If I weren't in a serious relationship with Tanner, and if he had asked me to join him for a coffee, I'd say yes in a heartbeat."

I swallow the food in my mouth. "Sorry."

"You are not."

I smile, drink some water.

"I wonder where he banks. I've never seen him in mine," she says. "Maybe he needs a loan or something. I could give him my business card, and if he comes in I could kind of casually mention you. Maybe set up a date."

"Do not!"

She waves that away. "I just might. Did you know he's the director of the search-and-rescue group in the southeast and southwest areas of the province? He took over a few weeks ago when Greg Morton retired."

I pick up a fry and pop it in my mouth. "I actually met him at the command centre a couple of days ago, so I knew he was a member of the search team. But I figured he was a volunteer."

Mal widens her eyes. "You already met him?"

"Yes. So?"

"Anyway, as I was trying to tell you, he came here to care for Della when she was ill. After she died, he stayed, told people he loved it here. I heard this from Trish Carew, whose husband Finn is a search-and-rescue volunteer. She said Landry isn't one to stay at the command centre giving orders. He's been out in the field every day, searching through rough terrain and in bad weather since the first day."

I'm impressed, but I hide it from Malin. "He gave me a tour of the command centre tent, but he never let on that he's the director of the SAR group."

"Maybe he was going to do that today and that's why he asked you to go for a coffee, Dummy."

"Where did he live before he moved here?" I ask. "What did he do?"

"Winnipeg, although I'm not sure what he did there." She grins. "But I'd put my money on him being a male model."

I have to smile at that.

We eat in silence for a moment, then Malin frowns at me. "I heard him talking to you about Della's obituary. Sounded like he enjoyed it."

"Yes, apparently. I have to say, though, her life was kind of sad. She never stepped foot outside of Nova Scotia. She lived in the same house she was born in... in fact, she lived her entire life in this bleak little town. Her life was depressingly bland."

Malin stiffens. "I was born in Blackheart Bay and have lived my entire thirty-three years here in this 'bleak little town,' other than for my time away at university. I'll die here too, Raine. Does that make my life depressingly bland and boring to you? Am I less of a person in your eyes?"

I feel my face flush. "No. Of course not. You live here, sure, but you travel. You've been to the Bahamas, Cuba, Mexico, and Europe. It's not the same. Not at all."

"I don't know about that. I'm thinking you'll feel my obituary needs some spicing up, too, and you better not. Because I love this town and the people who live here. I am happy, Raine. And where have you lived besides Halifax, Ms. World Traveller? To be honest, you don't seem very happy despite your leaving town as soon as you could move to the city."

I drink some water and am about to counter that when I see her look over my shoulder. Her face flinches.

"What is it, Mal?" I turn my head and follow her eyes to the parking lot.

Aubrie, Jarrod, and Cormac Skinner are sitting in a sand-coloured pickup truck parked in the lot facing us. Jarrod's behind the wheel, staring at us behind dark sunglasses. Aubrie's next to him and Cormac sits by the passenger door.

"Now what do they want?" I say.

Malin nods uneasily. "I don't know, but I think they're watching us. They're looking this way and there's no one else in their line of sight."

The Skinners climb out of the truck and cut across the lawn toward us. Jarrod's step is brisk while Aubrie limps alongside him. Cormac saunters casually behind, his eyes never leaving us.

Malin's face sets in a thin, tight line. "They're coming."

"Girls, you're finished your lunch, aren't you? Why don't you go play for a little while?" I point towards the playground on the other side of the lawn. "Stay in our sight, though."

Pell looks down at her fries. "But I'm not finished."

"Me neither," adds Brie.

"Fine. But eat up fast and then go play."

Jarrod and Aubrie walk around the table and stand beside Malin, obstructing the sun. Cormac stops at the side of the table. Jarrod and Aubrie both take their sunglasses off and stare at us with sour expressions. Aubrie is smoking a liquorice-scented cigarillo. He takes one last drag and drops it to the ground, grinding it out with his boot heel.

"What do you guys want?" I ask.

"We heard you're telling everyone in town that you think we're responsible for Quinn's disappearance?" Jarrod says, his tone furious. "Is that true?"

I nod. "Yes. So what?"

He pulls on the lobe of his ear. "So we want you to stop. It's not true. We never touched your brother."

"Fine. You've said what you came to say." I give them all a hard look. "Now you guys can go. You're upsetting my nieces."

"They're not upsetting me, Aunt Raine," Brie says boldly. "I'm not afraid of them."

"Me neither," says Pella, trying to be as brave as her sister.

Malin smiles at her and puts an arm around Pella's shoulders. "Nor am I."

"And I certainly am not," I say coldly, directing it at the brothers. "So leave us alone."

Jarrod twists his lips up in a cruel smile. "We'll leave when we're good and ready, not before."

Cormac looks up from staring at the ground. "Jarrod, come on. Let's go."
Jarrod ignores him.

Aubrie steps around the table and points a finger at me. "We didn't have anything to do with your brother disappearing. Everyone in town knows he either flew the coop or took a dive off the cliff."

I hear Pella let out a soft cry.

"Brie, please take your sister over to the playground," I say. Brie nods, takes Pell's hand, and leads her across the lawn to the swing set. I turn back to Jarrod. "I think you've done something horrible to Quinn. Like I told your father, you won't get away with it."

Jarrod's nostrils flare. "Where's your proof?"

"The police will find the proof," I counter.

"No they won't, 'cause there's none to find."

Aubrie snickers and Jarrod's cruel smile never leaves his face. Cormac is staring at something over my shoulder and won't meet my eyes, not that it matters much with his dark sunglasses.

While Aubrie's peculiar laugh is unsettling, there's something equally disturbing about Jarrod's constant smile. Aubrie's eyes are empty and Jarrod's are cold and detached. And Jarrod's ears are strange-looking; his left ear is bigger than the right and the lobe is an odd colour, and misshapen. It looks like a blob of purple jelly.

The Skinners are a nasty, frightening bunch.

Jarrod releases a breath, then turns his head and stares out over the harbour. The sound of the mower grows louder as it moves closer.

"I'm done talking to these fools," Jarrod says finally.

The three brothers turn and walk back to the truck in the parking lot. I watch them walk away. Before they get to their truck, though, I notice Landry Storm nearby. He's leaning on the hood of a grey SUV, watching all this. Once the Skinners drive away, he straightens up and heads toward us.

Landry stands at the end of the table and studies us closely. "Is everything okay?" he asks. "Looked like you were having a heated exchange with those guys."

Malin sighs. "Well, no, they—"

"Everything's fine," I say coldly.

"You're sure?" he says.

"We're entirely sure," I snap. "We may be women, Mr. Storm, but I can assure you we can take care of ourselves. No chance of any of us here fainting from fear."

Malin winces. "Raine..."

A hint of a smile hits Landry's eyes. "I have no doubt, Ms. Hunter, that you can take care of yourself just fine."

"Not me," Malin pipes up, giving him a helpless look. "I nearly fainted."

"Would you like some water?" he asks her.

"Yes, thank you so much," Malin says, in a fake weak voice.

I look at her in disgust and point to the bottle of spring water she's been sipping from ever since we sat down to eat. "Mal, you have water. There's a bottle right in front of you."

"Oh, right, so I do." She glances darkly at me, embarrassed. "So I do."

I look up at him. "Did you follow us here from church?"

He blinks. "Did I *what*?"

Malin catches my eye and shakes her head vigorously.

I ignore her and narrow my eyes at him. "Did you follow us here? Are you some kind of stalker?"

Mal mouth falls open. She stares at me, mortified.

Landry hesitates, then nods his head to the right. "No. Actually I'm here for a family picnic."

"Mm, a family picnic," I say, doubtfully.

Malin releases a long despairing moan.

His eyes linger on me. "I'd better get over there. Enjoy the rest of your day."

We watch him walk across the lawn and over to a group of people gathered around three picnic tables set up under the shade trees. I notice quite a few of them look suspiciously like him.

Malin swings her head back to me with a look of profound disbelief. "Followed us here from church?" she says, incredulous. "You accused him of stalking us?"

I feel extremely embarrassed, but I won't let on. "Well, it seemed like way too much of a coincidence to me."

"Are you mental?"

"That's not nice, Mal."

She stares at me. "I thought you couldn't do or say anything more to shock me, but this time you outdid yourself. What is it like living in la-la land? Can you tell me?"

"It's not lonely, trust me on that. And what about you, Mal? What was up with that helpless voice?"

"He was only showing concern... concern toward you, I might add. Thought I'd help you out by keeping him here." She lets out a long breath. "I don't understand you..."

I hold up a hand. "Don't say it, Mal."

"I think he likes you. Why are you so rude to him? Wait, never mind. I know why."

I snort. "You do?"

"You're scared to start dating again."

"I am *not* afraid. I'm just not interested."

"Bull. You like him. That's why you're trying as hard as you can to push him away."

"Do I pay you now or at the end of this therapy appointment?"

She's quiet for a few seconds. "I understand your fear, but he seems like such a nice guy. I mean, clearly he doesn't take offense easily. I really believe there's nothing to be afraid of with him."

"Mal, please, drop it."

"Fine." She shrugs irritably. "It's not like anything I say will make a difference anyway. Never has, never will."

CHAPTER TWENTY-FOUR

Malin pulls up in my dad's driveway. His two-storey house is slate-blue with a closed-in front porch. It faces the sidewalk of Harborview Street; its back, the harbour. Its cedar shingles are grey with age, salt, and weather, yet it looks to be in good shape. A lime-green car is parked next to Dad's car and I figure it must be Lena's.

"Grampy, Grampy!" Pell and Brie shout when he answers the door.

We enter the foyer and he drops to his knees, holding out his arms as they run to him.

"How are my girls?" He hugs them tightly. "Oh, I've missed you."

"We missed you, too, Grampy." Pella lays her head down on his shoulder for a long time.

Malin watches them, her eyes moist. She's such a softie.

I gaze idly around the place, at the black leather couch and loveseat in the living room. The coffee and end tables are black, too, wrought-iron with glass tops. A wide bookcase against the wall overflows with books. It's cosy, bright, and clean.

Dad is dressed in pyjamas and housecoat. I know Malin is right, that he's missed church because he isn't feeling well, but I'm irritated being around him so I don't bother to ask how he is. Lena, still wearing a light jacket, is holding a pot. I figure she's only just gotten here and has brought lunch.

Mal and Lena take the girls into the kitchen so Dad and I can talk about Quinn without upsetting them.

"I'm so happy you came over," Dad says when he and I are alone in the living room. He moves unsteadily to embrace me, but I dart back. He drops his arms. "Why don't you and the girls stay for lunch? Lena made squash and sweet potato soup. It's delicious."

"We already ate."

"Well, come over tomorrow night for supper then?" His voice fades when he sees the look in my eyes. "Or maybe not."

There's a moment of uneasy silence. I hear the girls, Lena, and Malin laughing in the kitchen. That irritates me, too.

Dad clears his throat. "I was going to ask you and the girls to stay here with me, but I imagine the answer is no to that, too."

"You're right."

"I just thought the noise of the search helicopter, the four-wheelers… it must be upsetting for the girls, and you."

I shrug benignly, but in truth the constant *thump-thump* of the helicopter has been disturbing.

"For the first few days, I kept the radio or television on to drown it out when the girls were home," I say. "But the search has moved farther away from the house now and the noise is much fainter."

"All right then. I spoke with Sergeant Flynn earlier."

"I know. She told me. She called me before we left for church."

His face brightens. "You went to church? I'm happy to hear that, Raine."

"Don't get excited, Dad. Mal and the girls dragged me there."

He sighs softly. "Anyway, when I spoke to Sergeant Flynn she told me this is still a missing persons case, not a criminal investigation. There's still no evidence to show that the Skinners are responsible. Nothing at all to suggest anything criminal happened to him."

"She told me pretty much the same thing. There's no crime scene, no evidence, and no witnesses," I say, frustrated. "And even if they do find Quinn's body in the water, there aren't any signs of a struggle along the cliff to prove he was pushed off…"

Dad draws in a deep breath through his nose. "It's the not knowing that kills me. Wondering if he's alive or dead. Wondering if he tripped… if he got lost or is hurt in the woods… I'm worried sick that the Skinners abducted him, that they're holding him somewhere trying to get him to agree to sell his place."

I've had the same worries.

"Or… was he really so depressed over Holly's death that he took off? Or jumped?" Dad says. "That's harder to deal with than the things we know for sure."

A gust of wind wails in off the harbour and slams into the back wall. The house shudders.

I wait for the wind to die down. "Dad, will you stop staying that! Suicide is the easy answer, but it's not the right answer. Quinn would never leave Brie and Pella. He would never kill himself."

"In my heart, I know that." He lifts a shoulder in a miserable shrug. "But that's what the police think. So do a lot of people in town."

"Ignore it, Dad. They're all wrong."

We fall silent. The strong wind whips up off the harbour again and lashes the windows. I look out the back window to the choppy water and watch a blue and white lobster boat steam back in, heading for the wharf, its hull low, its deck full of traps.

"It's under terrible circumstances, but I'm glad you came home and that we're talking again, Raine," he says softly.

I give him a sharp look. "We're talking about Quinn, that's it. Nothing's changed between us, Dad. You blamed me for Natalie's death. Have you forgotten that?"

A shadow slides across his face. "No, of course I haven't forgotten. You have no idea how deeply I regret my words. I regretted them the moment I spoke them. I'm the one who took the family to a dangerous land, put you in peril to live my dream. And look what happened—"

"Really, because you pretty much said it again after Mom died. Do you remember that, the day I left?"

Tears of remorse well up in his eyes. "The day Nat died, in the heat of the moment, I blamed you. But I was wrong, so wrong. I couldn't live with my own grief. You were just a child. But I never truly blamed you, Raine. And when you were eighteen and we had that terrible fight… no, Raine, I did not say it the day you left."

"You did," I accuse, raising my voice.

"You misunderstood or heard what you wanted to hear."

"That's not true!"

Lena enters the room and her gaze passes from Dad to me. She looks unsure whether to stay or leave.

When Dad next speaks, it's with love and remorse in his eyes. "It is true, Raine. Can't you see that it's your own guilt eating you up?"

"I don't feel guilty," I say. Lena's eyebrows shoot up like she's caught me in a lie. I glare at her. "Do you mind, Lena? This is private."

She reaches out and touches Dad's arm, then turns and leaves the room.

Dad sighs. "Raine, please, listen to me. I worry about you. You've held anger toward me and guilt over Nat's death in your heart since the day it happened. It's consumed your life, made you a hard woman, turned you away from God."

"Stop it, Dad," I shout. "Don't go there. Don't you dare."

"Go where? I'm your father. Of course I'm concerned about your soul."

"Don't worry about my soul or me going to hell, Dad. I live in my own personal hell. I went there the day I watched that crocodile drag Natalie away. Have you forgotten that I was in shock? I was devastated. I couldn't eat or sleep for days after she died. It still haunts me. I relive the terror daily. It's like a horror movie playing in my mind over and over again."

"I know that. I've always known that. But Raine, you don't have to live with it. God will help you."

"Do you hear yourself? So righteous… wow. Don't forget that *you* left the ministry after Nat died."

"Not because I blamed God. Your mom and I needed to come back home, and New Hope already had a pastor. In fact, there were no open positions in any church around here. Being a lightkeeper was supposed to be temporary, but when your mother fell ill I stayed on because it allowed me to work and stay home to care for her. I could never have done that as a pastor shepherding a flock. After that? Well, it was too late. I was old." His voice sounds so wretched. I hold back my biting reply and only shrug. "And it's not my intention to sound righteous. I'm just trying to help you understand that if you'll allow Him, God will bring you comfort and help you to forgive yourself."

I smile bitterly. "Forgive myself, ha! Despite your words, you've never even forgiven me. I hear it in your voice, see it in your eyes even now."

"When will you ever believe me?" Exasperation rises in his voice. "I do not blame you. You've never forgiven yourself, Raine. You're tormented by your own personal guilt and sorrow."

"I know that. But there's a difference in our grief, Dad. For you, you lost your daughter, and I understand that's the most profound suffering and unnatural grief a parent can endure. But for me, I was there. I heard her cry out to me for help, plead with me to save her. I looked right into her eyes and saw the terror and pain in them. I was holding her arm when the crocodile ripped her out of my grasp. I was the last person to hold her, the last person she saw. My grief is unfathomable, except to those who have experienced it. And then to have you blame me? Can you imagine what that does to an eleven-year-old? Every day of my life I relive Natalie's horror-filled death knowing, feeling, believing that *I* am responsible for causing it."

"You're not responsible, Raine, you never were," he says, his face deeply remorseful and broken. "I put my family in peril. Put you in peril, too. It could have been you. It could have been both of you. Please believe me. I didn't mean a word of what I said in grief back then. I've told you again and again how wrong I was, how sorry I am. You're my daughter and I love you. Please forgive me."

"Dad!" I shout, angrily. "How can you—"

Mal enters the room and steps between us. "Stop, both of you. Please. Brie and Pella can hear you and you're upsetting them."

There's a brief, tense silence before Dad and I nod.

Then Brie walks in. "What's wrong?" she says with a worried expression. "Why are you fighting?"

"We're not fighting, sweetheart." Dad scoops her up in his arms. "We were just talking about how we'd love some ice cream. How about you? Feel like going out for an ice cream cone?"

Pella walks in and pumps the air with her arm. "Yay!"

"But you're wearing pyjamas, Grampy," Brie says.

"That's fine. We'll eat in the car." He steps over to Pella, picks her up in his arms, and carries her out the door. The rest of us follow them, and I feel Malin's eyes on me all the while. I avoid looking at her, even when she reaches out and touches my arm.

"Hey, you need to speak kinder to your father," she admonishes me. "He's said he's sorry more than once. Your words can be mean and unforgiving. They can bruise like rocks."

I open my mouth to argue, but she just shakes her head. I shrug and walk out of the house.

Later, as Malin drives the girls and me back to Quinn's place in the fading light, I have to admit that Malin may be right. My dad's remorse seems sincere, his love for me genuine, and though I try to fight it, his words have touched my heart.

CHAPTER TWENTY-FIVE

There's no school on Tuesday due to a teacher's workshop. Malin has taken the day off work and she and I spend the morning in the kitchen making split-pea soup for lunch.

"I can't believe it's been a week, and still not a trace of Quinn," I say, bristling. "And now the Mounties are talking about scaling back the search again."

Malin gets a bag of rolls out of the cupboard and sets them on the table. "I know it's upsetting," she says in whisper, pointing upstairs in a gesture that means I should keep my voice quiet so the girls don't hear.

I nod as I walk out of the kitchen and into the living room. I was so sure my brother would be home by now that I can hardly bear the disappointment and worry.

It's a sunny, pleasant day. The first warm gusts of spring are coming off the water and entering the house through the open windows. I wander over to the front the window and gaze out just in time to see a woman walking down the lane. She looks cheery and carefree, wearing a butter yellow sundress, high-heeled sandals, and big gold earrings that glitter in the sunlight. She's carrying a blue shopping bag in one hand.

The woman stops at the end of the driveway, places her hand over her eyes to shield them from the sun, and studies our house. I release a small gasp. Her hair is no longer fiery red—she's got brown hair with blond highlights, and it's cut shoulder-length—but I recognize her.

Surprise rushes through me. My mind is in a whirl. What is she doing back in town?

I watch Holly's sister, Piper, take a few steps onto the front lawn and stare into the windows. I jump back, then lean forward to peer around the edge of the drape. She strolls up to the front step, sets the bag down, and chews the inside of her cheek. Then she smiles—a dark, calculating smile I don't like.

Abruptly, she turns and strides back down the lane. I watch until she rounds the bend and disappears.

I run outside and jog down the lane, coming to the shoulder of the highway. I look left and right, but she seems to have vanished. But then, in the not-too-far distance, a silver convertible climbs the hill, heading toward town. She must have had a car parked out by the road when she walked up the house.

I run back down the lane to the lighthouse and jump into my Jeep, thankful that I have the keys in my pocket. I start it up and take off down the road, speeding up until I see the silver car up ahead. I lose sight of it for a minute as it crests a hill, so I hit the gas.

Once in town, I cruise down Harbourview Street until I see the car parked in front of Driscoll's Pharmacy. I park and get out, spotting a grey-haired man wearing sunglasses in the driver's seat. Through the pharmacy's plate-glass window I spot Piper standing at the counter, smiling at the cashier.

I quickly walk away, turning into the alley between the pharmacy and library. I duck behind a big recycling bin and peer around it out to the street.

After a few minutes, Piper walks out of the pharmacy and gets into the silver convertible. Her hair lifts in the wind as she and the grey-haired man drive by.

I jump back into my Jeep and follow them, my stomach roiling. The traffic is quiet today and they drive slowly, so I have to stay well back to avoid being spotted.

I follow them out of downtown and down Sea Spray Lane, which runs parallel with the harbour. Soon they pull into Bennett's Cottages and park into one of the farthest cottages from the road. It sits back from the dirt lane under a copse of pine trees.

I pull into a nearby empty driveway, shut off the car, and run over to the side wall of the cottage. Creeping around to the front porch, I duck behind the wooden step and inch my head up a little. Piper and the man get out of the car, and now I can see that the man is Brad Milson, a dentist who used to have a practice here years ago. A big white purse swings from her right forearm, along with the shopping bag. Her sandals click loudly on the sidewalk with each jaunty step she takes.

The man takes the shopping bag from her and she smiles lovingly at him. She looks like a happy, devoted wife—but I know she isn't. Her so-called boyfriend is as old as my dad.

But the thing that sends a blaze of annoyance through me is that she looks so happy and carefree… as though she doesn't care one bit that she was too selfish to come home for her only sister's funeral.

———————————

When I get home, I see Brie biking over to the mailbox. She stops in front of the box, but the flag isn't up. But that doesn't mean anything; our mail carrier, old Mr. Grinnell, often forgets to put it up. As I watch, Brie pulls out a white envelope, reads it, and lets out a little whoop. Then she folds it in half and stuffs it into the back pocket of her shorts.

I go over to the shed and pick up a watering can. I fill it with water from the faucet, then walk up the steps to the porch

"Brie!" I call before she pedals back towards the road. "Where're you going?"

She brakes, turns the bike around and looks at me. "Nowhere. I was gone. I just got back."

"Good. Don't go anywhere else. Lunch is almost ready."

"Okay."

"What's that thing on your head?" I ask.

She lifts her eyes. "You mean my bike helmet?"

I bend over and water Quinn's potted yucca plants on the steps. "Why are you wearing it?"

"Dad said to. So if I wipe out I don't crack my skull open."

"I never wore one and I'm alive, aren't I?"

"Yeah, but that was forty years ago. Everyone wears one now."

I straighten up and scowl. "Forty years ago? How old do you think I am, anyway?" She shrugs. "Listen, don't wear that thing. That's just for chickens. Are you a chicken?"

"No, but I'm pretty sure it's against the law not to wear one."

"Ahh, most laws are just suggestions." I wave my free hand airily. "Take it off. Let the wind blow through your hair. It won't kill you to live a little on the edge."

"Okay," she says uncertainly. "I don't think Dad will like me not wearing it, though."

"Well, that figures. Your dad's always been too overprotective."

"He is not. He said it's because the road to town is in bad shape. There are tons of heaves and potholes and there's no shoulder or bike lane to ride on."

I spin my head to look at her, and I can see she's a bit angry. But I'm pleased she has the gumption to stand up for her dad.

"Well, just keep your eyes open for them then. Pay attention and ride alert," I say. "Listen, it doesn't do a kid a bit of good to be mollycoddled. Until your dad gets home, I'm in charge. And I will not coddle you or Pell."

"Not much chance of that," she mutters. And she leaves her helmet on.

"Pardon me?"

"Nothing."

"Come in now. Lunch is probably ready."

Suddenly, I remember the bag Piper left on the step. I wait until Brie is pushing her bike over to the shed, then skip back down the steps and grab it.

Once back in the living room, I look inside the bag and find two wrapped gifts, one with Brie's name on it and another with Pell's. I pull them out and rip some of the wrapping paper so I can see what's in them. Pell's gift is a small doll, and Brie's is a video game. Taped to Brie's gift is a folded sheet of paper with her name written on it. I rip it off and stuff it in my pocket, then throw the gifts back in the bag and go into the kitchen to hide the gifts in the cupboard over the fridge that no one uses.

"Where'd you go?" Malin asks, stirring the soup on the stove.

"Had to do something quick," I say, unsettled about Piper suddenly showing up in town. "I'll tell you about it later."

She frowns but lets it go.

Brie then steps into the kitchen.

"Well, look what the cat's dragged in," says Malin. She always says that when Brie or Pell come into a room. It never seems to get old for them. I guess it's better than the greetings I give, which Malin says are squinty looks and vague hellos, like the kind you'd give the furnace repairman when he comes up from the basement, wrench in hand, and you'd totally forgotten he was down there.

"Soup's ready," I tell Brie. "Wash your hands and go get your sister."

She steps up to the kitchen sink and squirts handsoap into her palms and scrubs them clean. Then she walks out to the hall and bellows up the stairs, "*Pellllll! Lunnncchhh isss reeaaddyyy!*"

When she comes back into the kitchen I put my hands on my hip. "Gee, do you suppose she heard?"

"You sure have an awesome set of lungs on you, girl," says Malin, grinning. "I think you're going to be a famous opera singer someday."

Brie snorts a laugh at that. Malin always says stuff like that to her and Pella, telling them they're a couple of brains, that they can be anything they want, do anything they set their hearts to… but then, Malin is kind, patient, and generous while I'm kind of cranky, impatient, and stingy with compliments. I've always been like that, but moving back to Blackheart Bay hasn't helped my naturally moody disposition.

While Malin seems to truly care for Brie and Pell, sometimes I'm afraid I mostly just tolerate them. Malin and I are so different. She has a cheerful personality, is short and plump, and her thick blonde hair and dimples make her look pretty when she smiles, which is often. I'm crabby, I've been told I'd be pretty if I ever did smile, which is seldom. But then, I'm trying to be nice to the girls. Take today, for example. I told Malin to go ahead and make Brie's favourite soup today even though I don't really like split-pea at all.

I sit at the table, grab a roll from the bowl on the centre of the table, and start buttering it. Brie joins me and does the same. One thing she doesn't seem to mind about me is that I don't pray before I eat—and I don't make the girls pray either. If Quinn was here, Brie probably wouldn't have dared taking a bite before we prayed.

Pell joins us, and we begin to eat.

After a few minutes, Malin smiles at Brie. "I saw you checking the mail. Any news from that children's book publisher?"

Brie sneaks a glance at me. There are things I can't tolerate—and children's chitchat is one of them. However, because I'm an avid reader and a published author, literary news is an exception to the rule. I look back at her expectantly.

She pulls out the letter, beaming. "They're going to publish my story in next month's issue."

"All right!" shouts Malin, pumping her fist in the air. "Congratulations, Brie!"

I eye her for a moment, then nod. "Good girl. Excellent. Your writing talent is a gift you got from me." Malin rolls her eyes at me. "Well, it is!"

"But you're not writing anymore, Raine. You haven't written a book in a few years now. You write obits."

I grin. "Correct, and I find it quite enjoyable."

Malin shakes her head. "I can't help noticing that what you find enjoyable, no one else does."

"Correct again."

"You remember my uncle who owned the funeral home in town when we were little? He had the same disturbing sense of humour as you."

I howl with laughter at that. From the corner of my eye, I see that even Brie smiles. It strikes me that she does seem to take after me. Pell favours Quinn with her height, auburn hair, and green eyes. She's a math whiz and has said she wants to be a doctor. Brie, on the other hand, wants to be a writer. More than once, I've heard Quinn mumble under his breath that she's too much like me for her own good. Privately, this has always pleased me to no end.

"Can I read the letter?" Malin asks.

Brie passes her the letter and watches as Malin reads it, her face glowing, her dimples becoming more pronounced as her smile widens. "That's just wonderful, Brie. Congrats again."

She passes it to me, and I read it. But I only nod and say, curtly, "Good." Then I hand the letter back to Brie and ask Malin how the soup is, duty done, the conversation with me over.

"It's tasty, Raine," Malin says.

"It is, but not as tasty as the bowl of termite soup I once ate in Australia."

Malin leans her head back and huffs out a disbelieving breath. "You did not."

"I did, too. The termites were so bad that year—a plague, really—so the ranchers around town started collecting them and making soup. Louisa, who owned a diner in town, made a big pot of soup with them and asked if I wanted to try some. So I did. It had carrots, potatoes, turnip, garlic, onions, thyme, termites, and a buttery cream base. It was actually quite tasty."

Pell makes a face. "Ew."

"You need to stop it," Malin scolds me.

"Stop what?"

"You know what. Termite soup, sure. Get over your writer's block and start a new book. Get this pathetic need to tell fiction out of your system."

I smile, unfazed, and go back to eating my soup.

"Aunt Raine?" Brie says.

I snap my head around and eye her darkly. She has committed the heinous felony of talking at the table. "What?" I growl.

"I saw Aunt Piper out in front of the house earlier," she says worriedly.

Malin drops her spoon and it hits the table with a clatter.

Brie's words hang in the stunned silence.

"A lot of people look alike," Malin says. "Maybe it was just someone who resembled her."

Brie shakes her head. "Her hair's different, but it was her."

I huff out a breath. "It was her, Malin. I saw her, too. I was going tell you later." I start from the beginning and tell the story without stopping for breath, including the part about her being driven around by old Brad Milson. When I'm finished, I make eye contact with Brie. "Where were you when Piper was in the yard?"

"Hiding behind the shed. I saw you come out and follow her in your Jeep."

I sit motionless, staring at Brie, my soup forgotten. Malin has stopped eating too; she's shocked, not only about Piper being back in town but the fact that she's skulking around the house.

"I don't believe it," Malin says. "What is she doing back here?"

I push my bowl away. "Good question. How can she even show her face in town?" I say through gritted teeth. "And to come out here and gawk in the windows? Wow, that woman has some nerve. Terrific."

"It is?" Pell says, smiling.

Brie catches Pell's eye and shakes her head in warning. Pell's smile turns to a puzzled frown.

"I wonder where they're staying," Malin says.

"I know where," Brie says nervously. She looks at me like she's afraid I'm going to hit the roof. "I followed them, too"

I jerk my head back. "You did?"

"I saw you going after her, so I pedalled as fast as I could after you. I caught up with you in town."

"Good job!" I say. "I never saw you at all. You get your sleuthing genes from me, too."

Malin smacks me on the arm. "No, that was not a good idea at all. And why would she get that from you? You're nosy as all get out for sure, but that doesn't make you a private detective."

I dismiss her words with a wave of my hand. "So tell Malin where they're staying."

"At Bennett's Cottages off on Tidewater Lane," Brie says. "They went into the one with the number seven."

"Correct!" I nod, pleased with my niece.

Malin's voice rises in alarm. "You didn't knock on the door, did you? You didn't go in to see her?"

Brie snorts into her soup. "No."

"Good girl." Malin shoots me a reproving look.

I ignore that, too, and drum my fingers angrily on the table. I look out the window to the trees in the backyard, then purse my lips.

"Why is she back?" I ask, blowing out a loud breath. "She couldn't have cared less when Holly died. She told Quinn she was too busy to come home for the funeral, but apparently she came slinking around here a few days after, asking Quinn if Holly had left her anything. Didn't she serve jail time once for stealing from Holly? And now she's here with that Milson guy? Wasn't he married when she first started up with him?"

Malin smiles wryly. "Yes, Brad Milson left his wife and kids for her. They were older, of course, and one was married with children. But he was a grandfather, for goodness sake! And Piper was what, twenty? Gross."

"Does that woman have no shame?" I say. "I should drive over there right now, grab her by the throat, and shake her until her head falls right off."

Pell makes a frightened choking sound.

"She doesn't mean that, sweet pea," Malin assures Pell, who nods but looks unconvinced.

"Maybe she's changed and really just wants to see her nieces," Malin says.

"I want to see Aunt Piper. Can we all go see her?" Pell blurts. She's too young to understand.

"No," I say.

"But why not?" Pell persists.

"Because I said no!" I shout.

Pell's eyes well and her chin quivers.

"My soul, Raine," Malin says, exasperated. "Don't yell at her like that. She's just a child."

I breathe out through my nose. "Sorry, Pell."

Malin leans over, gives Pell a comforting hug, and tells her to finish her lunch.

Pell digs back into her soup and starts telling us a story she learned in school about penguins, her favourite animal. I notice that although Malin's looking at Pell and nodding, she's only half-listening. She has sunk into a troubled mood. I'm not listening at all, and I'm not even irked with Pell for talking at the table. I stare at the floor, sipping my coffee, quietly smouldering. Piper's arrival is both infuriating and unsettling, and I decide not to tell Brie or Pella about the gifts she left on the step.

Brie puts her spoon down, and I can see by her expression the tension in the room has killed her appetite. "May I please be excused?"

"Me too," says Pell.

I nod and grunt a yes. Malin forces a smile.

Pell and Brie stand up and put their dishes in the sink. Pell goes back upstairs to play with her dolls while Brie, not a girl to play with dolls or stay inside unless she has to, goes outside.

"Quinn's disappearance is a big story," I say to Malin after I'm sure the girls are gone. "But why would that bring her back here? She didn't love her own sister, so why would she care about Quinn?"

"Maybe she's moved home and it has nothing to do with Quinn. But it's odd. She never made any bones about despising this town."

I hear a noise at the open kitchen window and see a tuft of dark hair. "Brie! No eavesdropping!"

I go over to the window and catch Brie jogging across the yard and then down the trail to the beach.

CHAPTER TWENTY-SIX

The weather has done a complete turnaround: the wind is cold and raw, tearing off the water, slamming into the house. The rough seas bash the cliffs repeatedly with a boom that echoes and rolls throughout the house.

It's a gusty spring morning, and I feel like staying under my warm blankets. But then I think of Quinn, maybe lost and freezing in the woods, and a wave of sadness and guilt washes over me. I throw back the blankets and swing my legs out onto the floor.

There's a lull in the wind, and in the brief silence I hear someone moving around the kitchen—the clank of a pan, Malin's voice singing quietly. The smell of coffee and eggs drifts up the stairway to my room.

I wake Brie and Pella, then head down to the kitchen where I find Malin at the counter whisking eggs and milk in a bowl.

"Good morning," I greet her, yawning. "I don't remember hearing the doorbell."

She turns, smiles. "I didn't want to wake anyone. I used the spare key your dad gave me."

"Oh, okay. That's good."

"Want a cheese omelette?"

"No thanks."

"Why not?"

"I don't like omelettes, cheese or otherwise."

"I don't like omelettes, cheese or otherwise," she mimics, shaking her head. "You are fussier than a toddler."

"I know it," I admit. "I'll make some toast."

"Make enough for everyone. And did I just hear you yelling at Brie and Pell to hit the deck, that it's chow time?"

I pick up a mug and carry it over to the coffeemaker where I pour a cup. "Yes, why?"

"Why? They're not in the Navy. They're little girls."

I look at her, baffled.

She closes her eyes briefly. "Next time, how about saying 'Good morning' or 'How did you sleep?' You know, something warm and loving."

I nod. "I can try that, sure."

That's just one of the things I love about Malin. She understands children because she has the heart of a child. She loves completely and unconditionally, and when wronged she forgives unreservedly. I wish I was more like her.

"And another thing," she says, sitting down at the table and looking at me.

"What now?"

"For a bedtime story the other night, did you tell the girls some yarn about a kangaroo attacking you and Quinn when you were in Australia and it kicking you so hard that you broke your wrist?"

I nod. "Pell's not a big fan of stories involving reptiles, so that one seemed mellow enough."

"No, it was not mellow enough. Why in the world would you think it's okay to tell a story like that to Pell before bed? It's guaranteed to give her nightmares. You forget she's only six? Listen, promise me: no more horror stories before bed, or any other time."

"I promise."

"Did a kangaroo really knock you to the ground and break your wrist?"

I grin. "No. I read a story about it happening to a man who surprised a family of kangaroos. The male kangaroo was protecting its family."

She points a finger at me. "I know I've said it before, but it's worth saying again: write a novel, please."

Outside, I hear the crunch of car tires on the scallop shells in the driveway.

"I wonder who that is, coming by so early," I say.

I set my coffee cup down on the table and go to the door. There, I watch as Piper climbs out of her convertible. The top is up and Brad Milson is wearing a long-sleeved dress shirt and silver-framed aviator sunglasses. He's staring out through the windshield at me.

At least I think he is. It's hard to tell for certain with the sunglasses.

Piper's wearing a cotton top under a brown leather jacket, white denim jeans, and sandals. She stands for a moment studying the property, then shares a conspiratorial smile with Brad.

My stomach goes cold. Piper is not a person to be trusted. She has a history of fraud. In the past, she was caught forging cheques and stealing money from seniors she'd been looking after while working as a caregiver. And she'd stolen from Quinn and Holly once. She'd served a year in jail for those offences.

I hurry back into the kitchen. "Mal, go upstairs and keep the girls in the bedroom."

"What's wrong?"

"Bonnie and Clyde are outside."

Mal frowns. "What?"

"It's Piper and Brad Milson. They just drove onto the yard."

Malin nods, turns off the burner, and heads for the stairs.

I open the door and step out on the porch. Piper stops at the bottom of the step and looks up at me.

"Hello, Raine," she says.

"Piper."

"I heard about Quinn. It's horrible. May I come in?"

"No, you may not."

"Just for a moment, please. I want to see Brie and Pella."

"It's not a good time. They're getting ready for school."

A flicker of irritation crosses her face and she puts a hand on her hip. "Come on, Raine. Just for a minute. I won't stay long."

"No, I'm sorry. Not today."

"Tomorrow then?"

I shake my head. "No, that won't work, either. You're not allowed on Quinn's property. It's a parole violation. You forget that?"

"My parole is over. I've changed, Raine. I'm not the same person I was back then. Please, bring the girls out here so I can say hello. I miss my nieces."

I snort. "Do you?"

"Yes, I do. Very much."

"All of a sudden? You haven't shown any interest in seeing them since the day they were born."

Piper's smile disappears and she shakes her head angrily. "You're not their only aunt. I have as much right as you to see them. Besides, with my parents in Florida—and remember those are Brie and Pella's *grandparents*—there's no one from our side to be here for them. I'm the only one in town. It's what Holly would have wanted."

"I highly doubt that."

Her pale brown eyes narrow disconcertingly. She smiles, a slow sly smile that sickens me. "Raine, with their father missing, they need family now. Like it or not, that includes me."

I fold my arms over my chest and shake my head.

"Raine, please, I'm so upset about Quinn. I need to see them." Her chin quivers and she swipes at her eyes even though there are no tears. Then she opens her purse and pulls out a white envelope. "I have a letter here I wrote to the girls. Will you at least give it to them for me?"

I take it, knowing that the only place it's going is in the trash.

Piper gives me another pleading look. "You won't let me see them, Raine?"

"Look, for the last time, I don't know what you're doing or what you're really up to, but you're not seeing them today or any day after that."

"You can't keep them from me."

"Yes, I can."

We stare angrily at each other for a moment—and then I see a muscle at the corner of her right eye twitch.

"Fine, but I'll be back, Raine. I'm going to see a lawyer. There's no legal reason why I can't see them. You can't stop me. This isn't the end of this, not by any means."

With that, she stalks back to the car, tight-lipped. I watch her get back in the car, her lips moving as she speaks angrily to Brad. Before driving away, he smiles darkly at me.

The vultures are circling.

Vexed, I puff out my cheeks and blow a hard breath.

Later that day, I go down to the beach and sit on a large bone-white log. I pull out the note Piper wrote to the girls and stare at it. As far as I know, she's never sent Brie or Pell a card, letter, or gift before. Quinn had made it clear that Piper didn't care about her own sister, let alone her nieces.

I think about tearing up the letter without reading a word, but curiosity gets the better of me. I open the note and read.

Dear Brie & Pella,
My beautiful nieces, I am so sorry about your dad. I decided to come home now because you need me. I know I haven't been much of an aunt to you in the past, but that is all going to change now. I am back in town for good and would love to see you both. Please believe me when I say that I love you both deeply and have missed you.

I hope that you will forgive me for what's happened in the past. I have changed so much since then. I hope you will want to see me, too. My cell number is 902-555-5555. I'm staying at Bennett's Cottages on Tidewater Lane, number seven. Please call me at any time so that we can meet.

Your loving aunt,
Piper Matheson xxoo

My stomach twists in a knot. That liar!

I stand, pick up a rock, and whip it out across the water as hard as I can. Then I sit back down and stare at the letter again. Anger surges through me. My hands tremble.

She's asking Brie and Pell to understand and forgive her, to meet up with her after what she's done? The thought leaves a sourness in my stomach. The realization that I might not be able to stop it from happening is utterly distressing.

I look down at the note and decide to keep it, at least so I can show it to Malin and Dad… and Quinn, when he gets home. I remain seated on the that log for a long time, staring out at the water but not really seeing anything.

I can't sleep. I'm tired, but waves of anxiety roll through me. My brain churns with all sorts of thoughts; I'm worried sick about Quinn and troubled by Piper's visit. I know I likely can't stop her from seeing the girls. What is she really up to? With her history of fraud and theft, I'm sure whatever she's planning is bound to be criminal.

I get up and step outside on the widows walk and lean against the railing. The moon is up, casting a wide swath of silvery light across the dark water. I inhale deeply and allow the fresh ocean air to clear my head and ease my tension. It's a quiet night, the usual boom of the sea exploding against the rocks below has become more of a soft thump. I see a flash of heat lightning in the distance and hear the rumble of thunder.

I'm about to go back inside when a noise catches my attention from around the side of the lighthouse. I freeze and listen hard, but all I hear are the leaves brushing against the house in the light breeze. I relax.

And then I hear what sounds like the crunch of a footstep on loose gravel.

I strain to hear over the barking of a dog, either one of Gloria Jean's or one of the Skinner's.

Another crunch perks my ears; it's the scrape of a shoe on gravel. It's probably just an animal. A deer likely.

Still, I slip back inside and walk out to the hall to peer into Brie's bedroom. She's lying on her back, her left arm hanging down over the side of the bed. Pell is spooned up against her, her stuffed pink turtle, Pinky, clutched in one arm, her other arm flung over Brie's chest. Surprisingly, rather than the usual surge of panic I feel when I watch them, this time I feel a surprising trace of tenderness.

I pad down to the first level and into the kitchen. Through the windows, I look out to the driveway and side yard. They're dark and empty. Far out to sea, I hear the clang of a buoy bell, the blare of a foghorn.

And then a harsh scraping noise comes from behind me and I spin around and face the living room, heart thudding in my throat.

I hold my breath as I hear a shrill rasp at the living room window. I duck down behind the kitchen island just as a dark shape whips past the windowpane. It's a tree branch from the birch that grows close to the outside wall.

I stand, laughing at myself.

Then the wind shifts and the smell of smoke carries in through the windows. Briefly, I think it's wood smoke from a bonfire on the beach. But then I realize it's cigarette smoke… liquorice-scented cigarette smoke.

I look outside again and see, under a tree at the back of the property, a glowing red ember—the tip of a cigarette. It moves up through the air and stops. Behind, I can make out the dark silhouette of a man standing motionless under the tree.

I hurry over to the window and smack right into a dining room chair, knocking it over on the wooden floor with a bang. Wincing, I limp over towards the window and stare at the man. The sound of the falling chair must have carried, since he suddenly turns around and limps toward the treeline.

I run to the patio door and dash out onto the deck. My heart races as I watch the man limp away, the snap of his footsteps ringing through the air as he steps on dead branches and twigs.

As he disappears into the woods, I fight the urge to go after him. I don't want to leave the girls home alone. But it doesn't matter: I know who it is. I couldn't see his face, but Aubrie Skinner smokes liquorice-flavoured cigarillos and walks with a limp.

I go back inside just as Brie comes down the stairs.

"What's wrong?" she asks. "I heard a crash."

"Everything's fine, Brie. I came down for a glass of water and didn't turn the light on. I smacked right into the chair."

I step into the dining room and stand the chair back up.

Brie narrows her eyes and points to the right. "The sink's that way, though."

My face burns and I'm glad it's dark. "Yeah, I know. But I couldn't sleep so I decided to watch TV for a little while," I say. "Before I got the water, I mean."

"Uh-huh," she says in a tone of disbelief.

Why do I try? She's too bright to be fooled so easily. "Come on now, back to bed," I say as I usher her back up the stairs.

But I'm shaken, and once Brie is back in bed I slip back downstairs and spend the rest of the night sitting guard by the living room window—in case he returns.

CHAPTER TWENTY-SEVEN

The next morning, after the girls have left for school, I follow the path from our yard through the woods to Gloria Jean's house. The ground is covered with soft and fragrant pine needles, the air fresh and salty and warm. The sky is a cloudless blue, promising a glorious spring day.

No Trespassing signs are nailed to many of the trees, and other signs say things like *Keep Off My Property Or I'll Shoot* in clearly printed black marker. I feel suddenly uneasy.

A low growl causes me to turn and see a cute honey-blonde Pomeranian with its teeth bared, racing toward me, ready to chew my leg off. Behind it I see a big black Lab loping toward me with a goofy expression, ready to lick me to death.

"Stop right there!" Gloria Jean shouts.

And there she is, standing in the doorway of her house, wearing men's trousers and flannel shirt, and the same black rubber boots she wore the last time I saw her. Her hair is wild and frizzy as she stands there pointing a gun directly at me.

The Pom chews on my pant leg and tries to drag me away while the Lab slobbers all over my hand in greeting.

"I had no idea you were blind, Raine," the woman says.

I lift an eyebrow. "What?"

"You couldn't see all the no trespassing signs?" She waves the gun barrel up and down as she speaks.

I shrug a shoulder, feigning calmness when in truth I'm unnerved. "I did, but I wanted to drop off some food for Bella and Ben." The dogs smell the stew and start jumping up to get at it.

"I don't need your charity, Raine," she says, but I see her gaze move to the stew and then to the dogs. I know she wants it for them, but her pride stops her from saying so.

"It's not charity, Gloria Jena. Not at all. We were given more food at church on Sunday. We have way too much and none of us like beef stew, so it's only going to go to waste. And you did say you were having a hard time feeding your dogs."

She lets go of the rifle stock and settles it under her armpit. Then she slaps her hand, palm down, on the door. "I never said any such thing!"

I pause, letting out a soft breath. "All right, you didn't. Would you put the gun down, please?"

She watches me for a time and then sets it stock-down against the wall of the house. She points to the ground in front of me. "Since you brought it over, you might as well leave it right where you stand." Then she calls out at the dogs: "Bella, Ben, get over here and sit!"

The dogs turn and trot over to the step and sit obediently down on the ground, staring at me, panting steadily.

I set two large containers of beef stew down on the grass and place a bag of white rolls on top. "There's some homemade rolls for you... ah... for the dogs."

"All right then," she says. "Thank you and goodbye, Raine."

I nod, turn, but then look back over my shoulder and see her picking up the shotgun again. "I thought the Mounties took your gun?"

"They did—my sixteen-gauge shotgun. This here's my late husband's old twelve-gauge. When I saw them coming down the lane, I hid it in the cellar."

I walk away on shaky legs, almost able to feel the shotgun aimed at an imaginary bullseye in the centre of my back. I decide to leave any extra food for Gloria Jean out on Quinn's step from now on.

I reach the house but keep going, following the path that starts at the tree line and leads through the woods to the Skinners' place. After a while I come out into the open area where the search-and-rescue command centre had been for the first week. The clearing's empty now. No surprise, since Sergeant Flynn had called to tell me they'd finished searching the area and were going to move the command centre to the other side of the Skinners' property to search there. Now there's only a flattened rectangular area on the grass where the tent stood, and tire tracks from the police, rescue vehicles, and four-wheelers.

I'd told Flynn about Piper's sudden return to town and her snooping around Quinn's place, but she didn't seem to think it meant much. Later, I plan to go to the new command centre to find out about how the search is going there. And I want to know if she's followed up with Piper.

First though, I need to take care of something.

Minutes later, I stand in the front yard facing the Skinners' wood-sided bungalow. The old house faces the ocean like Quinn's but has a narrow, rocky beach that isn't safe for swimming. The air is heavy with the smell of seaweed and dead fish, and I see gulls diving towards the beach.

Over the sound of waves, a low snarl makes me turn my head. A brown pit bull with white down its snout trots slowly toward me, tail low, teeth bared. I hear more growling and then see three more dogs approaching, another pit bull and two brown boxers—one in front of me, another to my left, and the third slinking up behind me. They've effectively got me surrounded, cutting off any escape. Their lips pull back as snarls erupt came from their throats.

The dogs move in, one boxer growling louder than the others, sounding like a small engine. All four dogs slaver, long strings of saliva swinging from their open mouths.

My heart seizes for a second. I love dogs, but these ones have bad owners and appear to have been trained to attack. I'm in trouble.

Suddenly, the front door swings open and Loretta Skinner sticks her head out. "Get! Go on! Get away from her, you rotten dogs!"

All four dogs whip around and take off running across the lawn. They disappear into the woods.

I let out a long breath as my heartbeat steadies. In the silence, I hear them panting in the shadowy tree line—still close, watching me.

"Hello, Raine, how are you?" Loretta calls out, stepping onto the porch and holding the outer screen door open. She wears a faded yellow house dress and soiled white slippers. She's aged hard. The skin around her tea-brown eyes is heavily wrinkled and there are dark shadows beneath. Her mouth hangs downward, giving her a haunted look. Behind her, through the open door, I see pine cupboards and an old gas stove.

"Hi, Loretta. I'm fine. How are you?"

"Can't complain. You haven't changed much. Recognized you right away."

It amuses me whenever someone says that, since aging is a moot point when it comes to me. It would be hard to not recognize me with my horrible scar.

"I'm sorry about Quinn," Loretta adds. "Karl and I have been praying for him. The boys, too."

I can barely keep from rolling my eyes, but I offer a lukewarm nod.

"Sorry about your Dad, too. He's doing better, though?"

"Yes," I say. "He's out of the hospital and on the mend."

Her hair is grey and cut short to the ears, parted like a man's. I know she's close to my dad's age, but she looks much older. Her skin puckers like a chicken's and sags at the chin and neck. I notice a faint custard yellow and violet bruise at the corner of her left eye. No surprise. I feel a wave of pity for her.

"Glad to hear it," Loretta says. "He gave us quite a scare. Grabbed his left arm and sank down to his knees right about where you're standing. Cormac called 911, and I brought a blanket out. We covered him up and stayed with him until the ambulance got here."

"Thanks."

Although I'm thankful Cormac helped my dad, I also know that her husband and sons are the cause of all this.

She picks up on my tone and folds her arms over her chest. "So how can I help you?"

"I'm looking for Aubrie. I'd like to talk to him."

"Aubrie? What do you want with him?"

"He was in Quinn's yard last night around two o'clock in the morning. I want to ask him what he was doing there."

She pauses for a moment, staring at me with intense bewilderment. "Why would you think he was in Quinn's yard last night?"

"I saw him."

"You saw Aubrie in your yard last night?"

I try to be patient. "Yes, I did."

"At two o'clock?" She frowns. "It would have been dark. How can you be sure it was him?"

"The moon was bright. I smelled his liquorice-flavoured cigarillo and watched him limp away. In this direction." I soften my tone. "Loretta, it was Aubrie."

"Still, Raine, that don't mean a thing," she says with thinly veiled scorn. "He was likely just on his way home from town and cut across your property to save time."

"He walks home from town late at night?"

"Sometimes, if he's been at the pub."

"That's more than two kilometres," I say doubtfully.

"Well, I imagine a two-kilometre walk is better than a big fine and losing his licence," she says in a tone that implies she can't believe how stupid I am.

"Loretta, I saw him standing under a tree in the backyard staring into my living room window."

She smiles and shakes her head. "So what? Even if he was in your brother's yard, like I said, that don't mean nothing. His foot hurts him bad sometimes. I'm sure he just stopped there to rest it and have a smoke. He wasn't looking in your windows. My boy's not a peeping Tom."

"Maybe he's not a peeping Tom, but he was prowling around Quinn's yard and up to no good, that's for certain. And you and I both know he and his brothers had something to do with all the vandalism on Quinn's property—and very likely Quinn's disappearance."

Deep sorrow crosses her face. "No, Raine. As I told the police, Karl and my boys were home all that night. I swear it. They wouldn't hurt Quinn."

"Then go get him for me, Loretta. I want to talk to him. Is he home?'

"No, he's not."

"Where is he?"

She shrugs. "He left with his brothers early this morning. They're men now; they don't tell me their business."

"Men?" I snort in irritation. "Don't they all still live at home?"

Her face tightens. "Okay, that's enough, Raine. You're being rude now. You need to go home."

"When Aubrie does get home, tell him I was here. Tell him I said to stay off Quinn's property or I'll be back with the cops to talk to him."

But Loretta only turns and steps inside, letting the screen door bang shut behind her. She slams the inner door hard and I hear the click of the lock.

And all my empathy and compassion for her slides away.

I walk back home thinking of my encounters with Gloria Jean and then Loretta and vow that I will never again feel sorry for either of them—or any other crazy old woman in this town.

CHAPTER TWENTY-EIGHT

"Hello, Raine," Piper says.

I step out onto the front step of the house, closing the door behind me. "Back again?" I say in a clipped tone.

"Yes, I want to see Brie and Pell."

"No. I told you, it's not happening."

"I had a feeling you'd still say no, so I spoke to a lawyer before I came here and he said you can't stop me from seeing them."

"Did he? Well, I can and I am. You got a paper to say I have to let you see them?"

"No, I don't. But I *will* get one, and I *will* see Brie and Pella. They're my nieces and I love them and miss them dearly."

I study her face. There wasn't a trace of emotion in her expression when she said the girls' names. She cranes her neck to peek around me trying to spot one of the girls.

"Goodbye, Piper."

"Raine, you have to let me in," she says with an air of barely controlled anger. "If you refuse to let me see Brie and Pella, this lawyer said I can file for visitation rights and take you to court."

"Go right ahead and try that. But until that happens, if it ever even happens, I'm caring for them. And I say no, you can't see them."

"You're caring for them?" Piper laughs. "Everyone in town is talking about how hard you are on them. And how irresponsible you are, letting them ride their bikes down Widow's Hill without wearing helmets. That hill lives up to its name. It's full of ruts and potholes. They're going to get seriously hurt."

I give an impervious shrug. "I believe in letting the girls learn how to stand on their own feet."

"By letting a five-year-old and nine-year-old ride their bikes down Widow's Hill at thirty miles an hour with no helmets?"

I snort. "Brie's ten and Pella's six, but then how would you know that? You've never shown the slightest bit of interest in them before."

"You're one to talk," she retorts. "They're too young to know any better. But you should. You don't let children do dangerous thing like that."

"Quinn and I did it as children and it never killed us."

"Then your parents were as crazy as you. I guess that just proves the apple really doesn't fall far from the tree."

I shake my head slowly. "You're still not seeing them."

Piper looks like she's going to cry. "Raine, have a heart. Let me speak to Brie and Pella. They need all their family now. They must be so frightened. I want them to know I'm here for them, too."

"After the fraud? After stealing from their parents…? I said no and I mean it. The last thing they need is you in their lives."

Piper wilts under my harsh stare and tone. "Raine, please. I'm devastated about Quinn and I miss my nieces."

I laugh derisively. "You're devastated about Quinn and you miss your nieces? Ha, that's rich."

"I understand that sounds insincere, but I do mean it. I may not have liked Quinn, but I loved Holly and I care deeply for Brie and Pella. I know I haven't been a good aunt in the past, but I want to be one now. I want to explain that to them." We both fall silent for a moment. "No matter what you think, this is about Pell and Brie. And they should be with *all* their family at a time like this."

"They're doing fine with me."

"Ha! You're not a good role model for them. Not by any means."

I cross my arms over my chest. "Piper, the answer is no."

"All right, Raine. If that's the way you want it, you leave me no choice. Brie and Pell are my nieces, too. I'll go back to my lawyer and get visitation rights. You listen carefully. If something bad has happened to Quinn, if he's dead, then I'll file for custody of them, too. You live and work in Halifax and I know you won't move back here. A judge would never uproot the girls. Your dad is too ill and too old. That leaves me. I'll win custody of them and have you thrown out of here."

"Vulture."

Piper pulls her mouth back into a cold, devious smile.

"Leave now," I say, then turn and go back inside, shutting the door firmly behind me.

———————

After Piper leaves, I swallow my pride and bitterness and call my dad, asking him to watch the girls for a few hours. He eagerly agrees. I also tell him that Piper is back in town and that she's come by to see us twice. He's a bit surprised but doesn't think it's a big deal; he even suggests that maybe she's changed.

"Piper is as much those girls' aunt as you are," he tells me. "You'll likely have to let her see them at some point."

Despite my annoyance at this, I jump in the car with Brie and Pell and drive them to Dad's. Winter has finally capitulated and it's a bright and sunny spring morning, gorgeous really—as hot as a summer day. The sea in winter is a surly gunmetal blue, but in the spring and summer it's a vibrant shade of turquoise. The sun's rays blaze across the surface. I wear shorts, a T-shirt, and flip-flops.

My mood is buoyed by the thought that this warm weather will also help Quinn hang on until searchers find him.

I don't go inside Dad's house when he opens the door and steps out onto the front porch. He gives me a big smile and wave, but I only give him a tepid wave back.

After dropping the girls off, I drive to Molly's Café. I buy two large coffees and two sesame seed bagels with plain cream cheese, then head out to Malin's little cottage on Periwinkle Cove Road.

I go up her walkway and stop in front of the front steps. She bought this place years ago, but I haven't seen it yet—other than the pictures she's shown me.

The pictures don't do it justice. It's painted a pretty lavender shade with white sills and white shutters and doors. She has flower boxes under the front windows, and pots of pastel-coloured pots line the front porch, each with a plant; they don't have any flowers yet, but I imagine they'll be lovely when in season.

She has put a lot of work into fixing up the place, and it shows. I'm impressed. I step into the beautiful garden to have a look at it, when suddenly I hear a clicking sound behind me.

"Well, well, talk about finding Lucifer in the garden," says Malin.

I laugh. "Good morning. I figured you'd sleep in on your day off, so I brought breakfast. Sesame bagels with plain cream cheese. Your favourite."

"Come on in. I'll show you around before I get dressed. Let's eat in the garden. There's nothing much to look at there yet, but it's a beautiful morning."

After Malin shows me around the place, I go back outside while she dresses. I take a seat in one of the yellow plastic lawn chairs set up around the rectangular patio table under the shade of a big elm tree. I set the cardboard coffee tray and bagels on the table.

Wearing stylish black shorts, a white silk top, and silver sandals, Malin comes outside in a few minutes and joins me at the table.

"This is a gorgeous garden," I say, handing her a coffee and bagel. "And it seems warm enough today for you to plant some flowers."

She takes a sip of her coffee, a bite of her bagel, and shakes her head. "Not while there's still danger of frost."

Overhead, a blue jay scolds us from the bare tree branches.

Malin chews the bagel, then swallows. "So are the girls at school?"

"No, they're with my dad. We haven't heard from Sergeant Flynn since yesterday morning, so I told him one of us should drive over to the new command centre and get an update on how the search is going. I'm going to do it. Anyway, the girls were feeling a bit down today, missing Quinn a lot. I decided not to take them to school. Dad's taking them to the park and then they're going to meet Lena at her shop and go for pizzas after."

"That should cheer them up a little."

"Yes, I hope so," I say. "They're seeing a child counsellor later today, too. It's their second appointment with Dr. DeWitt. Sergeant Flynn recommended her."

Malin nods. "That's great. I'm so glad for them. I've heard of Dr. DeWitt. She's supposed to be wonderful with children."

I swallow some coffee. "Oh, I nearly forgot. Piper came back to the house just before we left for Dad's."

Her face falls. "Did she talk to Brie and Pell?"

"No, they were out on the deck eating breakfast so I don't think they heard her or knew she was there, thank goodness."

"What did she want?"

"To see them. I refused and she told me she had spoken to a lawyer. She said she's going back to see this lawyer and she'll get a court order to force me to let her see the girls. And she said that if Quinn's dead, she'll fight for custody and kick me out of the house..."

"Let her try. She's their aunt, so she could get visitation rights, but I don't think, with her criminal record, a judge would ever give her custody." I nod. "But if something bad has happened to Quinn, *and it hasn't*, you and I and your dad will fight her every inch of the way."

I smile, relieved and glad for Malin's friendship and advice. I always feel better after talking to her.

"Are you going to the command centre now?" she asks. I swallow some bagel and nod. "Do you want some company? I took the day off in case you needed me for anything."

"Sure, thanks. You're a good friend, Malin."

"I know it."

I vow to myself that I will be a better friend to her.

"You can treat me to lunch after," she says.

"I just bought you breakfast."

"So? And we're taking my car. I don't want to drive in that rough old Jeep of yours."

"All right," I say with a soft laugh.

CHAPTER TWENTY-NINE

A s Malin turns onto a dirt lane that leads to the command post, a sense of foreboding fills my chest. Nine days and not a sign of Quinn. It's frightening.

She pulls up into a circular area where police vehicles, search-and-rescue trucks, and news reporters' vehicles are parked. She shuts off the engine and we get out and walk over to the command centre tent. Wind rustles in the trees as the tide roars in. Over that, there's the static of radios; above us, a woodpecker hammering; and over by the tent, a dog barking—a big glossy black Labrador retriever with a streak of white on its snout.

That's when Landry Storm sees us and approaches. "Hi, Raine… Malin. How are you two today?"

"I'm all right," I say, trying to sound like I am.

"Hi," Malin says, smiling.

"That looks like a different breed of dog than you were using the last time we spoke," I mention uneasily.

"Yes, it is," he says, watching me carefully. "That's Kita, the RCMP cadaver dog. They brought her in earlier this morning. The search-and-rescue dogs are gone now."

"I figured." My voice cracks.

I notice Sergeant Flynn about twenty feet to our left. She's speaking to a group of reporters. As I walk up behind her, Malin and Landry Storm join me on either side.

Malin looks at me, nods her chin slightly to Landry, and whispers in my ear. "Since when are you two on speaking terms?"

I shake my head; I don't want to talk about it.

"Why not use the search-and-rescue dogs *and* the cadaver dog?" I hear a reporter ask. "I don't understand."

Sergeant Flynn draws in a breath. "Search-and-rescue dogs bark and claw if they sense someone in need, so they're used more if we think someone is lost or hurt. Cadaver dogs, when and if they find human remains, will lie down or sit quietly by their find."

"I see," the reporter says quietly. "So you're looking for a body?"

She nods. "Yes, we are. Cadaver dogs can detect human remains through concrete, buried underground, or at the bottom of a body of water."

I feel sick to my stomach and Malin puts an arm around my shoulders.

"So you don't suspect foul play in Mr. Hunter's disappearance?" a bald reporter shouts out.

"We'll have to find the body first, and then an autopsy will reveal the cause of death," explains Sergeant Flynn. "If the autopsy reveals foul play, the body will often yield the DNA evidence we need to arrest and convict the perpetrators."

"And if the cadaver dog doesn't find anything?" another reporter asks. "What then?"

She scratches her forehead. "We have exhausted nearly all efforts in the search: our police helicopter, all-terrain vehicles, the K9 unit, and UAV. We'll be using the cadaver dog shortly. If nothing is found by the end of this week—say by Friday, late afternoon—I'm afraid we'll have to suspend the search."

The reporters all nod silently.

"What?" I say, my voice unsteady. "No. They can't do that."

The sergeant closes a notebook she's reading from and slides it and a pen into her jacket pocket. "We're asking people who have any information, no matter how trivial it might seem, to contact us. We're also asking people to keep an eye open and to contact us if they locate anything out of the ordinary that may be related to Mr. Hunter's disappearance. Mr. Hunter is five-foot-eleven and weighs approximately one hundred and sixty-five pounds. He has blondish-brown hair and wears glasses. He was last seen wearing blue jogging pants, a red hoodie, and red and white Nike running shoes."

When Flynn finished and the reporters scramble away, she turns. Recognizing me, she steps over.

"Why am I just hearing this now?" I stammer, so upset.

"Sorry," she tells me. "I did call your father just minutes ago and gave him an update before I spoke to the media. He said you were on your way here, and I wanted to wait for you to tell you... but as for the media..." She shrugs. "I couldn't wait any longer."

"You don't believe Quinn could still be alive?" I ask. "Some people survive longer than this in the woods."

"That's true, but your brother was dressed much too lightly for the cold temperatures we had the first few nights he was missing." Her voice is measured. "I know it's warm now, but the other nights were cold. The temperature fell to zero with heavy rain, and there were even some snow flurries. Also, he's been without food or water for nine days now. The infrared heat sensor on the helicopter hasn't picked up anything. I'm sorry, but as I told your father, I think you need to prepare for the worst."

She says all this with a cool, professional tone that masks the compassion I can otherwise detect in her eyes. But the harsh explanation nearly stops my heart. I swallow, look away.

"What about Piper?" I ask. "Have you spoken to her yet?"

She nods. "Yes, I called her and asked her and her boyfriend, a Brad Milson, to meet me at the police department. She met with me earlier this morning. She and Mr. Milson were at home in Mississauga, Ontario on the night your brother vanished."

I blow out a scoffing breath. "Who can verify that?"

"Their roommate. They were sharing a townhouse with a friend of Mr. Milson's. Piper provided his contact number and I spoke with him and he confirmed their story. They were both at home that night. This roommate also said he spoke with them both the following morning, and again before he left for work that evening. They weren't in Blackheart Bay the night your brother vanished."

I roll my eyes. "And then what? They suddenly moved out a few days later?"

"They explained that they had made the decision to move to Blackheart Bay a few months ago, but were unable to find someone to take over their lease until last week."

"Did she say why they were moving back to Blackheart Bay?"

"She says she wanted to be closer to family."

"Ha. She has none here… well, none other than Quinn, Brie, Pella and an uncle she was never close to. And she stole from them. So why come home now?"

Flynn lifts a shoulder in a shrug. "People change."

"Not her," I say, unconvinced.

"Her concern for your brother and her nieces seemed genuine. Her alibi's solid. I'm sorry. There's nothing there that will help find your brother."

We fall silent. Even the woodpecker is quiet.

Quinn, where are you, what has happened to you? I ask myself, filled with despair.

The silence is broken by the sudden roar of four-wheelers starting up and searchers shouting to each other.

"Any other questions?" Flynn asks kindly. The way she says it, it seems she's done talking.

I shake my head. "No."

She walks away, calling out and waving her arm at the RCMP dog handler.

"I'm so sorry, Raine," Landry says with kindness.

I look at him, desperate. "Quinn is tough. He could still be alive, couldn't he?"

"Yes, he could," he says, but with a cautionary look in his eyes. "People have survived in these same circumstances. But I don't want to give you false hope, either. The odds are not in his favour. I'm sorry."

I let out a long breath, deflated.

"If there's anything I can do, feel free to call me." He hands me a card with his name and phone numbers on it.

I take it. "Thanks."

He smiles compassionately, then nods and walks over to the command centre tent.

"Let's go, Mal," I say, tears stinging the corners of my eyes.

We drive back to town in sombre silence. She pulls over and parks against the curb next to Molly's. I look out through the windshield to the restaurant. Through the big plate-glass window, I can see that it's packed with the lunch crowd. I feel my chest constrict.

"I'm not going in after all," I say. "I'm not really hungry."

Malin follows my eyes to the restaurant and nods in understanding. "Me neither. But we're here now, so let's go in and get a quick café mocha."

"I don't know. Look at all the people in there. Some of them are already staring at us."

"When did that ever stop you from doing anything in this town? And remember, most of the people in there are good, kind people who would give you the shirt off their backs. That's the great thing about living in a small town, something you haven't yet realized or appreciated. The majority of the people will support and help you if you're going through a crisis. In fact, the majority of the people in Blackheart Bay are supporting you right now. So come on in with me, say hello, be gracious. I need my caffeine fix. *And* I want to know more about how you and Landry came to be on such good speaking terms."

I shake my head, my face flaming.

She grins. "Ha, you like him! That's wonderful, Raine. Landry's a good, kind man."

I nod, realizing that his kindness has drawn me to him. "I feel so comfortable when I talk to him." I lift a hand and run a finger along my scar. "And I completely forget about this… I don't feel disfigured and ugly around him. I've never experienced that with any other man before."

Malin squeezes my forearm and we climb out of the car to walk along the sidewalk towards Molly's.

Before we get there, we find our path blocked by Karl, Jarrod, Aubrie, and Cormac standing in front of the door.

"So we meet again," Karl says with his chill smile.

Aubrie erupts in a jarring laugh. He puts a cigarillo to his lips and lights it with a plastic disposable lighter. Cormac slides his sunglasses on his nose, watching us.

Malin's normally cheery face goes dark and her posture stiffens.

I feel my own heartbeat quicken. "What do you guys want?" I ask as firmly as I can.

"Mom said you were looking for me," Aubrie says, exhaling smoke in my face. "What do *you* want?"

I make a face and move my head out of the way. "I saw you lurking around Quinn's property the other night. I wanted to tell you to stay off it."

"Lurking?" Karl echoes. "Nice choice of words."

"It's not a big deal," Aubrie says. "Sometimes I take a shortcut home across your brother's property. That's all I was doing."

I give him a sardonic smile. "Really? And while you take this shortcut, do you stand under a tree and look in Quinn's windows while you have a smoke?"

"Don't be so foolish."

I can hear the blood rushing in my ears. "Step on Quinn's property again and I'll call the cops."

He laughs. "Go right ahead. That wouldn't stop me."

Karl raises his eyebrows. "Aren't you forgetting that I own the police, Raine?"

"Maybe the old town cops, but not anymore. And you certainly don't own the RCMP. I'll get a restraining order against you and your sons."

"A restraining order?" he says. He, Aubrie and Jarrod all laugh at that.

Cormac, however, lets out a quiet breath and looks down at the ground.

Jarrod reaches out and pokes me in the arm. "Go right ahead. You'll only be wasting your time. Piper's back and the cops are using a cadaver dog to look for Quinn. So he's dead for sure."

"What does Piper being back here have to do with anything?" I ask.

Karl smiles cunningly. "I guess you'll find out."

I stand utterly frozen, ice seeping into my bones. Did Piper talk to them?

"I will find out," I say, but in truth I'm badly shaken. "And I'll make sure she doesn't see Brie or Pella or set foot on Quinn's property again."

"What you should do is start packing your bags," Karl tells me with a mean smile. "And say goodbye to your nieces."

Jarrod snickers and Aubrie erupts into a queer laugh.

Karl gives me an indolent stare. "There are two kinds of people in the world, Raine: predators and prey. Your brother was prey. Think about that." Then he turns and starts off down the sidewalk. "Let's go, boys."

Jarrod and Cormac follow. Aubrie tosses his cigarillo on the ground, grinds it out with his boot heel, and limps past us. As he does, he leans into Malin's face and whispers something in her ear. Then he raises his eyes and lets out that horrible laugh again. A chill shivers up my neck.

Malin shudders, her face draining of blood. Her colour frightens me.

"Mal, are you okay?"

"I'm fine," she says a bit hollowly.

"What did Aubrie say to you?"

"Nothing I'd repeat." She makes a face. "Ugh, he makes my flesh crawl."

"Mine, too."

"Maybe I was wrong about them. Maybe they *are* more than just small town thugs. I always found them repugnant, but now they seem so evil."

"It's not so much that they seem evil; it's that they love evil."

She nods in solemn agreement. "Yes, that's it."

"Piper must have talked to Karl. If Quinn is dead, maybe she'll try to fight for the girls and then move into the lighthouse. In time, she'd sell it to Laramount and leave town. Mal, she might take Brie and Pell with her to who knows where. She doesn't love them like we do. She'll mistreat them."

As I say this, it strikes me that I've come to love Brie and Pella deeply.

"I know. The woman is an iceberg." Malin reaches out and squeezes my arm again. "We won't let that happen."

I nod firmly. "No, we won't."

"Now, let's go inside. I need a café mocha so bad after that, don't you? It's my treat."

"In that case, make mine an extra large."

We laugh softly—defiant laughter in the face of adversity.

CHAPTER THIRTY

On Saturday morning, I look out the kitchen window towards the ocean. The water glistens under bright sunlight and gulls dive into the froth. The breeze is pleasantly warm and floods the room with the scent of wild rose and salt.

Suddenly, the wind changes direction and a wide band of dark clouds moves across the sun. The waves rise, topped with white caps, and the trees and shrubs in the backyard whip back and forth.

The girls are with Dad at his house again. Lena picked them up early this morning and took the morning off from her store to look after them with my dad, who wasn't quite up to looking after them alone for more than a couple of hours. Although I'm glad for the break, at the same time, to my surprise, the house seems a little quiet and empty without them.

I decide to walk over to the command centre to get an update. My heart quickens at the thought that I may see Landry, so I change into a plum-coloured silk top, one nicer than I usually wear.

I freeze. What am I doing? I'm about to kick myself when my cell phone rings.

"Hello?"

"Ms. Hunter? This is Sergeant Flynn."

My heartbeat wobbles. "Is there news?"

"Yes, there is. We've found some clothing in a cabin about five kilometres from the Skinners' place. It's a man's shirt and hoodie. There's also a pair of men's running shoes. I wonder if you could come over now and take a look at them. I want to know if you recognize any of the items."

"You think they're Quinn's?"

"They match the description of the clothing Brie and Pella said he was wearing that night."

"Where's the cabin? There must be a road in."

"About five kilometres down the highway past the Skinners' place. Turn left onto the Cormorant Road. Do you know it?"

"Yes."

"Drive down the lane for about a kilometre and you'll see police cars and other vehicles there. I'll have someone meet you and walk you in. The cabin is set back in a thick copse of woods and isn't visible from the road. You have to walk in to get to it."

"All right," I say, my heart spiralling with hope. "I'll be there shortly."

When I arrive at the location, I park behind an RCMP cruiser and see, to my surprise, Landry Storm standing there waiting for me. He smiles and waves, and my heart flutters a little. He's wearing blue jeans, knee-high rubber boots, and a sky blue T-shirt under a cotton long-sleeved shirt. He's rolled the sleeves up and I find myself staring at his tanned forearms.

Don't be so foolish, I tell myself. *Get a grip.*

"Hi, Raine. Sergeant Flynn asked me to guide you in to the cabin. Hope that's all right?"

"That's fine," I say, walking toward him. But I worry for Quinn and what the clothing might mean. It keeps me from smiling back.

It doesn't seem to bother him, though. He immediately starts into the woods. I follow, keeping one arm up to push away the branches and brush that grows over the narrow dirt trail.

He glances back over his shoulder, his blue eyes holding kindness. "How are you doing?"

"All right."

"How's your dad and your nieces?"

"They're holding up. Hoping to find Quinn very soon."

He nods and gives me a compassionate smile. "We will. Keep hope."

We walk along in silence for a time. The air is saturated with the scent of pine needles. Birdsong fills the air from the branches above. It's a gorgeous section of woods, a splendid day, so incongruous with what's happening at the cabin.

He stops and looks at me. "I heard you're a published author. That's something. Are you working on a novel now? Oh, wait, sorry… that's a stupid question. I was trying to take your mind off things. I imagine that must be impossible with all that's going on."

"It's not a good time right now to sit down and write a novel, no." I keep my tone gracious to show I don't take offence.

I meet his eyes and we hold each other's gaze for a time. I finally look away, disconcerted by how much I'm drawn to him.

He clears his throat. "We should get going."

Sergeant Flynn comes out of the cabin carrying two plastic evidence bags. One holds red and white running shoes. The other holds a red hoodie. She stops me at the bottom of the steps.

The sunlight breaks through the canopy of trees overhead, its warm rays pouring down on my head, but as I look at the evidence bag I feel cold. Landry stays beside me and I'm glad, for I find his presence a comfort.

"Do you recognize this hoodie?" she asks, holding the bag up so I can see the front of it.

I study the hoodie and grow suddenly still. It's cherry red with the words *Pensacola Bible School* printed in white letters across the chest. The hem is badly frayed at the collar… and it's identical to the one I saw him wear when he'd visited me in Halifax last year. It's Quinn's. It's old, but he'd loved it and always said he'd never throw it away. The Nike running shoes look like the same ones he wore that day, too.

I draw in a breath to calm my breathing. "That's Quinn's hoodie, but I'm not positive about the running shoes. They look like a pair he was wearing when he visited last year, but I can't be sure. My dad would know for certain."

Flynn nods. "I'll bring them over to your dad's place later."

"So he was definitely here." I feel a vein in my temple pulsing. "Who owns the cabin?"

"An older couple by the name of Chester and Ellen Holmes. We've contacted them. They're in Four Lakes, Florida, where they've been going every winter for the past fifteen years. They closed the cabin up in October and left for Florida on November 1. They said they haven't been back since then."

"The cabin is pretty far from the ocean. It's beyond the land Laramount wants, isn't it?"

She nods. "It is."

"Did you see anything in there? Rope? Handcuffs?"

She pauses. "No. We're gathering fingerprints and other evidence. Whoever was here didn't stay long. There's canned food in the cupboards that wasn't touched. The shower and sink in the bathroom weren't used as far as we can tell. There's a woodstove and it's clean inside… hasn't had a fire in it for some time."

"When are you going to arrest the Skinners?" I demand. "It had to be them. If Quinn had come here alone, he'd have lit a fire and then only stayed long enough to wait out the rain and cold. The Skinners must have been holding Quinn captive here, and when they heard the searchers getting close they moved him somewhere else."

"That's possible," Sergeant Flynn says. "However, we need to find some evidence before we can question them or anyone else." She juts her chin toward the cabin. "I'll let you know as soon as I learn anything. You'll be the first I call."

"So that's it?"

She nods. "Yes, for now that's it."

I let out a shaky breath, my eyes locked on Quinn's hoodie and shoes, my stomach queasy. "All right."

I turn and start toward the trail to go back to my car.

"I'll walk you back if you like, Raine," Landry offers.

I hold up a hand without looking at him. "No. I'm fine."

When the girls get home from my dad's that afternoon, we start making chocolate chip cookies in the kitchen. Brie and Pell are kneeling on chairs pulled up to the kitchen counter.

Suddenly, I hear a car pull into the driveway and stop.

"Add another egg to the batter and keep stirring, then add the chocolate chips," I tell them. "I'll see who it is and be right back."

I go to the door and look out to find Dad and Lena, and a few seconds later Malin pulls up in her convertible. They all climb out and walk up the path to the house. Dad and Lena are in front, holding hands. Normally cheerful and unflustered, Malin follows behind looking forlorn and anxious.

I run back into the kitchen and check my phone. There are two missed calls from Sergeant Flynn. The sound of the dishwasher and electric egg beater must have drowned out the rings.

I hurry back to the door and step out into the bright afternoon sunshine.

"Hi," I say apprehensively.

"Hi, Raine," Malin says, her voice cracking. She has tears in her eyes and she's clenching a tissue.

I look at my dad. His eyes are red-rimmed and puffy, his face a sickly grey. Lena gives me a sad smile.

Clearly they've all been crying. Shock and understanding hits me like a kick to the chest and I lurch backward.

"It's Quinn, isn't it?" I say, my blood rushing to my head with such force that I feel nauseous.

Dad hesitates. "It is. Let's go inside so you can sit down first, Raine."

I open the door and hold it for them as they step into the foyer. The girls are chattering and laughing in the kitchen.

"Just tell me here, Dad, and keep your voice down," I say, forcing down the coffee that rises in the back of my throat.

"Sergeant Flynn called to say that they found a letter in the cabin," he says hoarsely.

I shake my head, my fear mounting. "A letter?"

"A letter that was written by Quinn and addressed to all of us," he explains in a quiet voice. He pauses, watching me. "It's a suicide letter."

I stagger back and hit the foyer wall with a soft bump. I feel lightheaded, like my heart is falling down inside me. Dad reaches out and gently steadies me.

"How do they know Quinn wrote it?" I ask frantically.

"They also found a notebook filled with his thoughts, prayer lists, and church events. They compared the writing and it's the same," Dad says. "Sergeant Flynn called me about a half-hour ago. I was going to call you but then I decided to tell you in person. I figured you'd want Malin to be here with you."

I look at Malin and give her a weak but thankful smile. "I'm glad you did."

Dad inhales a shaky breath. "Sergeant Flynn is going to bring the clothing and other items so we can positively identify them, but I'm sure they're Quinn's. The running shoes had neon pink laces, the same as Quinn's. Brie and Pella gave them to him for Christmas."

I'm trying to grasp what Dad has just told me. "Oh, Quinn… no…" I begin to cry, and my throat aches. Tears pour down my face.

"I know. It's horrible," Dad says, his own eyes filling up.

"Brie and Pell are in the kitchen?" Malin says.

My entire body quivers. "Yes. We're making chocolate chip cookies…"

"We can't tell them any of this, not yet," Dad says.

I shake my head. "No."

We all walk slowly down the hallway and step into the kitchen, wearing fake smiles. Brie and Pell look up, and their faces brighten when they see the visitors.

"Grampy, Lena, Malin!" they shout happily.

"We're making cookies," Pella tells them. "Want some when they're ready?"

Dad smiles. "Sure we do, but first I wonder if we could all pray for your daddy right now?"

Brie and Pella nod their heads vigorously.

Malin whispers, "Oh, yes, let's do that."

"Will you pray too, Aunt Raine?" Pella asks.

"Yes, you should pray for Daddy, too," Brie says bluntly.

"From the mouths of babes," Malin whispers softly beside me.

And to my surprise, I feel a cold spot in my heart soften… and a desire to pray for my brother. It's not some foxhole desire to pray, but a genuine longing to pray to my Heavenly Father, to draw close to Him.

CHAPTER THIRTY-ONE

Sergeant Flynn comes to the house a couple of hours later, followed shortly after with Pastor Henderson and his wife. Once Malin, Lena, and Mrs. Henderson have taken Brie and Pell upstairs, Dad positively identifies the hoodie and running shoes in the plastic evidence bags as Quinn's.

The sergeant reiterates most of what we already know. They discovered the cabin and, upon looking in the windows, spotted the red hoodie hanging on the back of a kitchen chair. She said they discovered this on their second sweep of the area, having missed it the first time by about a hundred feet. The door and windows were locked except for one at the side, and when the sergeant and her constables went inside they found the running shoes and the letter.

"You were within a hundred feet of finding Quinn?" I say to Flynn, incredulous. "How could that happen?"

She nods solemnly and takes her time answering. "I know that's upsetting to hear, but you need to understand that the cabin was set back in a thickly forested area and concealed by heavy foliage. The only reason the searcher did spot it is that he tripped on a tree root and fell flat on his face. When he raised his head, he saw the base of the cottage. Also, we were using the cadaver dog at the time, not the search-and-rescue dog. The SAR dogs would have found Quinn's tracks or scent right away."

My chest feels tight as I struggle to understand this.

Flynn pauses, watching me. "Your brother was gone by the time we got there. But we'll find him. The tracking dog arrived around noon today and picked up a scent."

"And?" Dad and I say together.

She makes a wry expression. "He followed Quinn's tracks from the cabin through the woods and out to the highway. Then he lost the scent. We don't know which night he was there, or how many nights he stayed… although we're certain it wasn't for very long. He must have left at night when we weren't searching."

I look at her numbly, my heart crushed with sorrow for what Quinn must have been going through to hide from us, the ones who loved him most.

"There is something else." Flynn reaches into her jacket pocket and pulls out a small red spiral notebook. "We found this notebook in the other pocket of his hoodie. He wrote names in the notepad. It looks to have been used to write down prayer lists, sermon notes, and reminders of church events. Only he would have known about the things written in this notebook—names of parishioners, the church schedule, private thoughts, etc. We'll have the writing examined by an handwriting expert, but we are certain he wrote it."

I look at her numbly, my mind reeling with shock and horror. "And he wrote us a farewell message."

Dad lets out a small moan, a sound that makes me think of a baby kitten mewling in pain.

"I'm so sorry," Flynn says, looking from me to Dad.

Tears stab my eyes. "No, no…"

The sergeant watches me steadily, then pulls out a sheet of paper that's been folded in half and holds it up alongside the notebook. "We need to keep the original letter, but I made a copy for you. Would you like it, or would you rather I give it to your father? It's addressed to you, your dad, and Brie and Pella."

"You read it, Raine, please," Dad says, his voice breaking.

I swallow hard. "I'll take it."

I reach for the letter as casually as I can, though my hand shakes horribly.

"Again, I'm sorry," Flynn says. "Don't give up. We're searching for your brother and will continue to search, using every available resource we have. I will keep you informed daily."

She gives us a sympathetic nod and then goes out of the house.

I slump down into a chair at the table, feeling weak with nausea. I set the notebook down on the table and then slowly and carefully unfold the letter.

Dear Dad, Brie, Pella and Raine,
I'm so sorry but I just can't go on. Every time I look at Brie and Pella I feel so guilty, I can't bear it. They are growing up without their kind loving mother because of me. I can't look at them one more day and think that. I miss Holly so much I can't live another day without her by my side.

Please tell Brie and Pella that I love them so much. Tell them I pray they grow up to be kind, compassionate, strong women of faith. Tell them I pray they can one day forgive me for this.

Dad, Raine… I love you both. Please forgive me.

Love to all, Quinn.

A painful lump grows in my throat and a rush of tears fills my eyes. I squeeze my eyes shut for a moment, swiping the tears away. Then I take a breath, stand, and pass the letter to my dad. Feeling shattered, I sit down again.

Dad takes a chair across the table from me and reads the letter silently. He folds it and sets it down on the table without raising his eyes. We both sit there, staring at the notebook, shattered with grief.

I pick up the notebook and thumb through the pages. It's used mostly for Quinn's prayer lists. He likely wrote in it during his morning devotions at home, for each page contained names of people in his congregation, as well as Brie and Pell, Dad, and me. My name appears on every prayer list, and to my shock it is, without fail, the first name on every list. This knowledge is heart-breaking.

After we pray together, the Hendersons, Malin, and Lena go home, and Dad and I put Brie and Pell to bed for the night. I read them a story and Dad reads them a Bible story. I think about leaving the room, but I decide not to and instead listen to my dad read a passage from Luke. In this moment, I'm swept back in time to when he did the same thing with me and Nat. I always loved when Dad read Bible stories to us.

I feel like crying and look away fast so Dad won't see. But he has sensed it and reaches over to give my hand a loving squeeze.

Dad goes up to bed in Quinn's room and I shut off all the lights and go into my bedroom. But I lie awake, unable to sleep, haunted by the thought of Quinn's body floating in the sea or lying somewhere in the forest and never being found.

Overcome with fear, tension, and grief, I put my face in my hands and release great sobs.

I hear my door open and Dad comes in, wearing a pair of Quinn's pyjamas and housecoat. He sits down on the side of the bed and pulls me into his arms.

"There, there, Raine," he says, soothingly. "There, there."

"Oh Dad, I let my bitterness keep me away from Quinn. Sometimes when he called, I wouldn't even pick up. Other times I'd lie and tell him I was busy and couldn't talk. I should have visited, should have talked to him. I was selfish and stupid, yet he never gave up on me. Do you know my name was at the top of his prayer lists? He prayed for me first every morning."

"I know he did," Dad murmurs. "He worried about you. He missed you. He loved you. As do I, Raine. I pray for you every day and love you so much. I've missed you all these years. I can't tell you how much I've missed you."

I press my face against his chest and weep, my tears spilling onto his housecoat.

CHAPTER THIRTY-TWO

The woman drives through the cold pouring rain. It's nearly 3:00 a.m. and the houses are dark, the sidewalks and streets empty. Shaking with anger and gripping the steering wheel tightly, she drives fast. Rain streams in through the open driver's window, wetting her face, but she's too focused on her task to care.

The man next to her swears under his breath and shakes his head back and forth. A second man lies quietly in the backseat, wearing only a white T-shirt, blue jogging pants, and white socks. A long canary yellow scarf is tied around his mouth and his hands and feet are bound by a soft nylon rope.

Behind the wheel, the woman holds her head high, her back erect. Her shoulder-length hair lifts in the breeze as she drives determinedly down the main street of town.

She reaches the entrance to the old wharf road and looks at the man beside her. "Here?"

He shrugs unhappily as she turns down the road. She hardly notices the noise when she drives over an empty pop can, the sound breaking the night air.

She presses on, passing the lobster boats bobbing at their moorings on the water. She doesn't look at them; she doesn't have to. She grew up in Blackheart Bay. Her grandfather and great-grandfather were fishermen. In fact, she recognizes a couple of the older boats—the Cierra-Caylin, the Linda-Darlene, the Katherine-Joanne.

She reaches the end of the T-shaped wharf and stops, looking around even though she knows the fishermen won't be down to the wharf for another hour or more. She takes her foot off the brake and steers purposefully over to the wooden railing that faces the southern end of the harbour.

She sits in the car, calm under a pool of light thrown down from a street lamp. She looks left to the lighthouse on Puffin Island at the harbour entrance. Its revolving white light usually calms her, but tonight it only increases her anxiety. She peers out through the windshield at the water, dimpled by the steady rain.

Her passenger shifts uncomfortably next to her. His breathing is ragged. "I don't know about this."

"We have to do it. We have to do it now."

The man nods and wipes a sheen of sweat from his forehead.

She turns and looks over the seat to the passenger in the back. He's lying on his right side, facing her. He stares back calmly yet boldly, and she responds with a cruel smile.

Turning her attention to the back window, she takes in the backs of the buildings that line this end of Harbourview Street: Molly's Café, the Lobster Pot Restaurant, Rumrunner's Pub & Grill… businesses she knows. The owners, like everyone in this town, are people she despises.

She faces the inky black harbour again, the water seeming impenetrable and icy. The nearby boats creak in their moorings, the tide sloshes against the wharf pylons, and a bell clangs from a buoy at the harbour mouth. Then a sea gull swoops over the car, shrieking into the waning night, nearly stopping her heart.

She draws in a deep breath to steady herself. "Come on, let's get do it and get out of here."

They both get out and reach in for the tied-up man's legs. He begins kicking at them with his bound feet, his cries muffled by the scarf.

"Stop it!" she yells at him, then addresses her accomplice. "Hold his feet!"

They finally get a hold of his feet and pull him out of the car. He hits the wharf road with a hard thump.

"You get his legs," she says. "I'll get his shoulders."

Together they carry their captive over to the wood railing despite his fierce but futile struggles to free himself. The woman's accomplice takes a knife out of his pocket and opens the blade, then kneels on the man's legs to pin him to the ground and quickly slices the ropes around his hands and feet. He slides the blade between the man's cheek and the scarf and slices it free, too. He slips the scarf and ropes into his jacket pocket, then grabs the man by his ankles.

"On three," the woman says, laughing darkly. "One, two—"

"Hey, what are you guys doing?" calls out a male voice.

The woman whips her head to the right just as a figure steps out from the shadows at the side of the weigh station office. It's a man wearing blue coveralls and yellow raincoat with the hood up over a dark ball cap.

"What's going on?" the figure says.

A jolt of angry frustration hits her. It's Jack O'Hara, captain of one of the lobster fishing boats. A husband, father, grandfather… someone one of her uncles once described as a good brave man who had gone out in bad storms to rescue fellow fishers who were in trouble at sea. She knows he'll try to stop her.

"What are you guys doing?" the fisherman calls out again.

"Help!" the captive cries out, but a gust of wind kicks up at the same time and drowns out his voice.

Resolute, the woman looks at her accomplice and nods. "He can't see us clearly. Let's do it fast and get out of here."

"Three," she says, and they swing the man left and heave him over the railing.

Their captive sails through the air, hanging briefly in the air before dropping into the water. He hits the water with a huge splash. Without waiting a second longer than they have to, the woman and her accomplice run back to the car and jump in. She hits the gas, backs up with a screech, and speeds away, tires screeching.

Jack O'Hara runs down to the wharf railing and sees the man thrashing in the water as the tide comes in; he's flailing both arms, trying to stay afloat.

"Help, help! I can't swim!"

"Hang on! I'm coming!" Jack fishes deep in his pocket for his cell phone while he pushes off his boots. He finds his phone and punches in a number, keeping one eye on the man's head bobbing in the water. "Grab onto the ladder!"

"I can't swim!"

"Kick your legs and grab the ladder!"

Within seconds, the man's arms and legs stop flailing. His cries grow weak, become frail, and then his movements cease as water slips over his mouth.

Jack O'Hara, rain streaming down his face, cell phone to his ear, swiftly but cautiously steps down the slippery iron rungs of the ladder, horror-struck as the man's white face stares up at him and sinks into the frigid depths.

My phone rings at three-thirty in the morning, jolting me awake. I turn on the lamp and see that it's Sergeant Flynn.

"Raine?" she says.

"Yes, speaking."

"It's Sergeant Flynn. I have some news."

My heart begins beating so hard I'm afraid it will explode.

"Tell me," I say, a tremor in my voice.

"We've found him," Flynn says. "We've found your brother and he's alive."

"Where is he?" I shout, fighting back instant tears.

"He's in an ambulance on his way to the hospital as we speak. Call your father and meet me there. I'll fill you both in."

"My dad's here with me. I'll wake him and we'll be there as soon as we can get someone to come over to stay with the girls."

I vault out of bed and run out into the hallway. "Quinn's alive! Dad! Brie! Pella! Wake up, wake up! They've found him and he's alive!"

CHAPTER THIRTY-THREE

"Daaaaadddd!" Brie and Pella scream as they jump up onto the bed and get on top of Quinn. He holds his arms open for them, tears streaming down his face. Dad and I stand back with Sergeant Flynn, letting the girls have some time alone with him.

Flynn nods toward the hall and we follow her out into a quiet room down the hallway, where she tells us the entire story. Apparently Piper and Brad Milson grabbed him while he was walking through the woods between the lighthouse and the Skinners' property. They'd heard on the news about Laramount's planned resort and Quinn's refusal to sell, then hatched a plan to kidnap him and force him to write a suicide letter and sign the deed of the house and land over to her. Piper then planned to sell it all to Laramount.

The sergeant further explains that Piper and Brad had paid their roommate in Mississauga to say they'd been in the apartment with him the night Quinn was kidnapped, while in reality they had already arrived in Blackheart Bay.

But when they tried to grab Quinn, he escaped into the woods and kept going until he found the old cabin. He'd gone in through the window to hide, but Piper and Brad found him there and made him write the suicide note. They then put it in the pocket of the hoodie and left it behind for the searchers to find. They also left his shoes, mostly so he couldn't run away again, before walking him back to where they'd hidden their car. Ever since, he'd been held in the cottage they'd been renting under a false name.

They had planned to throw Quinn into the harbour to make it look like he had committed suicide.

Of course, this seems to mean the Skinners had nothing to do with the kidnapping, but Dad and I aren't so sure. Someone had told them about Quinn's habit of taking his walk after supper every night. And I'm also bothered that we don't know what Piper and Brad planned to do with Brie and Pella once the lighthouse was sold and they had custody.

But Jack O'Hara saw them tossing Quinn into the water and ruined their plans. The deed hadn't gone as intended and now they were on the run.

"We've issued Canada-wide warrants for them on the charges of kidnapping and attempted murder," Flynn tells us before leaving the hospital. "We have their pictures up everywhere, along with a description of the vehicle they're travelling in. They won't get too far."

It hits me later that Brie and I came close to finding Quinn the day we followed Piper and Brad to their rental cottage.

Lena and Malin take the girls to the cafeteria for lunch, leaving me and Dad alone with Quinn. He sits up in bed, clutching his head between his hands.

"It was stupid of me to leave the house without my cell phone," Quinn says, shaking his head. "But the battery had died and it was charging. I was only going to take a short walk. I thought it'd be fine." He shrugs uncomfortably. "I wasn't thinking straight. What if something had happened to the girls? They wouldn't have been able to call me."

My dad reaches out and gives his forearm a squeeze.

"I need to tell you both something," Quinn says quietly. "I know a lot of people thought I abandoned Brie and Pella because I've been kind of low since Holly died…"

"We knew you'd never do that," I assure him.

He nods. "No, I would never, but I have to be honest—I thought about it. One night back in early December, I packed a bag and left a goodbye note on the kitchen table asking you guys to take care of Brie and Pella." He swallows hard. "But Brie heard me leaving. She called to me from her bedroom window, crying. She was shattered. I couldn't leave. I went back inside and ripped the note up."

"Holly's death hit you that hard?" Dad says with deep concern.

Quinn draws in a breath and gathers his composure. "There's something I've been carrying in my heart that I haven't told anyone about. In the first year after she died, the guilt was like a worm eating away at my soul, and my faith."

Dad sits on the edge of the bed. I shift in my chair, and we both wait for him to continue

Quinn runs his fingers through his hair. "I pushed Holly to go on that missions trip. She didn't really want to go. She had a bad feeling about it. But I wouldn't listen to her. I even laughed at her. I just kept pressuring her until she agreed to go."

Dad and I exchange surreptitious glances.

"There's something else," Quinn says uneasily, looking at me. "That night when Natalie was killed?"

I lift my brows. "What about it?"

"I told Mom and Dad I fell asleep, but I didn't really. I heard you guys calling out my name, but I ignored you. Then I went downstairs and looked out through the window on the back door and saw you and Nat start running down the path towards the river. I ran outside and went after you… to stop you… but you were long gone. I tried to catch up with you guys, but I heard the whispery sound of a snake brushing up against a dead branch and got scared." He pauses and draws in a deep breath. "I went back in the house and stayed there till Mom and Dad got home. I told them where you guys went, but it was too late. It was all my fault. First for hiding in the closet and then for chickening out and going back into the house instead of going after you guys and stopping you from going all the way down to the river."

I flick my eyes to my dad, who gives a regretful shake of his head.

"No, Quinn, you were only six," I say gently. "It was not your fault, not at all."

"Your sister's right, Quinn." Dad then looks me in the eyes. "It was no one's fault, not yours, and not Raine's. If it's anyone's, it's mine. I was the adult and I reacted badly. I blamed Raine because I couldn't deal with my own guilt of bringing my family to the Outback and claiming it was God's will when in my heart I knew it was more my own desire." He lays a hand on Quinn's shoulder and squeezes it tenderly. "I'm so sorry, Quinn."

I get up and sit on the other side of the bed, then put my arm around Quinn.

Quinn shifts uncomfortably. "I couldn't tell you guys about Natalie or Holly and what I'd done. I was too ashamed. And I'm a pastor, for goodness sake."

"Pastors aren't perfect. Christians aren't perfect," Dad says. "If anyone has learned that, it's me. It took me a long time to forgive myself for the horrible way I treated Raine after Nat died."

I give Quinn an understanding and comforting smile. "And I'm just now beginning to forgive Dad for that."

Quinn looks me in the eye. "You need to forgive yourself, too, Raine. Let God heal your heart."

I lift a shoulder in a shrug. "It's easier to forgive Dad than it is to forgive myself."

Quinn smiles. "I know. It took me a long time to forgive myself after Holly died. But God promised us that He's forgiven us for all our sins, Raine. And he tells us we must forgive others, and ourselves. Let Him help you."

I avert my gaze to the window and look out without seeing anything.

We sit in silence for a time. Then Dad gets up and stretches. "I'm going to get a coffee. Anyone else want one?"

I shake my head.

"Sure," says Quinn. "One milk, one sugar... Thanks, Dad."

"Listen to him, Raine, please," Dad whispers in my ear before he exits the room. "Quinn will help you."

CHAPTER THIRTY-FOUR

A sliver of sunlight slips in through a gap in the blinds, falling across my face and waking me. It's almost nine o'clock, but I'm not surprised; I was exhausted when I went to bed. The house is quiet. The girls and Dad are still asleep. Outside I hear the slow roar of the sea, the screeching of gulls, and the wind rattling a window in the kitchen.

I make a cup of coffee, then carry it down to the beach and sit on the log. The breeze coming off the water is warming up, so salt-laden that I can taste it on my lips. The tide's coming in and each foamy wave breaks over the pebbles and pushes them up the beach. The repeating rhythm of it is like the tinkle of broken glass. Some might find the noise irritating… I find it strangely calming.

I think of Quinn, of his deep faith and calm in the aftermath of a terrifying situation. He's found the strength to trust in his Heavenly Father and know that he's been forgiven for Holly's death. With that, he can forgive himself.

I've felt drawn back to God these past few days, but another part of me feels like a fraud and rebukes myself for feeling so. Though I want more than anything to forgive myself for Nat's death, I still struggle with guilt.

Feeling confused and unsettled, I walk back up to the house just in time to see a man getting out of a grey pickup truck. At the sight of him, my heart tumbles in my chest. It's Landry Storm.

Landry lifts his hand in a wave and walks toward me. "Hi, Raine. Beautiful morning."

"Hi," I stammer, thinking he sure doesn't give up easy. "Yes, it's gorgeous."

He holds up a plastic food container. "I wanted to come over to tell you how glad I was to hear about your brother. And I brought you guys some of my famous chili. Thought you might need a break from your own cooking."

I allow a small smile. "Your famous chili? Why haven't I heard of it before now?"

He grins. "Famous in my own, rather small family."

The patio door opens and I glance sideways as Brie and Pell come out onto the deck, still wearing pyjamas, their hair mussed.

Landry smiles broadly. "Hi, girls."

They both smile shyly and say hi back in unison.

My dad pushes open the door, sticks his head out. "Morning, Landry."

"Morning. Thought I'd bring over some chili. I meant to bring it long before now, but with the search…" He shrugs apologetically.

"That was kind of you," Dad says. "Have you eaten yet? I was just about to scramble some eggs."

"I've eaten, thanks," Landry replies.

I shoot my dad a murderous look, but my dad ignores it. "Would you like to come inside for a cup of coffee then?"

Landry flicks his eyes from my dad to the girls, then to me, and quickly shakes his head. "Ah, no, I'd better not."

"Are you sure?" my dad says.

"Yes. I was just dropping off the chili. I should get going now."

"All right then. Another time." Dad ushers the girls back inside.

Landry holds the container of chili out to me and I accept it with trembling hands.

"Goodbye," Landry says. "It was nice to see you again under happier circumstances, Raine. Again, I'm glad your brother is safe and sound."

I nod and watch him walk to his pickup. I take a breath and then call out, "Um, Landry?"

He keeps one hand on the door handle and turns his head sideways to look at me. "Yes?"

"I think I'll take Dad up on that coffee. Why don't you come in and have one, too?"

He hesitates, watching me steadily. "Well then, all right."

We sit at the kitchen table alone, drinking our coffees. My dad has talked the girls into eating their breakfasts out on the deck with him. The worst fool in the entire world would know what he's up to.

"How is your brother doing?" Landry asks.

"He's fine. Had some hypothermia, but he should be released in another day or two."

"Good." He nods in understanding. "When I was twelve, my little brother went missing for twenty-four hours when my family was camping in a provincial park in Alberta. Not as scary as what you've been through, but I remember being terrified until they found him."

"Is that why you became a search and rescue tech?"

He smiles. "Yes. In fact, it is."

Our eyes meet and hold. I feel a catch in my throat.

Then I hear a giggle and look over at the open window to see Brie and Pella peeking in at us. I scowl at them and they flinch and move away.

Landry sees the girls, too, and laughs. A minute later, we see the tops of their heads poking up from the window sill again. I hear Dad move past the kitchen doorway very slowly and catch him peeking into the room, too.

"They're back," Landry says, grinning.

"Not their fault. They get their nosiness from their grandfather."

We both laugh together.

"Maybe next time we could go for a walk?" Landry says a bit tentatively. "Might be more private."

My heart begins thumping merrily in my chest. "How about after we finish our coffees? We can walk along the beach below the lighthouse. It's a pretty walk."

He lays his hand over mine. "I'd love to."

I smile and don't move my hand away.

CHAPTER THIRTY-FIVE

Later that morning, Dad goes to town to get a haircut. Lena and Malin arrive shortly after and we clean the kitchen together. The girls are playing in the front yard, and once Dad gets back we'll all go visit Quinn in the hospital.

Through the open window, I hear the wind in the pines and the continuous roar of the sea. Over that, I make out the familiar voice of Karl Skinner. I head into the living room and look outside and see Karl and Cormac in the yard talking to Brie and Pella.

The hair stands up on the back of my neck. "What are they doing here?" I gasp.

I storm out of the house to the yard and place myself in front of Brie and Pell.

"You girls go inside with Lena and Malin," I tell them, noticing a white ceramic dish in Cormac's hand.

Karl lifts a hand in a wave. "Raine."

"What do you want, Karl?"

"We just came to give you this food." He juts his head toward the covered dish in Cormac's hand. "Loretta made a ham and macaroni casserole for you."

Cormac steps forward and holds it out to me. I don't accept it and instead fold my arms over my chest. Cormac sets the dish down on the ground.

"We wanted to tell you how glad we were to hear that Quinn was found and that he's okay," Karl says.

I look at him. "Tell Loretta thank you, but I don't want the food and I don't believe for one minute you are glad Quinn's safe."

Karl scowls. "Why are you talking to us like this? It's bad enough you and your dad had half the town believing we were responsible. We had nothing to do with your brother's disappearance. You know that now."

"I don't know that. How did Piper know it was Quinn's habit to walk on that trail each night after supper? A trail that leads right to your place?"

He shrugs. "I didn't know Quinn walked there at night, so how would I tell Piper?"

"Then it was your sons." My eyes go to Cormac, and I clarify myself. "I mean, Aubrie or Jarrod."

"You're dreaming."

"Whatever, Karl. You and your sons have been harassing Quinn, trespassing on his land, and damaging his property for a while now."

Karl shakes his head, his smile bitter. "Come on now. That's ridiculous."

"Just go. Take your food and leave, Karl."

He looks me in the eyes. "Not until we talk about something."

"We have nothing to talk about."

He scratches his neck and eyes the house. "Yes, we do. I was hoping you'd have more sense than your brother and you'd talk to him about selling it to Laramount."

"You *what?*"

"Just talk to him. He's keeping me from making three-quarters of a million."

I shake my head. "No, I will not talk to him. And he'll never sell to Laramount."

Karl's face darkens as his temper rises. "The deadline is next Friday at midnight. If he doesn't agree to sell by then, Colin Laramount is going to cancel the development."

"Then it will be cancelled because Quinn isn't selling. So get back in your car and leave."

"Listen to me…" Seething, he reaches out to grab my arm but I backpedal out of the way and he misses.

"You heard her, Karl," shouts Gloria Jean, emerging from the trees with a shotgun in her hands. "Leave now."

"Don't you point that at me, you lunatic," Karl says.

Gloria Jean walks toward him, the shotgun held out in front of her, shoulder high, aimed right at his heart.

"Gloria Jean," I caution her. "Put that down, please."

"You wouldn't shoot me," Karl sneers.

She lifts the shotgun and squints down its sight. "Want to find out?" Karl goes silent, his jaw tensing. "Get in your car and leave."

Karl releases a dry, uneasy laugh. "You wouldn't shoot me, you crazy old thing," he says, stepping closer, though warily.

Gloria Jean points the barrel to the sky and pulls the trigger. The boom shatters the morning air, startling a group of squirrels that scurry away through the trees.

My heart pulses in my throat, my ears thrum from the echoing blast of the gunshot. "Gloria Jean, put that down now."

"Are you crazy?" Karl shouts at her, his face white.

Cormac looks a bit shaken, but he remains as silent as ever.

Gloria Jean smiles and lowers the shotgun just as Malin bursts out of the house.

"What's going on?" Malin says, her eyes wide when she sees the shotgun in Gloria Jean's hands. "Whoa."

I turn to her. "It's all right, Mal. Karl's just leaving. Gloria Jean just gave him a little encouragement."

Malin smiles at Gloria Jean. "Good morning, Gloria Jean. How are you?"

"Couldn't be better," the woman replies without taking her eyes off Karl.

Malin gazes at the three of us for a moment, then up at the sunny sky. "Isn't it just a magnificent morning?" With that, she turns and goes back in the house.

I face Karl and Cormac again. "You guys had better leave," I say seriously.

Karl's face contorts and his clenched fists shake at the realization that he's lost. I find his cold black rage unsettling, but Gloria Jean appears unfazed.

"Leave now, Karl." Gloria Jean lifts the shotgun a few inches, her lips firmly set.

As Karl glares at her, a vein throbs in his forehead. When the shotgun doesn't waver, though, he looks away and blows out a breath so hard that his lips flutter. He whips around and stomps to his car.

Cormac starts to follow, but then he stops and walks up to me.

Gloria Jean goes stiff again, and I touch her on the arm. "It's fine."

Cormac removes his sunglasses. "Raine, I'm really glad things turned out good for Quinn. I mean that. Tell him that for me. He's a good man and I always liked him."

His eyes hold compassion, and I wonder for a moment whether he had a part in the trespassing and vandalizing of Quinn's property. From his words and expression, I surmise that he likely didn't.

"Thank you, Cormac. I'll tell him." I watch as he nods and walks to the car. Suddenly, I call out his name one last time. He stops and glances back over his shoulder. "You're not like your father or brothers."

"Don't be so sure of that."

"I am sure. I think you have a good heart."

His face colours. He casts his eyes down.

"Why do stay here?" I ask. "Why don't you leave?"

He lifts his eyes. "I stay for Mom. She needs me."

"Take her with you."

He gives me a small, sad smile. "It's that not simple, Raine."

"Someday in the future then?"

He exhales heavily. "Maybe someday."

Then he climbs in the car and shuts the door. Karl starts the ignition and backs up so fast that dirt and shells go flying. The car speeds away with a roar.

"Nothing more enjoyable than running Karl Skinner off," Gloria Jean says, smiling to herself as she cradles the shotgun under her arm.

I smile. "Thanks, Gloria Jean."

"You're welcome. Don't worry. I wouldn't have really shot Karl."

"Well, that's good. How'd you know he was here?"

"I was out doing yard work and all of a sudden it felt like someone just walked over my grave. That always means a Skinner is around."

"Ahh."

"How's Quinn?"

"He's coming along. Should be released in a day or two."

She averts her gaze to the trees. "Good. I was worried about him. I like your brother a lot, considering he's a Christian and all. He's like your mom. He's always been so kind to me. Doesn't judge me like a lot of people in this town. I kind of went off the deep end after Eric died. Shocked me so bad I never was the same again. People can be so cruel with their talk. But not your mom, and not Quinn."

I nod with compassion.

"You're not so bad yourself, Raine."

I smile. "I don't know about that, but thanks."

She clears her throat, her face red. "So tell Quinn hello for me, will you?"

"I will, Gloria Jean."

I pick up the casserole dish from the ground and hold it out to Gloria Jean. "Do you want this for Bella and Ben?"

She scowls at me, clearly insulted. "From the Skinners? I can't believe you would even offer that to me, Raine. I wouldn't feed that to my babies even if it was the last drop of food on this earth."

I walk over to the trash barrel by the shed, lift the lid, and almost drop it in. But then I remember that Cormac has a good heart, something he's gotten from Loretta, and she's been kind enough to make this meal. I decide to keep it.

"I'm going to have a cup of coffee, Gloria Jean. Why don't you join me?"

She goes still, stares at me, then shakes her head.

"You're sure?"

"I'm not much for chinwagging," she says uneasily.

I smile. "I'm not either, nor is Brie. Have to warn you, though, Malin and Pell have no problem keeping a conversation going. They can talk the ears right off your head. Come on in and join me for a quick cup. I'll dig out some of the ton of food we have in the freezer and you can take it for your dogs. We really will never be able to eat it all."

She watches me some more. "All right, but I can't stay long. Quick cup, as you said. I'm a busy woman."

"Great. Oh, wait… you can't bring the shotgun inside, Gloria Jean."

She frowns. "Why not?"

"I don't like guns in the house."

She looks at me with immense astonishment. "You don't like guns in the house?"

"No, never did, never will. And especially not now with Brie and Pell in there. Why don't we lock it in the back of my Jeep for now?"

"I suppose that's fine," she grumbles. "Can't say I understand your thinking one bit, but it's your house."

———————————

I need to get away by myself, so I leave the house and go down to the beach. I stand on the hard-packed sand at the water's edge and look out to the horizon. The sun is descending, blazing the sea in a wide swath of molten red, filling the sky with streaks of pink, mauve, and crimson.

What a gorgeous sunset. I've missed that, Lord, I pray. *I've missed fifteen years of Quinn's life. I've missed fifteen years of my dad's life. I've missed out on being there on Quinn's, Brie's, and Pella's birthdays… Easters… Christmases. I've missed so much because of my guilt and anger and bitterness. I feel only regret now.*

"Are you okay, Raine?"

I turn to see Dad coming down the path. I let out a breath. "Yes. I was just thinking of Quinn and how much I've missed of his life."

He gazes out at the steadily advancing water, the gulls swooping down into the swells. "It not too late, not for Quinn or Brie or Pella."

"Or you," I say quietly.

He doesn't answer, but smiles lovingly.

"Dad, I keep thinking about Quinn. How brave and strong he was through what must have been a terrifying ordeal. And how he found the spiritual strength to forgive himself after Holly died."

"Quinn is a man of great strength and tremendous spiritual strength. I'm sure he was scared but at the same time found comfort and strength to bear his captivity. And though he, too, struggled with finding forgiveness, he was able to find it in time. And I'm not just giving you some Christian platitude."

I don't speak for a moment. "I think you're right, Dad. I only wish I had the same spiritual strength."

"You do, Raine. You'll find your way back to God, to find the strength and trust to forgive yourself. I think you've already started. Don't you?"

"I think so. I feel different. It no longer feels like bitterness and faith are at battle in my heart."

"That's so wonderful to hear, Raine," he says in a joyous whisper. I nod, swallowing down my tears. "So what are you going to do when Quinn comes home tomorrow? Are you going to go back to Halifax?"

"Not right away. He might need help with the girls for a few days. Plus, I want to spend some more time with him."

"Good."

"I've actually been thinking about moving back here."

His face lights up. "Really?"

"I'm not sure. I love Halifax, so I'll see."

"If you do, that will be wonderful, Raine. You loved this town once. Maybe you'll come to love it again."

"I don't think I really ever stopped loving it," I confess. "Or stopped loving you, Dad, though I know I didn't show it."

His eyes well up and he turns to embrace me. And this time I wrap my arms around him and embrace him back.

CHAPTER THIRTY-SIX

I open the small cardboard box and pull out the novel, look at the front cover…

Tears in the Desert
By
Raine Vivian Hunter

I open the book to the dedication page and read it slowly.

This book is lovingly dedicated to my sister, Natalie,
February 1982–February 1996
And to my mother, Vivian Rose Hunter
October 1960–June 2002
And for my father, my brother, and my precious nieces,
Brie and Pella.

I turn to the middle of the book and gaze at the gallery of photos of our whole family in Australia. A lump fills my throat and tears spring to my eyes, but they're no longer tears of blame and anguish.

I slide the novel back into its cardboard carton and put it in my tote bag. I pick up my phone and purse, slip the handle of the bag over my shoulder, and get into my car.

The sun is rising quickly and burning off the low-lying fog over Halifax Harbour. Soft orange and mauve streaks fill the dawn sky. The briny air mingles with the scent of my rosebushes and the newly cut grass from my neighbour's backyard, an altogether wonderful scent. Birdsong rises from the trees and a container ship's horn blasts as it passes George's Island.

I start the ignition, put the car in gear and back out of my driveway. I drive out of Halifax, my heart light, and head southwest. Three hours later, I arrive in Blackheart Bay where the water in the harbour glitters under the brilliant morning sunshine. The sea breeze is fresh and invigorating.

I've decided not to move to Blackheart Bay after all. Halifax has been my home for sixteen years and I love it too much to leave. Besides, it's only a three-hour drive to Blackheart Bay, an easy commute to visit all the important people in my life—my dad, the girls, Malin, and Landry. I've vowed to keep up these visits twice a month, and so far I've kept that vow. I drive up on a Friday, stay at Quinn's, attend church services, then lunch with my friends and family before leaving mid-afternoon on Sunday.

It isn't difficult, and I find that I can't wait for the weekend to arrive so I can see everyone, especially Landry. He comes to the city twice a month to see me, too. He loves Halifax and has applied for a position there with Halifax Search and Rescue. If he gets it, and it looks good, he'll soon be moving close by.

Dad and Lena are getting married on October 6, and Malin and Tanner are getting married on October 27. I'll be maid of honour for Malin, so I've planned to go home for the entire month of October. I'm looking forward to both ceremonies.

Piper and Brad Milson are both in jail, serving long sentences for the kidnapping and attempted murder of Quinn. Piper will be almost fifty before she's eligible for parole. Brad will be in his eighties.

Colin Laramount is building a big seaside resort over by Digby. The Skinners, mercifully, stopped harassing Quinn and no longer blatantly trespass on his property.

I drive slowly along Harbourview Street. It's noon and the downtown area is busy—businesses are open and the sidewalks are full of townspeople and tourists. I keep going, heading out of town. I turn off onto Lighthouse Road and follow the newly paved lane to Quinn's place. I pull into the driveway and park behind Dad's car. Quinn's, Malin's, and Landry's vehicles are parked over to the side. We've all planned to get together for lunch.

The door bursts open and Brie and Pella run out to my car. I drop to my knees and hold my arms out. They crash into me.

"How are you two?" I ask, embracing them tightly. "That was a long week. I missed you both so much."

"We missed you, too, Aunt Raine," they say in unison.

I can smell the scent of food cooking on the barbecue, and it's coming from the patio around the back of the house.

Dad opens the door and steps out onto the front porch. I walk up the steps with Brie and Pella.

"Glad you made it safe," he says, smiling. "The others are all out on the deck, getting things ready. We were waiting for you before we started to eat." He looks at the thin cardboard carton in my hand. "Is that it?"

"Yes," I say, pulling out the book and passing it to him.

He studies the cover and then reads the dedication page. He looks a long time at the photos and his eyes grow moist. He swallows hard.

"Brings back memories," he says, his voice cracking.

"I know."

He sniffs. "Raine, I'm so proud of you. Natalie and your mom would be so proud of you, too."

"Thanks, Dad."

"Are you crying, Grampy?" Pella asks, frowning up at him.

"No, no," he replies, self-conscious, and clears his throat.

"Yes, you are," she says in her frank way. "Just admit it, Grampy."

"Well, maybe a little," he admits with a chuckle.

Brie sighs. "I knew it."

Landry opens the door and comes out on the step. Our eyes meet and my heart does that little tumble down in my chest it always does when I see him again.

"Who's hungry?" Dad says as he leads the girls into the house. "I know I'm starving. Let's go inside."

"I'm glad you made it," Landry says with a warm smile once we're alone. "It's been a long week. I've missed you."

"I've missed you, too," I say.

He puts his arm around me, gives me a tender squeeze, and together we go into the house.